Palace
OF
Spies

Palace

OF

Spies

BEING A TRUE, ACCURATE, AND COMPLETE ACCOUNT
OF THE SCANDALOUS AND WHOLLY REMARKABLE
ADVENTURES OF MARGARET PRESTON FITZROY,
COUNTERFEIT LADY, ACCUSED THIEF,
AND CONFIDENTIAL AGENT AT THE COURT OF
HIS MAJESTY, KING GEORGE I.

SARAH ZETTEL

HOUGHTON MIFFLIN HARCOURT
Boston   New York

www.hmhbooks.com

Text set in 12 pt. LTC Deepdene
Design by Christine Kettner

LIBRARY OF CONGRESS CATALOGING-IN-PUBLICATION DATA
Zettel, Sarah.
Palace of spies: being a true, accurate, and complete account of the scandalous and
wholly remarkable adventures of Margaret Preston Fitzroy, counterfeit lady, accused
thief, and confidential agent at the court of his majesty, King George I / Sarah Zettel.
pages cm. — (Palace of spies ; book 1)
Summary: In 1716 London, an orphaned sixteen-year-old girl from a good family
impersonates a lady-in-waiting only to discover that the real girl was murdered,
the court harbors a nest of spies, and the handsome young artist who is helping
her solve the mystery might be a spy himself.
ISBN 978-0-544-07411-8
[1. Spies—Fiction. 2. Courts and courtiers—Fiction. 3. Love—Fiction. 4. Orphans—
Fiction. 5. London (England)—History—18th century—Fiction. 6. Great Britain—
History—George I, 1714-1727—Fiction.] I. Title.
PZ7.Z448Mo 2013
[Fic]—dc23
2012046366

Manufactured in the United States of America
DOC 10 9 8 7 6 5 4 3 2 1
4500437607

To my husband and son,
as always

CHAPTER ONE

‑ꞏꞏꞏ‑

London, 1716

IN WHICH A DRAMATIC READING COMMENCES,
AND OUR HEROINE RECEIVES
AN UNEXPECTED SUMMONS.

I must begin with a frank confession. I became Lady Francesca Wallingham only after I met the man calling himself Tinderflint. This was after my betrothal, but before my uncle threw me into the street and barred the door.

Before these events, I was simply Margaret Preston Fitzroy, known mostly as Peggy, and I began that morning as I did most others—at breakfast with Cousin Olivia, reading the newspapers we had bribed the housemaid to smuggle out of Uncle's book room.

"Is there any agony this morning?" asked my cousin as she spread her napkin over her flowered muslin skirt.

I scanned the tidy columns of type in front of me. Uncle Pierpont favored the *Morning Gazetteer* for its tables of shipping information, but there were other advertisements there as well. These were the "agony columns," cries from the heart that some people thought best to print directly in the paper, where the object of their desire, and everybody else, would be sure to get a look at them.

"'To Miss X from Mr. C,'" I read. "'The letter is burnt. I beg you may return without delay.'"

"A Jacobite spy for certain," said Olivia. "What else?"

"How's this? 'Should any young gentleman, sound of limb, in search of employment present himself at the ware-house of Lewis & Bowery in Sherwood Street, he will meet a situation providing excellent remuneration.'"

"Oh, fie, Peggy. How dull." My cousin twitched the paper out of my hands and smoothed it over her portion of the table.

As I know readers must be naturally curious about the particulars of the heroine in any adventure, I will here set mine down. I was at this time sixteen years of age, and in what is most quaintly called "an orphaned state." In my case, this meant my mother was dead and no one knew where my father might be found. I possessed dark hair too coarse for fashion, pale skin too prone to freckle in the sun, and dark eyes too easily regarded as "sly," all coupled with a manner of speaking that was too loud and too frank. These fine qualities and others like them resulted in my being informed on a daily basis that I was both a nuisance and a disappointment.

Because I was also a girl without a farthing to call my own, I had to endure these bulletins. As a result, I was kept at Uncle Pierpont's house like a bad-tempered horse is kept in a good stable. That is, grudgingly on my uncle's part and with a strong urge to kick on mine.

"Perhaps it's a trap." I poured coffee into Olivia's cup and helped myself to another slice of toast from the rack. I will say, the food was a point in favor of my uncle's house. He was very much of the opinion that a true gentleman kept a good board. That morning we had porridge with cream, toast with rough-cut marmalade, kippered herrings, and enough bacon to feed a regiment. Which was good, because that regiment, in the form of all six of Olivia's plump and over-groomed dogs, milled about our ankles making sounds as if they were about to drop dead of starvation. "Perhaps the young man who answers the advertisement will be tied in a sack and handed to the press gangs."

"There's a thought. They might be slavers and mean to sell him to the Turks. The Turks are said to favor strong young English men."

It is a tribute to Olivia's steadfast friendship that my urge to kick never extended to her. My cousin was one of nature's golden girls, somehow managing to be both slim and curved, even before she put on her stays. She possessed hair of an entirely acceptable shade of gold and translucent skin that flushed pink only at appropriate points. As if these were not blessings enough, she had her father's fortune to dower her and a pair of large blue eyes designed solely to drive gallant youths out of their wits.

Those same gallants, however, might have been sur-prised to see Olivia leap to her feet and brandish an invisible sword.

"Back, you parcel of Turkish rogues!" she cried, which caused the entire dog flock to yip and run about her hems, looking for something very small they could savage for their mistress's sake. "I am a stout son of England! You will never take me living!"

"Hurray!" I applauded.

Olivia bowed. "Of course, Our Hero kills the nearest ruffian to make his escape, the rest of the gang pursues him, and he is forced to flee London for the countryside—"

"Where he is found dying of fever in a ditch by the fair daughter of Lord . . . Lord . . ."

"Lord Applepuss, Duke of Stemhempfordshire." Olivia scooped up the stoutest of her dogs and turned him over in her arm so she could smooth his fluff back from his face and gaze adoringly down at him. "Lady Hannah Applepuss falls instantly in love and hides Our Hero in a disused hunting lodge to nurse him back to health. But Lord Applepuss is a secret supporter of the Pretender, and he means to marry his daughter off to a vile Spanish noble in return for money for another uprising—"

"And as she is forced onto a ship to sail for Spain, he steals aboard for a daring rescue?" One of the dogs decided to test out its savaging skills on my slipper. I gave it a firm hint that this was a bad idea with the toe of that selfsame slipper. It yipped and retreated. "Can there be pirates?"

"Of course there are pirates." Olivia nipped some bacon off her plate with her fingers. "What do you take me for?" She turned to the dogs and held the bacon up high so that they all stood neatly on their hind legs, and all whined in an amazing display of puppy harmony.

"You really should write a play, Olivia," I said, addressing myself once more to my toast, coffee, and kippers. "You're better at drama than half the actors in Drury Lane."

"Oh, yes, and wouldn't my parents love that? Mother already harangues me for overmuch reading. 'A book won't teach you how to produce good sons, Olivia.'"

"That just shows she hasn't read the right books."

Olivia clapped her hand over her laugh. "You outrageous thing! Well, perhaps I shall write a play. Then—"

But I never was to know what she would do then. For at that moment the door opened, and to our utter shock and surprise, Olivia's mother entered.

My aunt Pierpont declared she could not bear the smell of food before one of the clock, so she daily kept to her boudoir until that time. My throat tightened at the sight of her, and my mind hastily ran down a list of all my recent activities, wondering which could have gotten me into trouble this time.

My cousin, naturally, remained unperturbed. "Good morning, Mother. How delightful of you to join us." Olivia possessed admirably tidy habits when it came to other people's property and forbidden literature. She folded the paper so its title could not be seen. "Shall I pour you some coffee?"

"Thank you, Olivia." Aunt Pierpont had been a celebrated

beauty in her day. She still carried herself very straight, but time and four babies had softened and spread her figure. Twenty-odd years of marriage to my uncle had wreaked havoc upon her nerves, and she was forever clutching at things: a handkerchief, a bottle of eau de toilette, an ivory fan. This morning it was the handkerchief, which she applied to her nose as she drew up her seat next to mine.

"Good morning to you too, Peggy. I trust you are well this morning?"

"Yes, Aunt. Quite. Thank you for asking." I slipped a glance at Olivia, who was busy pouring coffee and offering it to her mother with sugar and cream. Olivia shook her head, a tiny movement you wouldn't catch unless you were looking for it. She had no notion what occasioned this unprecedented appearance either.

"Isn't the weather fine to-day?" Aunt Pierpont's hands fussed with her lacy little square, as if about to pull it to bits. "Olivia, I think a stroll in the garden will be just the thing after breakfast."

This was too much for even Olivia's composure. A flicker of consternation crossed her face. "Yes . . . certainly. We'd be glad to, wouldn't we, Peggy?"

"Erm, no, my dear. I thought just you and I. Surely, Peggy won't mind."

"No, of course not." My mind was racing. What could Aunt have to say to Olivia that I couldn't hear? Had Olivia received a marriage offer? Her looks and her father's money meant she had cartloads of youths chasing after her. Worry knotted in my stomach. What would I do in this house without Olivia? Uncle Pierpont often grumbled about sending me off to Norwich to "make myself useful" to his aging mother, thus saving himself the cost of my keeping.

"Well." Olivia delicately blotted her mouth with her napkin. "Shall I fetch my bonnet, then?"

"Yes, yes, do."

Olivia scurried from the room, the canine flock trailing behind. Left alone with my aunt and my now thoroughly queasy stomach, I found it difficult to fit words to my tongue.

"Peggy, you know we are all very fond of you." Aunt Pierpont squeezed the much-abused handkerchief in her fist.

"Yes, Aunt." I stared at that strangled bit of lace and fancied it might soon yield some milk, or a plea for help.

"And we've always had your welfare at heart."

This is it. I am bound for Norwich and a damp cottage and a deaf old woman who can pinch a sixpence until it screams. I'd been there once before, one interminable, gray winter, to nurse the dowager Pierpont through a cold. She'd made up her mind that if she was to have nothing but gruel and weak tea, no one else need have anything better. I must have written a thousand murder plans in my diary in those months. Had her serving girl been able to read, I would have been hanged straightaway.

"I was very fond of your mother," my aunt added suddenly. "You have grown to be very like her. Did you know that?"

"No." In fact, she never spoke of my deceased mother. No one did.

Aunt Pierpont gave the handkerchief a fresh twist. "Well, you have. Just as pretty, and just as willful. You must . . ." She bit her lip, and another ripple of fear surged through me. But before she managed to continue, the door opened to admit Dolcy, the parlormaid.

"I beg your pardon, ma'am." Dolcy bobbed her curtsy to us. "But Master says Miss Fitzroy is to join him in his book room."

So, the end had come. I rose to my feet. My aunt smiled encouragingly at me and gave my hand a limp pat. *Norwich.* Empty. Gray. Flat. With a vicar whose sermons lasted a full two hours every Sunday and Thursday. My stays squeezed my breath, making me unpleasantly lightheaded as I walked to the door. No books in the cottage, no hearth in my bedroom . . .

Olivia stood in the dim hallway, bonnet dangling in her fingers.

"I heard everything." She seized my hand at once. "What have you done? Tell me quickly."

"Nothing, I swear." We were due to attend Lady Clarenda Newbank's birthday party that evening. I didn't care for Lady Clarenda, nor she for me, but the party would provide a welcome change of scene. Because of this, I had been treading very gently around my uncle so he should not be tempted to forbid my going.

"Hmmm." Olivia frowned. "Well, then, it's probably something trifling. About expenses, perhaps."

Neither one of us believed this, especially with her

mother waiting to have some urgent, private conversation in the gardens. I walked the narrow, dark corridors to my uncle's book room and found myself wondering if this was what it felt like to walk toward a trap one knew was coming. Unfortunately, unlike Olivia's imaginary hero, I had no way to fight back.

The dominant feature of my uncle Pierpont's book room was his desk. I had never once been in this room when the great ledger was not open on that gleaming surface, accompanied by bulwarks and battlements of letters and documents sealed with all colors of ribbon and wax.

Uncle Pierpont himself was a skinny man. He had skinny legs beneath his well-cut breeches and silk stockings. His arms had knobby elbows that always looked ready to poke through the cloth of his coat. The clever fingers of his hands seemed made for counting and writing sums. Slitted eyes graced his long face on either side of a nose at least as sharp as his pen. When I walked in, he was bent so close over his ledger, you might have thought he was using his nose rather than the goose quill to write out his accounts. His short-queue wig, a bundle of powdered curls, clung to the top of his head at a most dangerous angle.

I was determined to remain calm and resolute, but that room and the Desk had some magical power to them. By the time I crossed the long acre of carpet to stand in front of Uncle Pierpont, I was once again eight years old, alone, poor, terrified, and trying desperately not to fidget.

The great clock in the corner ticked, and ticked. My uncle continued his laborious writing without once glancing up. I valiantly battled against fidgets, against fear, and against wondering what Uncle would do when his wig slipped off his shiny forehead, which it surely must at any moment.

Finally, Uncle Pierpont finished his column and lifted his nose from the page. "Ah, there you are at last."

"Yes, sir," I replied meekly. The quickest way through these interviews was to agree with whatever was said.

"I have some good news for you, Peggy." Uncle Pierpont plucked a sheaf of documents bedecked with ribbons and red wax seals off one of his paper battlements.

"Good news? Sir?"

"Yes." Uncle Pierpont pushed the documents across the desk toward me. "You are betrothed."

—⚬⚬⚬✦⚬⚬⚬—

CHAPTER TWO

IN WHICH OUR HEROINE LEARNS
MUCH THAT IS UNEXPECTED, FINDS HOPE
UNLOOKED FOR, AND SHARES A SAD CONFIDENCE
WITH AN OLD AND TRUSTED FRIEND.

Betrothed?" I pressed my hand against my stomach and stared at the close-written papers. How was this possible? I had no suitors. I had nothing about myself to tempt any warm-blooded swain. I was going to grow old being Olivia's companion and nurse to her children. Or go to Norwich and die of the rising damps. "I . . . but . . . but . . . *who?*"

"It seems Lord Sandford, Baron of L——, wants you for his second son. Sebastian's his name. I think. In any case, he wants the boy married before he sends him back to the family's sugar plantations in Barbados. Thinks it will keep him out of trouble, or at least give him some legitimate offspring for a cover."

Barbados? I was betrothed to someone my uncle *thought* was named Sebastian, and who was expected in Barbados? It wasn't possible he could do this. Except, of course, it was. I was an orphan. I was a girl. As my legal guardian, Uncle Pierpont could dispose of me as he pleased.

"Almighty Heaven, look at her," said my uncle to his ledger, as if he expected it to sit up like one of Olivia's dogs. "Gawping like a codfish. What sort of thanks is that? You're coming off quite well, especially considering you've no dowry or family. The settlement's exceeding generous." He nudged the papers a little closer.

"But . . . but I don't want to be betrothed." Not to someone who would have me on my uncle's word. Not to someone I'd never before laid eyes on.

"And who d'ye think's asking what you want, you fool girl? It's not as if you're overrun with suitors."

"I'm only sixteen." That plea sounded weak even to me. But my wits had deserted me and taken my strength with them. The only things holding me upright were my corset stays. Those and the fear that if I fainted now, I might be shut up in the great desk drawers until it was time to be carried to church.

"You'll be seventeen by the wedding. That's plenty old enough." My uncle wiped his pen on the blotter and dipped it once again into the ink.

That, unmistakably, was the end of the conversation. My knees bent of their own volition to make the curtsy my uncle would not raise his eyes to see, and I left that room. The door closed behind me. I stood in the shadowed hallway, unable to think which way to go next.

"Peggy!" Olivia sailed up the corridor like a lost but very enthusiastic sunbeam and gave me an enormous hug. "Mother told me! How wonderful!" She grabbed my arm and drew me down the hall away from my uncle, and the Desk, and the betrothal contract I'd left behind in my shock. "You shall have your own house, and I'll come to visit every day. We'll have heaps of time all to ourselves, and you'll be able to take me anywhere we want, because you'll be a married woman! And . . . what on earth is the matter? Did you think I'd be angry because you're getting married first?"

"I've never met him," I whispered. "I've never even seen him."

"Is that all?" Olivia steered us into the breakfast room and shut the door. The sunlight of a clear May morning streamed through the windows, and her dogs flopped in their lacy baskets. The table had been cleared, and every other thing was in its place, as if nothing at all were wrong.

"All?" Disbelief melted the ice of my shock. "He could be a thousand years old and covered in shingles and swollen with gout and a drunkard and—"

"Actually, he's very handsome." Olivia settled herself in a round-backed chair next to her dogs and straightened her skirts.

I stared at her as if she'd just turned blue.

"With excellent legs," Olivia continued. "Very much the horseman, by all accounts."

"You *know* him?"

"No. But I know his sister Rosamond. Sebastian's nineteen years old, he's been in Barbados, but he was sent to Cambridge to finish his education, and he's got every girl in London sighing after him. *Including* Lady Clarenda Newbank. I can't wait to see the look on her face. Promise you'll let me tell her, Peggy, do!"

"I . . ." I sat down quickly. I detested girls who slumped into faints at the drop of a fan, but now I felt I might be about to join their ranks. "But . . . your father said he's to be sent out to Barbados after he's married. And I'm to go with him."

"Nonsense, Peggy. No one would dream of sending an English girl to the tropics. You'd be sick in an instant, not to mention brown as an Indian." Pale skin was regarded as one of the many signs of rank and virtue, and therefore must be strictly cherished. We good English girls were constantly warned that ruination accompanied turning the least bit brown. "Don't you see? It's perfect! You'll be installed in his London house and free to do whatever you like. And if any-one does entertain the idea of Barbados, you'll simply become ill. *Far* too ill to travel to such a harsh climate." Olivia tipped me a broad wink.

She meant a baby. I was barely able to comprehend that I'd been betrothed to this young man, and she saw me hav-ing his child. A strange, sick sensation bubbled through my mind. "This can't be happening. I'm not ready. I can't do this, Olivia. I can't—"

"Oh, Peggy, I'm sorry." Olivia folded me in her sisterly

embrace. "It's been a shock, hasn't it? Do you want to lie down?"

I grasped at this. "Yes, yes, I think perhaps I should."

My room was right next to Olivia's. My uncle grumbled at this, but Olivia had always insisted. It was furnished in the modern style, that is to say, hardly at all. I had a bed with a lace canopy, a wardrobe, a dressing table, a chair, a round table for a candle, and another chair for sitting beside the hearth and sewing. The floor was bare, but it was clean, and the maids liked me, so I always had plenty of coal for my fire and stout quilts in winter.

I had no window, nor any pictures for my walls, nor a desk where I could write in private. I was not allowed to keep more than one book at a time up here. None of this mattered at that moment. What mattered was the door I could shut against the rest of the house. Even against Olivia. I needed to be alone. I needed to think.

"You'll come to me at once if you need me?" asked Olivia anxiously. "Truly, you've turned a very odd color."

"I will. It's just the shock." Dutifully, I settled onto my coverlet. "See? I'm having a lie-down. I'll be right as rain in an hour or so." I made myself smile.

Olivia snorted at my exaggerated, wooden expression. "You'll like Sebastian when you see him, Peggy. I'm sure of it," she said kindly.

With this happy idea, she did leave me alone. The door

shut firmly behind her, and I lay on my back as stiff as Flossie, the porcelain doll Olivia had given me so long ago, and who still shared my pillow. I blinked up at my faded lace canopy. I was cold. What warmth May had to offer did not seem to have penetrated this deeply into the house.

I was betrothed. My opinion was not wanted or needed, because I was poor. Because I was orphaned.

According to our best novelists and playwrights, daughters loved their fathers unfailingly, be they present or absent. But I never had. From my youngest days, I had hated mine. My father's abandonment had been the source of all my troubles. I could remember quite clearly the morning I'd come into the parlor and seen Mother with her lovely face turned all red and blotchy.

"He's left us, Peggy." Mother held out her arms, and I ran into them at once. She hugged me too tight, her hot tears falling against my brow. "He's left us, and we must fend for ourselves now."

We must fend for ourselves now. I'd never forgotten those words, but I'd never truly considered them either. All I knew was that my father, in leaving, had taken my mother with him. Until then, Mother had come up to the nursery every night to play with me and read to me. We took breakfast together, and there had been excursions about the town. After Father left, Mama became a much-loved and beautiful ghost glimpsed on the stairs. If she came to me at all, it was for a fleeting kiss once I was tucked in.

Mama had died in her bed three years after my father's

disappearance. I hadn't been allowed to see her until afterward. Mama was delirious, the doctor had said, and I mustn't be exposed to her rantings.

When I finally was let in, I looked on her corpse and I cried, because that lifeless stock was not my warm, beautiful mama. She was gone, gone farther even than my father.

This memory finally brought the tears. They trickled down my cheeks and into my ears and nose, because I hadn't turned my head. I sneezed, and sneezed again, and it was all too ridiculous.

This realization dried up my self-pity and my tears. I found I was able to sit up, at which point I realized Flossie's dress was soaked.

"I'm sorry." I brushed out her old-fashioned flounces and smoothed down her hair. "I'm being silly. Really, crying over . . . nothing." The betrothal to Mr. Sebastian Sandford had already happened. I had to find some way to make peace with it.

"Olivia says he's handsome," I informed Flossie. "It might be he's nice as well. If he's been to Cambridge, he must like to read." Maybe he liked plays. We could go to the theater together. And the New Gardens. I'd always wanted to see a fireworks display at the gardens. My uncle expressly forbade it, but a young man from Cambridge, who had traveled, wouldn't be anything like so fastidious. "Anyway, once I'm married, I won't have to worry what Uncle Pierpont thinks."

Now, that was a fine thought. As a married woman, I not

only wouldn't be under my uncle's management anymore, but he could no longer scold me or order me about. That would be my husband's privilege. I could tell Uncle Pierpont he was nothing but a pinch-faced miser, and there would not be one thing he could do about it.

"Perhaps Olivia's right," I said to Flossie. "Perhaps this is for the best."

Flossie did not seem to have any opinion on the matter. I hugged her close and willed myself to believe it would be all right. There was, after all, nothing else I could do.

CHAPTER THREE

IN WHICH OUR HEROINE IS WICKEDLY
CONFINED, CRUELLY PROVOKED, AND COMMITS
SEVERAL ACTS OF A RASH NATURE.

I t should be more widely publicized that the nimble-fingered creators of ladies' attire are raised entirely by she-wolves. This infant experience leads them to conclude that the proper home for anything female is in a cage. It is the only conceivable explanation for the device known as the mantua.

For those among you who have been spared direct experience of the mantua, I shall describe this evil spawn of the dressmaker's art. It is principally, as I have said, a cage. The condemned prisoner stands shivering in her linen shift and gartered stockings, her breathing already constrained by the stays of her most confining corset. Wardens, in the form of ladies' maids, compel her to step into a round framework of willow struts, plainly modeled on the dimensions of the great bell at Bow. These struts are then laced firmly to her hips. The average weight of the cage is somewhere between one and two tons, and thus prevents her from moving quickly, or, indeed, breathing effectively.

The entire edifice, with the prisoner in it, is then concealed beneath layers of ruffled petticoats and damask satin of some shade deemed pleasing to the Masters of Fashion. It is further disguised with ribbons and furbelows and suchlike feminine decorations in one or more contrasting colors. The whole is then secured firmly with a broad, highly decorated stomacher in order to remove any lingering ability on the part of the prisoner to slouch, or breathe. If she is to attend court or a formal ball, a train may be added, which is a gaudy tail more unwieldy than that possessed by any prize peacock. The weight of this cloth and trimmings adds a further one ton to the cargo the Dainty English Beauty is compelled to carry.

Our prisoner is then handed a fan and exhorted to smile and act naturally.

The true indignity of this torturous device is not, however, found in its construction, but rather in the fact that the mantua-makers did not once consult the makers of doorways or sedan chairs when determining the proportions of their wearable prisons. If the prisoner's family have so impoverished themselves by their purchase of a proper mode of confinement for her that they cannot afford their own coach, she must be stuffed into the nearest chair and sit with her cage folded up around her body like the brilliant wings of some gigantic and demonic bird.

At which point, she is exhorted not to squirm, lest she accidentally crease her ribbons.

It is a great wonder that more ladies of quality do not commit murder upon the unhappy population of dressmakers. And ladies' maids. And chaperones.

I have, for the sake of brevity, neglected to this point to mention that the lady's face is painted over with white and red as thoroughly as that of any New World savage, then powdered with more white and stuck all over with black patches to cover any marks left by inconsiderate Nature. And then . . . But no. I shall stop here. If I am required to discuss at any length the process of being strapped into the powdered and sculpted horrors of the wig, I shall faint quite away.

For the occasion of Lady Clarenda Newbank's birthday party, my particular prison of a mantua was an ice blue damask silk with buttercup yellow bows, white petticoats, and ivory embroidery depicting birds in flight. Last year, it had belonged to Olivia. I was repeatedly assured no one would notice that, especially as it now had several rows of flounces added to accommodate the difference in our heights, and an entirely new color of ribbon for its trimming. I also had my mother's sapphire necklace and her sandalwood fan to call my own, but didn't hold out much hope for my pride in such details. There is nothing so much noticed or so long remembered as a girl's gown, especially by those who are not her friends.

I tried to tell myself that the girls at the party didn't

matter one whit. Sebastian Sandford had never seen this dress before, and I did look well enough. At least, I hoped I did.

Olivia certainly did. She had been imprisoned entirely in shades of pink: dusky rose petticoats, pale pink overskirt and bodice, with deep pink ribbons and silver embroidery. She wore pink tourmalines at her throat and in her wig, and in general, looked stunning.

We arrived together at the party during the fashionable window, that is to say, an hour after the announced time on the invitation. Footmen in the livery of the Earl of Keenesford—Lady Clarenda's father—threw open the doors for us, unleashing a flood of light and music. The butler announced us to a ballroom already well filled with young people in their brightest velvets and silks.

"Lady Trowbridge Preston Pierpont! Miss Olivia Preston Pierpont! Miss Margaret Fitzroy!"

Heads turned. I craned my neck, searching the faces of the young men who stood in clusters about the room. I had not the least idea what my betrothed looked like, but I searched for him all the same.

"Olivia!" Lady Clarenda sailed up to us. I swear, some mantua-maker had designed Lady Clarenda Newbank specifically to go with the current fashion in gowns. She was tall and willowy, with long white arms and long white hands, a slender throat, and no bosom to speak of. While the rest of us fought to breathe against our stays and struggled with swaying hoops, Lady Clarenda glided easily under her cream and gold skirts. "I'm so glad you could come!" She grasped Olivia's hands and kissed her cheeks carefully so nobody's face got mussed. "And Peggy! That's a simply delightful dress. Olivia, didn't you have something a little like it once?"

I returned her my sunniest smile. We'd had other such conversations, Lady Clarenda and I. I reminded myself I shouldn't knock the wig off her head. My betrothed might be here, and first impressions were important.

"Olivia, dear, there was something about which I particularly wanted to ask your opinion. You'll excuse us, won't you, Peggy?" Even as she said this, Lady Clarenda had already threaded her arm through my cousin's to draw her deeper into the heart of the gathering. Olivia had no choice but to go along, which left me there alone, with my skirts blocking the doorway of the ballroom.

I faded sideways and backwards to stand against the nearest wall. Lady Clarenda's mother, Lady Newbank, had decided to use the occasion of her daughter's seventeenth birthday to debut her new ballroom. For months, rumors about the cost of this addition to the London house had been running wild through the drawing rooms, which clearly demonstrates how little there was to talk about in those drawing rooms. It was indeed beautiful, with a dark parquet floor, cool blue walls decorated with plaster garlands, and gilded trim around the painted ceiling. They must have spent a small fortune on candles, and the air was filled with the scents of hot wax and smoke. Four musicians in matching gray coats played a decorous minuet for the line of dancing couples. At the back, French doors opened to show the small night-shrouded garden beyond.

I was still alone. All the young blades and young ladies had turned away to talk to their companions.

I tried in vain to stop my gaze from darting about the room. I counted at least a half dozen youths who were strangers to me. The fashion for young men this year was brightly colored silk coats cut with excessively full skirts at the bottom and yet extraordinarily tight across the shoulders. So tight, in fact, that if any of them did reach for the sword worn at his hip (assuming it could be found among the many folds of the coat), there would be a mighty and instant tearing of seams. Broad cuffs with embroidery or lace, or both, were a requirement. Coat hems, buckled velvet breeches, and silk stockings must be similarly adorned. Wigs were mostly powdered white, with either long or short queues at the back. I did note that Toby Blenham and his crowd had decided, for no earthly reason I could make out, to streak theirs with red and green.

But no youth from Toby Blenham's crowd or any other glanced in my direction. None moved around the dancers or got up from the little tables where youths and young ladies laughed and played at card games like ombre and piquet.

What were you thinking? I snapped open my fan and used it. Despite the open doors, the room was already far too warm. *Did you imagine he'd sweep across the room and take your hand? Perhaps he just should have ridden up to your chair disguised as a highwayman and abducted you.*

A flash of fresh movement caught my eye, and I turned toward it, my heart fluttering like my fan. But it was not my betrothed. Lady Clarenda Newbank had left Olivia behind and was now headed straight for me like a white, gold, and exceedingly peeved galleon. Olivia trailed the charging peeress, a look of uncharacteristic panic on her face.

"Peggy Fitzroy, you sly thing!" Lady Clarenda tapped me on the shoulder with her fan in that friendly way of hers. There'd only be a slight bruise later. "Is it true what I hear? *You*, betrothed to Sebastian Sandford?"

I hid my face behind my own fan to cover the fact that I couldn't muster the appropriate blush. "It hasn't been announced yet." I glowered at Olivia. She waved her fan helplessly back, which I took to mean that Lady Clarenda had already heard.

"You *must* be delighted!" Lady Clarenda said, loud enough to turn all the heads that had up until this moment been ignoring me. "And so *surprised!*"

I dipped my eyes and wished with all my heart that Lady Clarenda would shut her great, painted mouth.

Of course, she did not. "You must, indeed, wonder what Mr. Sandford thought when he heard what *sort* of prize he was getting." She smiled, showing all her perfect teeth. "But I wouldn't worry. I'm sure everyone understands you're only an orphan and not a —" She laid her dainty hand against her lips. "Oh, dear. I've spoken quite out of turn, haven't I?"

My hand was lowering my fan. I couldn't stop it. The

blood rose to my cheeks, but not from any emotion remotely related to maiden's delicate blush.

"*Lud*, Clarenda, have you seen Lucy DeLancy's new hair?" Olivia tried valiantly. "Has she told you—"

Lady Clarenda didn't so much as glance at her. "How thoughtless of me to go repeating baseless rumor!" she went on, just in case someone in that room wasn't yet paying atten-tion. "After all, the whole world knows you were born well before your father deserted your mother."

"The whole world knows it, as you say," I hissed back. "Just as they know your little walk with Lord Gunderson at the Mayday fete was perfectly innocent. Tell me, did you ever find the fan you lost? I heard he looked for it in all sorts of unlikely places."

Olivia was signaling "Don't." Olivia was signaling "Stop." But a terrible recklessness took hold as I watched Clarenda Newbank turn paper white and all her primped and powdered friends gaped wide-eyed at her. "Of course, I'm sure that has nothing to do with why *you've* had no offers yet. Neither could it be because of the walk you took with Jamie Finnmore at the Winstons' garden party last summer. Was it your handkerchief you'd lost that time? Oh, no, I re-call now, it was a ring. The kerchief was when you went walking with Sir Adam—"

Crack! The blow fell hard against my cheek and snapped my head back.

"You little brat!" Lady Clarenda lowered the fan she'd used against me. "How dare you?"

Oddly, I didn't feel anything. Even more oddly, I smiled. "Because everybody already knows what I am, Lady Clarenda. Now they know the same about you."

I wrenched myself and all my skirts around, and marched out the French doors. A sharp, stinging sensation spread across my cheek. At the same time, my hands began to shake. I'd just insulted *Lady* Clarenda Newbank at her own birthday party. If we'd been boys and drawn swords on each other, it could not have been more ruinous. I tottered down the terrace's curving steps to the garden. I was never going to live this down. Never. Barbados? I would need to go to the Antipodes to escape this night.

"Here! With me!" A hand grabbed mine. A young man's hand. He took off at a run and dragged me, stumbling, after him.

Was I being rescued or abducted? I actually didn't much care, so long as he stopped soon and let me *breathe*. My stays were cutting off my air, and the shadows swam past my eyes. "Please . . ." I panted.

The youth responded by dragging me around the corner of a brick and glass outbuilding. I hadn't enough breath left in me to do more than squeak as he started into the narrow space between its wall and the towering hedge. So I did the only other thing I could think of. I brought my fan down hard on his knuckles.

"Ow!" He came to a startled halt and turned to stare at me.

Now that I had a moment to examine him, my abductor

proved to be tall and young. Only a couple of years older than I, to judge by his thin frame and smooth chin. His pale coat was cut tight enough to show lean shoulders and well-made arms. His wig was of the latest style, with a plain ribbon tying its short queue in back, and only one small patch decorated his strong-boned face. But his most arresting feature was his eyes. Even in what dim light reached us from the house, I could see they were shockingly bright blue.

"Sir, you are too forward!" Hoops swaying gracelessly, I retreated, straight into the aforementioned, and very sloppily trimmed, hedge. "And we have not been introduced!"

"I am terribly sorry." My abductor plastered a woebegone look on his face, but his startling blue eyes glittered with suppressed mischief. "I've not made my bow, have I?" He did so right there, with great flourish. "The Honorable Sebastian Sandford, at your service."

CHAPTER FOUR

IN WHICH THE UNEXPECTED MEETING
PROVES TO HAVE SEVERE AND UNFORESEEN
CONSEQUENCES, AND OUR HEROINE
FINDS A PRACTICAL USE FOR HER FAN.

This time, I truly am going to faint. These words formed themselves in a distant and entirely calm part of my mind. At that same time, my body seemed intent on producing a string of embarrassing little hiccoughs as it attempted to draw enough breath to keep me from falling prostrate to the ground and—not incidentally—quite ruining my made-over skirts.

The Honorable Sebastian Sandford folded his arms, crossed one leg over the other, and leaned casually against the greenhouse window. "Do let me know when you've recovered, Miss Fitzroy."

The lazy words proved to have a most extraordinary effect. Knees and hands at once ceased their undignified trembling. Back and body straightened themselves within the cage of my corset.

"I am perfectly well, thank you, Mr. Sandford."

"Not perfectly, if I may say so." Mr. Sandford pulled a lace-edged handkerchief from his sleeve. "You're cut." He smiled as he stepped up to me, put his hand under my chin, and gently began to dab at my smarting cheek.

Whatever indignation I felt was entirely banished by the sudden intrusion of complete bewilderment. Separately, all things made sense. Sebastian's hand under my chin was warm. His eyes were blue. His brow, beneath the line of his tidy wig, was wide and clear. His mouth was inclined to smile. It was the details that threatened to overwhelm: how one corner of his mouth tipped softly upward, how his long, thick lashes curved as he half closed those blue eyes to concentrate on his task. The soft, persistent pattering of the linen against my face. The crook of his strong finger under my chin and the way in which he guided my head to turn slightly to the left so he could minister to another portion of my wounded cheek.

I had fallen madly in love once or twice when younger, so I recognized where this internal disorder sprang from. At least, most of it. Surely, I'd never felt my heart thundering in quite this fashion, or fallen to noticing such tiny details as the freckle at the corner of his jaw or how the shadows traced the sharp line of his chin. The muscle and motion of his throat as he swallowed. All these things combined carried me into a state of near-complete paralysis alternating with the need to shiver.

"No, it will not do." Sebastian stepped back and, as if I

had not enough confusion to contend with, he frowned. "We must have some water. Come on, in here." He grabbed my hand again, this time to lead me the rest of the way around the greenhouse, to its door, which he opened and walked straight through.

There were, of course, a thousand witty and sophisticated protests I could have advanced to this. Probably they should include some fluttering of my own eyelashes, to show he was not the only one in possession of this inexplicably attractive feature. Of course, the protest that actually reached my lips had nothing in common with any of these.

"You'll spoil my makeup."

"I'm afraid Lady Clarenda already saw to that."

The Newbanks' greenhouse seemed a typical example of its kind, with benches along the walls and down the center covered with pots, sacks of soil, and tools of the gardener's trade. It was warm and still. Scents of earth and greenery filled the close air. I could not help but notice how the potted seedlings that stood on shelves in the many windows made an effective curtain between us and any other party guest who might happen to be passing outside.

"We really should be getting back," I murmured. I couldn't hear any sounds at all from the house or the party. The only light came from the moon shining pale above the garden wall.

"Just as soon as we've cleaned you up." Sebastian stripped off his gloves and then dipped his handkerchief in a bucket of water some thoughtful gardener had left on a bench. "I'd rather my betrothed did not enter a ballroom looking as though she'd been in a brawl." He caught my chin again and applied the cold, damp kerchief, but somehow his touch failed to exert the same fascination as previously. "You know, this will go faster if you hold still."

But I didn't want to hold still. It was too quiet here with just Sebastian and myself behind the screening plants in this narrow aisle between the greenhouse workbenches. He was the man to whom I was betrothed. His strong hands, smiling mouth, fair hair, and fine eyes were points very much in his favor, as were the lace handkerchief and the concern he exhibited for my welfare. None of this made up for the fact that after all I had just said about Lady Clarenda going walking with assorted youths under dubious circumstances, here I was, without even a flimsy excuse.

"That's enough. Thank you." I pushed his hand away. The changeability that had taken hold of my mind was as discomforting as anything that had happened yet.

Sebastian sighed and shook out his bedraggled kerchief. "Look here, Miss Fitzroy . . . Margaret . . . I apologize, but I came to the party tonight with the express hope of seeing you." Really, it was most unfair of the moonlight to have settled into his eyes. "And after that scene you played with Lady Clarenda, I found I very much wanted to meet you properly. In private, if I could." His smile was rueful this time. If the shadows hadn't been so thick, would I have seen him blush? "We're betrothed, after all. It can't be wondered at that a man would want some conversation with his bride-to-be."

"I wanted to meet you as well," I said. "And I'm sorry about Lady Clarenda. I promise I don't normally behave so." *Outside my own thoughts,* I added silently.

"Don't be sorry." Sebastian smiled. "I enjoyed it. One doesn't get to meet many girls with spirit on the town."

My fingers, as unsettled as the rest of me, twiddled with my fan, folding it and unfolding it. "Perhaps that's because we're told if we show our spirit, no one will want us."

"Ridiculous." Sebastian laid his bared hand on my glove. "No man seeing you tonight could fail to find you anything but magnificent." His voice was low, and the sincerity of it ran through me like a current of heat. No one had ever called me magnificent, especially not a handsome young man who could capture the moonlight in his eyes.

His hand was under my chin again, lifting it. He was bending down. He was going to kiss me. He was very close now. I could feel his breath against my skin.

My hand acted on its own. It shoved up between us and snapped my fan open. Sebastian pulled back just in time to keep the sandalwood staves from tweaking his nose.

I started to stammer some apology, but it died before it could be fully formed. The change that came over Sebastian's handsome face was as sudden as any alteration my thoughts had undergone. His charming smile vanished, replaced by indignation and something far nastier.

"You've a taste for comedy, Margaret. Well. Such a scene needs two players."

Sebastian twisted my mother's fan clean out of my fingers

and slipped away between the benches while I was still gawking.

I am ashamed to admit it, but I shrieked, "Give that back!"

Sebastian's grin showed his teeth now, and there was nothing of good humor left in it. "Say please." He held my fan high overhead with one long arm, putting it as far out of my reach as the moon.

"I won't! Stop being childish!"

"I'm being childish?" He arched his brows. "You're the one stamping your foot."

If this was an attempt to put me out of my current humor, it failed miserably. "That fan was my mother's, and you will give it back!"

"I'll give it back, but you must pay a forfeit for being so careless with it."

"What forfeit?"

"You know what I want, Margaret Fitzroy. A kiss."

"No. It's not . . . it wouldn't be —"

"Wouldn't be, what? Oh, come, Margaret. Or perhaps I should call you Peggy. That's what my sister Rosamund said your friends call you. Mayn't I be one of those friends?" The words were spoken coaxingly, with the former sweetness creeping back in. But the effect was quite spoiled by the fact that he did not lower my fan a single inch.

"My friends do not steal my things."

"Oh, very well. If not a kiss, then let me hear you say my name. Say 'Please, Sebastian.'"

I did not like this game. I did not like the light in his eyes as he played or how he showed no sign of bringing my mother's fan down closer. Cold disquiet spread within me, but I also realized I'd only make myself ridiculous by jumping up to try for it. I gritted my teeth and tried to console myself with the fact that he had dropped his insistence that I give him a kiss.

"Please, Sebastian."

"There. Was that so very hard?" He smiled his brilliant smile, but this time it failed to set off any tremors in my bosom. He did, however, lower the fan enough for me to snatch away. "You'll find I'm a very easy man to keep in humor." Sebastian moved forward another step. I felt a bench pressing against my back, signaling I was cut off from further retreat, so I slid sideways.

"I'm going back now," I said, I hoped stoutly. "Olivia will be wondering where I've gotten to." Reminding Sebastian I was not friendless felt very important just then.

Impatience flickered across his face. As if to make up for that, he broadened his smile and softened his voice. "There's really no hurry. I'm not some stranger. I'm your betrothed. We can be as private as we choose, and no one will think anything wrong in it."

He moved forward again, sure-footed on the packed earth floor. The greenhouse's warmth had grown oppressive, as had the silence. Newbank house and its crowd of party guests seemed a thousand miles away.

"We may be betrothed, but we are still strangers." I was

fighting for calm. I would not be able to make him see any kind of reason if I gave way to the panic rising in my throat. "I know nothing about you."

"Well, you'll never learn if you keep cringing and mewling. You did say you wanted to meet me, didn't you?"

"This is not what I meant."

"But it is what I mean."

Sebastian lunged forward again. I tried to dodge, but my skirt and hoop caught on the corner of the nearest bench. All at once, Sebastian had hold of my wrists. He was grinning again, and the fresh light in his eyes had nothing at all to do with the moon.

"Now, now, none of that." Sebastian forced my hands down to my sides. "I only want to see more of this vaunted spirit of yours."

He yanked me forward to seize me around the waist and fasten his mouth over mine. It was hot and sickeningly soft, not to mention sloppy wet. His tongue shoved and stabbed at my teeth. In one breath, I was repulsed. In the next, I was horrified. In the third, I did the only thing I could think of.

I bit down. Hard.

It produced a taste of salt and copper, along with a most prodigious oath. Sebastian jerked backward, but he did not let go, and my heart shrank to a tight ball within me. Blood trickled down his chin, making an inky line against his white skin. "You'll learn to mind your manners with me!"

I don't know what he did next, but the world spun, and I was flat on my back, struggling for breath. Sebastian dropped down, trapping my skirts beneath his knees, pinning me under boning and damask. Then he was flat on top of me, his sloppy mouth slipping and sliding over mine. One hand pressed my wrists over my head while the other dug hard between my legs. Panic seized me. I couldn't even roll away because of the ridiculous hoops. And despite all my layers of satin and cambric, Sebastian found what he was looking for, and pinched. I screamed, but that just let his tongue stab into my mouth. I couldn't breathe. Sebastian scrabbled at my skirts. I was going to faint, and if I fainted he'd . . . merciful God . . . if I fainted, he'd . . . he'd—

Sebastian reared back. His Adam's apple bobbed vigorously in his white throat as he laughed. I felt his hot hands and the cold air. I also felt my fan in my fingers. He'd had to let go of one hand to get at my skirts and stuff his fingers between my bare thighs. There was no thought or plan in me, just the elemental force that is sheer desperation.

I jammed my mother's fan straight into the hollow of his throat.

Sebastian made an odd choking noise. At another time, I probably would have found the way his eyes bulged in their sockets most amusing. As it was, all that concerned me was that he had fallen back to the point where I could yank my skirts out from under his knees and scramble away.

"Oh, dear," said a new voice behind us. "Dear, dear, dear."

CHAPTER FIVE

In which there is an uncomfortable escape,
and an extraordinary assertion is made.

I seem to be intruding. It was unintentional, I do assure you. Yes. I do assure you."

A stout man wearing a coat adorned with enough embroidery and lace ruffles for three ordinary gallants bustled into the greenhouse. Without ceasing his stream of apologies, he helped me smoothly to my feet. He turned and held out a plump hand to Sebastian.

"You may take your leave . . . sir," growled Sebastian as he slowly straightened to tower over my stout rescuer, who, despite his high-heeled shoes, was not much taller than I. "You are not wanted here, as you can *clearly* see."

"Oh, no, no, I see, I see plainly." The man waved his gloved hand, fluttering a considerable amount of lace in the process. "I cannot apologize enough. Yes, yes." He had begun to mince backwards from Sebastian. I gulped air. He was going to retreat. He was going to consider this an embarrassing personal matter and, in the finest manner of our English gentlemen, take himself quickly out of sight. I had to get away. I had to find the breath in my body and the strength in my shaking limbs to run.

"But"—the man turned his watery eyes toward me— "are you quite certain I cannot render some assistance?"

I knew what was expected of me. I must avoid a scene. I could not further damage my reputation or Sebastian's pride. Such a thing was unthinkable. And may Heaven help me, part of me wanted this man to go. He might ask questions. He might blame me for luring Sebastian here. He would think I had brought this situation on myself, and he would say as much to whatever acquaintance he had back in the ballroom. Word of my being here, in such a state, would spread.

But I still felt the pain in my wrists and my arms from where Sebastian had pinned me down, and I saw the fury reflected in his blue eyes, and suddenly I did not care what anyone else had to say. I grabbed up my skirts and wrenched them, and myself, around to face the stout, ruffled man.

"Thank you, sir. I find I require an escort back to the house."

"Oh, most certainly. Most certainly. After you, my dear young lady . . . Yes, yes." The man bowed deeply to let me slip through the narrow passage between me and the bench, which had the very welcome effect of putting his bulk between me and Sebastian.

"You are making a mistake . . . sir." My betrothed did far too fine a job of looming over my rescuer and me.

"I think not," replied the gentleman. "I see we are destined to disagree on the subject, but I should be very sorry for it to become a quarrel between us." His voice remained soft, light, and calm. His repetitions had vanished. I also noticed that, despite our cramped quarters, he had raised his ribboned walking stick to make a surprisingly steady line pointing from his hand to the center of Sebastian's chest. This all had the effect of making him look rather less ridiculous than he had a moment ago. This impression was aided by the fact that the hand not occupied with his stick rested on the hilt of his dress sword.

Sebastian also noticed these interesting developments. In fact, he seemed quite immobilized by them. "You're making a mistake, Margaret Fitzroy," said my betrothed.

"Not this time," I answered. "And not again. Not with you."

My retreat would have demonstrated a great deal more dignity if I were not painfully aware that my wig had been knocked crooked. But I didn't slow down, and I didn't look back. I didn't dare. Not even as I heard my rescuer puffing to catch up.

"If I might . . . if you would . . . if you'd care . . . to

follow me." The gentleman gestured to our right, evidently meaning the shadows below the curve of the terrace, where there was a decorative alcove in the wall, complete with tidy marble benches. But I did not want to sit. I wanted to return to the brightly lit harbor of the ballroom.

Except now that danger had passed, I had begun to shake. My hands and feet had gone numb. I gulped air, trying desperately to regain my composure, but it had fled out of reach.

"I'm sorry. I'm sorry," I croaked.

"Not at all, my dear. Not at all. Here. Do sit down." The stout man bustled over to one of the alcove's benches. He drew out a lace handkerchief that had ambitions of becoming a tablecloth and spread it down for me. I sat gratefully. He also sat, at the exact opposite end of the bench. "You've had a shock," he went on. "You will be quite well in a moment. I've seen this before. Oh, yes. You must simply take your time and try to breathe normally." He folded both his heavily ringed hands on his walking stick and assumed an air that indicated he was prepared to wait all night if gallantry required.

Fortunately for my pride, it did not seem quite so much time would be required. As the gentleman predicted, my tremors soon eased and I was able to command body, breath, and voice once more.

"I've not even asked your name so I know to whom I owe my thanks."

He seemed to take a rather long time considering this

statement. "You may call me Mr. Tinderflint," he said finally. "And you, unless I am very much mistaken, are Margaret Preston Fitzroy."

This was the second time tonight I had been identified by someone to whom I had not been introduced. I was beginning to wonder if my particulars had been published in the *Morning Gazetteer*. "Do I . . . have we met?"

"No, no." Moonlight flashed on no fewer than four rings as Mr. Tinderflint waved his hand. "But I will confess I came to this party hoping that you would be here. I wanted to speak with you about a private matter. I blush to admit that when you . . . left the house, I followed with that aim in mind."

What on earth have I done to become so popular with highly questionable personages? My face must have betrayed something of this thought, because Mr. Tinderflint drew back so far, I feared he might fall off our bench.

"Oh, no, no. You mistake me, very much you do. I mean nothing improper. No, indeed. But I did wish to inform you of a . . . a . . . situation that could be very much to your advantage."

"Why would you wish to speak to me at all?"

"Because I was once a friend of your mother's."

The whole world stopped as he spoke these words. In fact, for a long moment it seemed that motion might never return. In all the years since my mother's death, not one relative or friend had come forward. How could it be possible that some complete and very fat stranger would appear tonight of all nights and declare himself her friend?

"You're surprised. Yes." Mr. Tinderflint bobbed his head several times. "Most natural. I'm sure she did not ever speak of me."

"My mother died when I was eight years old, sir. Why would she have spoken to a child of . . . you?"

"Yes, I did hear of her death." Mr. Tinderflint wagged his many chins. "So very, very sad. And I was deeply, yes, most deeply grieved by the news."

"But where did you . . . how . . . Are we related?" I knew I must have relatives somewhere, but none of them had ever made themselves known to me. England was endowed with a startling multiplicity of Fitzroys — that being the surname given to the bastard descendants of kings — without there being any genuine kinship between us.

"I am not aware of any direct relationship," Mr. Tinderflint said. "But, nonetheless, I knew her. She was a brave, intelligent, kindhearted woman, and I always had it in my mind that if I could do her daughter a good turn, I would."

"What sort of turn?" If there was more skepticism than politeness in my inquiry, I beg my reader to show forbearance and remember I had already been subjected to a somewhat trying evening.

Mr. Tinderflint drew himself up a little straighter. "I am in the position of being able to offer you a post in the court of His Majesty, King George."

"I beg your pardon?"

Mr. Tinderflint repeated himself. There in the darkened garden, with bruises forming on my arms and my head still swimming from my abrupt and violent encounter with my betrothed, I could not have imagined anything more fantastical being put in front of me. And yet here it was.

"The situation in this case is . . . complex," Mr. Tinderflint continued. "But the offer, and the post, are genuine, I assure you. I do. And the post comes with a salary. Enough to render a prudent young lady quite independent."

This was too much. My circumstances had traveled from frightening to the shores of madness. I lurched to my feet, and my wig lurched on my head. "You have my thanks, sir, for your previous assistance. I am returning to the house now."

"Of course. Allow me . . ." He reached toward me.

"Touch me, you overdressed pudding, and I will break your hand!"

We both froze, equally startled by the force of my outburst.

"Quite right," Mr. Tinderflint said calmly, placing the hand in question into his coat pocket. "Very proper too, when all circumstances are duly considered. But I do beg you, should those circumstances change, you will at least write to me." He held out a small card. "As a friend of your mother's, you will recall. A good friend. I will just stay here and make sure you return safely to the house. You might perhaps wish to tell your cousin you fell down into the rustic grotto Lady

Newbank most unwisely, most unwisely, has attempted to construct on the shore of her duck pond."

I took the card. I tucked it into my sleeve. I curtsied. He bowed. I turned and walked the length of the terrace wall and started up the broad stairs. All the while, I felt Mr. Tinderflint's mild eyes on me, watching and waiting for me to stumble.

Olivia—thank heavens—was on the terrace when I reached the top step. She plainly did not believe the story about a fall. Nevertheless, I stuck to it with a firmness of purpose that almost set me shaking again. Seeing my resolution, she did eventually go find her mother so we could all return home, where I was immediately put to bed with a hot water bottle on my supposedly turned ankle and a cold compress over my eyes to prevent any possibility of swelling.

Despite my exhaustion, it took a terribly long time to fall asleep. The events of the evening, from Sebastian's rage to the mysterious Mr. Tinderflint's assertions, played themselves over and over in my mind. Was it possible Mr. Tinderflint truly had known my mother? How? And this . . . story about a post at court, what on earth could that be? Surely nothing genuine. To send a girl like me—a poor relation without any title or special breeding—to court was as ridiculous as if he had proposed to outfit me with wings so I could fly across the channel to James the Pretender's court in exile.

What could this Mr. Tinderflint hope to gain by saying such a ridiculous thing?

Which led me back to how he'd helped rescue me from Sebastian and all that my betrothed had been after, which caused a fresh wave of fear to run through me, only to be stopped in its turn by a new barrage of questions.

What if Mr. Tinderflint had been my mother's friend? If the acquaintance was genuine, then surely he knew my father as well. What if . . . what if this Mr. Tinderflint knew where my father—the so thoroughly vanished Jonathan Fitzroy—was?

I suppose I must have fallen asleep eventually, because when I opened my eyes and removed my sodden compress, it was to see fresh daylight sneaking around the curtains. I was not much refreshed, but I did feel steadier in my mind, at least about one thing.

Whatever else had happened last night, I no longer needed to worry about marrying Sebastian Sandford. I had struck him. I had allowed a stranger to interpose himself into our . . . quarrel and to humiliate my betrothed by escorting me away. That, at least, was how the world and Sebastian would see the matter. That he had been attempting to force himself on me would not be taken into consideration. I had broken the rules of appropriate conduct. Therefore, a letter would arrive shortly from Lord Sandford to revoke the marriage contract. My uncle would, of course, be furious. I might even be banished to the cottage in Norwich. But Olivia would coax her mother to have me brought back as soon as she could. I just had to let matters take their natural course.

Norwich might even prove a blessing in disguise. It would remove all possibility of being tempted to find Mr. Tinderflint again. A man who would follow a young, unmarried girl about a party with an impossible proposition could not mean her any good, even if he had known her mother. Even if he might possibly know which corner of the earth her father had taken himself to.

These thoughts formed a comforting buttress against the night's fears, allowing me to bear the ritual of being dressed with patience. The upstairs maid efficiently laced me into a plain yellow morning dress with relatively few petticoats and a relatively loose corset. A cap with a lace ruffle covered my hair, and a cream silk housecoat would keep me from any drafts. A pair of simple earrings and a quick pat of powder, and I could make my way downstairs to the breakfast room. Olivia would already be there, of that I was certain. I'd have to decide how much to tell her. I couldn't face the possibility of actively lying to my dearest friend and cousin. I'd even tucked Mr. Tinderflint's card into my sleeve to show her. But did I need to tell her the whole truth? Yes, yes, I did. I had to tell someone, and Olivia would take my part, even if no one else did.

But I never reached the breakfast room. The maid, Dolcy, was waiting for me at the bottom of the stairs.

"You're wanted in the book room, Miss Fitzroy. At once."

Lord Sandford must have sent his letter shortly after daybreak. My brief betrothal was finished. The movement of the breakfast room door caught my eye, and I saw Olivia peering out, with at least three of the dogs struggling to escape around her skirts. I shook my head at her. It was better to get this over with. I could tell Olivia the whole story in one great lump then. I handed the maid my wrapper and proceeded down the hall to the book room. My uncle would rage and banish me to Norwich. I could bear it, and the sooner it happened, the sooner Olivia would be able to help me come back.

This was how I consoled myself as I knocked on the door. There was a grunt of acknowledgment from the other side, and I entered.

And froze in place, as stunned as if I had been slapped.

Uncle Pierpont was not behind his desk. The great ledger was closed, and the papers were scattered from their usual sturdy piles. My uncle stood at the window, his hands clasped tightly behind his back and his eyes swollen near out of their sockets with rage. Neither was he alone. Another man, dressed in a coat of russet broadcloth, white velvet breeches, and silver-buckled shoes, sat in the chair by the hearth. One gloved hand lay on his knee, and a smile of cold satisfaction rested on his broad, hateful lips.

"Good morning, Miss Fitzroy," said Sebastian Sandford.

CHAPTER SIX

THE WORST HAPPENS.

Fear hit me first, but anger followed fast on its heels. Anger cleared sight and sense and lent me the strength to turn my back and to spit out my next words to my uncle.

"What is he doing here?"

"*He* is waiting for your apology," declared Sebastian from behind me.

"*What?*" I swung around.

Sebastian's smile did not so much as waver. "It was with great reluctance that I felt I had to come speak to your uncle about your shocking behavior." Sebastian gestured languidly toward Uncle Pierpont. "But as you are still young and somewhat untutored in these matters, I am willing to overlook the incident, provided I receive an apology and your promise that you'll never behave in such a fashion again."

As Sebastian spoke, the entire room seemed to take on a scarlet tinge. I remembered each one of his pinches and his sharp-toothed grin as he held me down. The bruises on my wrists and my legs seemed to burn with their own fury. "You'll accept *my* apology, will you? When *you're* the one—"

Sebastian's eyes slid sideways. My uncle was close behind me. I could feel him there as if he were a fire burning at my back. My mouth shut tight. Sebastian settled more deeply into his chair.

"To answer your question, Miss Fitzroy, yes, I will accept your apology. I would be most grieved to have to tell my father, Lord Sanford, that you and I cannot agree."

What he should be doing was thanking Heaven there were no sharp objects near to hand. "You tell him that! Add that you are vile, cruel, and contemptible, and I wouldn't have you if you were the last man on earth!"

"Margaret Preston Fitzroy!" My name cracked over my head.

Shame and rage burned in my blood as I turned to face Uncle Pierpont. I was full ready to speak just as warmly to him, but my uncle wasn't even looking at me. He bowed toward Sebastian.

"Perhaps you'd be so good as to give me a moment in private with my niece, Mr. Sandford?"

"Of course, Sir Oliver." Sebastian stood and brushed past me. He took his time doing it, so I could get a good, long look at his toothy grin.

"Why are you doing this?" I demanded. "What is it you want?"

Sebastian's sly gaze cut into me as surely as if he held a knife, and although he spoke not a word, I understood. He was doing this because I'd dared to fight back. He could have just thrown me over, but what would that gain him? He might never find another bride so helpless, or whose only protectors were so eager to be rid of her. Not one his father was willing to accept, at any rate. Far better to threaten public shame and scandal. Then he'd have me forever, because it was a threat that could be repeated, and no matter what he did to me, the world would take his word over mine, because he was a man and the honorable son of a peer of the realm. I, on the other hand, was nobody at all.

Sebastian bowed, still smirking, and closed the door.

"Not one word, miss," said Uncle Pierpont before I could so much as open my mouth. "You will be silent until I bid you speak."

"Uncle—"

"Silence!" He slammed his open hand against the desktop, making the ledger, and me, jump. "I knew you for an ungrateful, ill-mannered brat. I knew your mother to be both sorry and shameless. I should have realized you would grow to be at the very least her equal."

The words, so bitter and unexpected, knocked me onto my heels as surely as if they'd been blows. "How dare you talk about my mother like that!"

"Because, my fine miss, your mother, my *dearest* sister, was a whore!"

I staggered. My balance was gone. He could not have spoken so. Not even he. No. I had misheard somehow.

But my uncle raised his slitted eyes, and I felt his gaze like a sword's point on my skin. "A whore," he repeated, as if he enjoyed the feel of the word against his clenched teeth. "Your mother dealt in men and illicit liaisons and died of it."

It was impossible. There was no circumstance under which this could be the truth. Except . . . there was Mr. Tinderflint's card in my sleeve. He'd spoken of knowing my mother, this strange, older, obviously well-off man. He said he'd known her well, but not where he knew her from or how they'd met. There was a roaring in my ears, and suddenly I wanted nothing so much as to creep away and hide.

Uncle Pierpont stalked around the corner of his desk until his skinny shadow slanted over me. His breath was oddly cold and smelled of onions and tobacco.

"If it had been up to me, you would have starved in a ditch," he said. "But your aunt, my wife, talked so much of appearances and Christian charity that I agreed to take you in. I've fed and clothed and sheltered you for eight years. I've kept my silence to spare my family's name, but I am done with it. You will take this marriage offer, or you may leave my house this instant and go to the devil, just as your mother did."

I closed my eyes and swallowed; swallowed tears, swallowed denial, swallowed the boundless anger raging through me. I had to be strong. I had to remember what was happening right this moment and what had happened the night before.

"No," I croaked.

"Speak up, miss. I did not hear you."

"I said no, sir." I lifted my chin and drew myself up to my full height. "Mr. Sandford is angry because I fought when he attacked me. Ask how that happened. I will tell you the whole of it. I will not be made into a liar by someone who would permanently shame me, and I most certainly will not marry him."

I'd done it. I'd spoken plainly and with dignity. My uncle, for all his faults, was a clear-eyed man. He would see by my attitude and bearing I told the truth. Then he would realize Sebastian had deliberately set out to defame me. He would not allow a man who so insulted the honor of a blood relation into his family, whatever he might believe about her —my—mother.

There may be a time when I am more profoundly mistaken, but it has not come yet. My uncle crossed the room in two strides. He grabbed my arm and, ignoring my cries, propelled me out the door and down the hall.

"Husband . . ." My aunt came running down the stairs. My uncle did not even break stride. He dragged me past the staircase, past the maid and the footman, who stared in equal confusion as I stumbled and squirmed in my uncle's grip. Olivia stood in the doorway to the breakfast room, open-mouthed. Even the dogs peeking around her skirts were stunned to silence. I was dragged past them as well. And finally, most terribly, past Sebastian Sandford, who stood smiling on the threshold of the blue parlor.

With an oath, my uncle opened the door to the street. He shoved me through. I staggered down three steps before I was able to catch the railing.

The door slammed shut.

"No!" I ran back up the steps, just in time to hear the clatter of locks being closed.

"Uncle! Olivia!" I banged on the door. I rattled the handle, but it was no use. My uncle had kept his word. I was out on the street, with nothing save the clothes on my back.

I had time to gasp only once or twice before the bow window on the second story banged open.

"Peggy!" Olivia leaned her head out, and I hastily backed down the stairs so I could see her better. "Has Father gone mad? Don't worry—"

She got no further. My uncle was beside her. He pulled his daughter inside the house as ruthlessly as he had pushed me out. With a look of contempt, he shut the casement. I watched, my heart in my mouth, as Olivia waved her hands and pointed her fingers at her father, clearly arguing forcibly. Her father didn't move until he recalled that I could see them. Then he reached up to twitch the drapes shut.

I heard the locks turning again. My heart in my mouth, I rushed to the top of the steps. Of course I needn't have feared. Of course Olivia had persuaded her father.

Of course it was Sebastian, whistling, as if pleased with

the outcome of his errand. Our eyes met. He bowed, still whistling, and walked on past me. The door slammed shut before I could so much as move.

I stayed on the stoop for a long time after this, twisting my fingers and trying to keep up hope that Olivia or my aunt would be coming soon to let me back in. The circumstance was so strange, I could not imagine what else might happen. But the time stretched out, and the square began to fill with carts and wheelbarrows and criers and people of all sorts. Not a few of them turned a questioning glance toward the girl standing on the steps before this fine, red brick house. I tried to straighten my cap and smooth my skirts. I tried to look as if nothing was wrong, but it was no good. I was loitering outside, alone, in a plain dress and cap not meant for anyplace but the house. I had no proper business doing such a thing, and even the scissor grinder pushing his barrow could see as much.

It began to dawn on me that the door might not open again. I descended the stairs as slowly as I could manage, just in case I was being too hasty. Perhaps, I thought, if I walked out a ways, I could go to the common green as Olivia and I did so often on fine mornings. It would give the house time to settle. Olivia could find me there and let me know I was allowed back in.

It is strange that when your mind seems completely empty, it simultaneously becomes difficult for any new thought to penetrate. Like the fact that someone was trying to catch my attention.

"Psst! Psst! Oh, for Heaven's sake, miss. Psst!"

"Templeton?" I hurried up to the area railing, where the stairs descended to the kitchen entrance. Olivia's maid stood on tiptoe on the other side, trying to watch me while at the same time looking back over her shoulder toward the kitchen door.

"At last! Here. From the young mistress." She thrust what she carried through the bars and into my hands. There was a leather bag that clinked, indicating coins inside.

"Quick now, miss," Templeton was saying. "You must go away from here before the master sees. Miss Olivia says—"

"Too late, I'm afraid, Templeton," said a gruff voice behind her.

Bromley, my uncle's butler, stepped out of the kitchen. Bromley was a tall, bald man with a sagging face and protruding belly who wore his livery with all the pride of a soldier in his red coat.

"The master has seen," Bromley informed us both sternly. "His orders are that whatever the young mistress sent out is to be retrieved. He further instructs me to say, Miss Fitzroy, that if you don't clear off immediately, I'm to throw you into the gutter."

"You can't do it, Mr. Bromley," said Templeton. I'd never noticed before that Templeton was older than I was, by a good ten years or so. She was grown woman, for all she was small and round-faced. I'd never given her any thought at all, and here she was taking my part in this disaster. "She'll have nowt!"

"You mind your tongue and be thankful there's no talk of turning *you* out." Bromley thrust his broad hand through the railing bars, like a prisoner reaching out of a cell. Or a warden reaching in. "If you please, miss. Templeton's already jeopardized her place. I'll not do the same."

I looked at stout, trusty Templeton and thought about how quickly she could be standing out here on the cobbles beside me.

"Thank you for your pains, Templeton." I handed Olivia's little purse to Bromley. The butler tucked it into his coat pocket, his stony expression softening just a bit.

"You best think on what you've done and repent, Miss Fitzroy. Let the master see you're truly sorry and that you'll be obedient. He might still be ready to settle the matter."

Bromley was right, of course. I must repent. As soon as I did, I'd be allowed to walk back into Uncle Pierpont's house. There, I'd be most generously permitted to marry where I was told and say nothing about anything for the rest of my days.

"Please give my thanks to Miss Olivia, Templeton," I told her slowly. "For all she has done."

I turned my back on the servants, the area railing, the house, and all it held, and walked away.

CHAPTER SEVEN

IN WHICH CERTAIN TRUTHS OF A SHOCKING
NATURE ARE REVEALED.

It took a long time to find a sedan chair willing to carry me to the address on Mr. Tinderflint's card. I had no money and could offer only a feeble promise that they would be paid upon my safely reaching my destination. Evidently the chair men who plied London's busy streets had heard such prom-ises before. I had to place my Belgian lace handkerchief and no fewer than six silver hairpins in pawn with the lead man before I was allowed to take my seat and be bumped and jostled through crowds and over cobbles in the direction, I assumed, of Mr. Tinderflint's house.

This was not where I wanted to go. Very far from it. My circle of acquaintances in town was small, and among them only the tiniest number might be ready, much less able, to take me in as I stood. But Kitty Shaw was in the country helping her sister with her lying-in. Honoria Dumont was sick with measles, and Liza Frank was accompanying her bilious aunt to Bath to take the waters. That left the address on the card and Mr. Tinderflint's vague and worrying declaration of an acquaintance with my mother.

My uncle's accusations would not leave me. All during that terrible, jolting ride through crowded streets filled with the stink and riot of London, not to mention the ankle-deep spring mud, I sat in dread of where I might be going, and what I might find when I got there.

As it transpired, what I found was an entirely respectable square of new terraced houses, part of the endless building and bettering happening at the western edge of restlessly expanding London Town. I also found rain and plenty of it. This turned the unfinished square to a mire and drew from my chair men some truly novel imprecations. Several of these were directed at me when I asked the lead man to knock at the door of the house and ascertain if Mr. Tinderflint was at home. I had no idea what I'd do if he wasn't, but I'd had enough of huddling on doorsteps for one day.

I craned my neck out the window and saw that the door was answered by a man in a black coat, who stared at the chair man, blank-faced. The chair man gestured and jerked his thumb at me with increasing energy. My heart shriveled. It had been some deception. I'd been given a false address for some reason. Or the chair man had brought me to the wrong house, or—

But Mr. Tinderflint's head poked around the black-clad man's shoulder and ducked back just as quickly. A moment later, my man squelched his way back to the chair, which was slowly settling up to its rails in the mud.

"She's to be delivered round back," he growled. "An' he better be payin' for it." The accompanying threat he uttered was physically impossible and unfit for publication.

The back garden was a square of sparse, limp grass with a threadbare lime tree doing its best to keep up appearances. The chair man wouldn't hear of my getting out into the rain, at least not until Mr. Tinderflint had laid several coins into his hand. Then he all but tipped me from the chair before he and his companion squelched away.

"Come in, my dear, come in, come in." Mr. Tinderflint bowed several times as I ducked into the doorway. "Just this way. Quickly now."

He repeated this admonition several times while ushering me through the surprisingly deserted kitchen, along a dim corridor, and into a sparsely furnished parlor. There was a fire in the shining grate, and the few furnishings were as new as the house. So were the thick green curtains, which Mr. Tinderflint immediately drew shut, plunging the chamber into a gloom my imagination at once labeled "forbidding." The young housemaid who sat in the chimney corner, quietly busy with some piece of mending, was some comfort, but not much.

"Do sit, please, Miss Fitzroy. I'm so delighted you've come." Mr. Tinderflint stooped to light a fresh candle from the fireplace. "Yes, yes. Delighted."

Between the candle and the fire, I finally was able to get a good look at Mr. Tinderflint. My impression from the previous night that he was simply stout and overdressed was proving somewhat mistaken. It is not often in life that one encounters an entirely spherical individual, but Mr. Tinderflint was apparently striving to achieve that perfection of form. This was greatly assisted by the fact that he was so short. His face was as round as his figure and covered with a solid layer of paint and powder. The equally well-powdered curls of a full-bottomed wig cascaded across his shoulders. His coat, waistcoat, and shirt were obscured by masses of braid, lace, buttons, and ribbons of all colors. Black velvet breeches and white silk stockings gleamed above high-heeled, gilt-buckled shoes. That such a very round man could balance so lightly on such stilts was impressive.

I did sit as I was bidden, taking care to rearrange my skirts so I had a moment to think. As I'd traveled here, my mind had been occupied by what I might do if I was turned away from the door or if I found myself facing some sort of ill-favored house. Now that I was in an entirely unremarkable parlor, I was at a loss to know how to speak with this man.

"You said, last night," I began. "You said . . . you . . . knew my mother?"

"I had the honor, yes," said Mr. Tinderflint. "You see, Miss Fitzroy, your mother, Margaret Fitzroy, nee Margaret

Hollingswood, was a correspondent of mine. During some of the uncertainty and, dare I say it, the unpleasantness that preceded the ascension of our current sovereign, King George, she kept me informed of those events in which we both took an interest and that might be of use to certain others of our, my, acquaintance."

It took me a long moment to untangle this statement, and when I did, what I saw caused my breath to come up short.

"You're talking about the succession," I said slowly. "About the rebellion in '08." In that year, the Jacobite rebels had declared that James Stuart was supposed to get the throne, instead of King George. Said and were still saying. In fact, in Scotland they had spent much of the previous winter up in arms over the dispute until the troops marshaled by our new king had put them down.

Understanding fell into place. Understanding pulled me up straight and brought out my next words in a most unbecoming shout.

"You—you're saying my mother was a *spy!*"

CHAPTER EIGHT

In which Our Heroine finds herself faced
with a most fateful decision.

"Shhh! My dear, a bit lower, if you please," cautioned
Mr. Tinderflint, even though the maid in her corner had not
so much as glanced at us. "I would not call her a spy, no, no,
no."

"Then what would you call her?" Considering that I'd
been dreading he would tell me he'd been what is politely
known as my mother's protector, I should have been relieved
to hear she'd merely engaged in political intrigue. That, however, was not my first reaction.

"A woman of letters with whom I corresponded," he
replied. "A woman of unimpeachable character, strong loyalties, and great learning, with whom one could share an ex-
change of views."

"And news?"

"Just so." Mr. Tinderflint got to his feet. "I understand that you have questions, many questions, but there is someone I must fetch before we go further. It would be best if you thought of him as my partner. Yes. Yes. Now, rest yourself and . . . when my partner arrives, my dear, it is not at all necessary to mention your mother." Mr. Tinderflint attempted to wink at me, but all he managed was a nervous twitch of one eye before he bustled out, leaving me alone with the maid.

I sat still, clutching my hands together and trying to make some sense of what I had just been told.

History taught us that in the life of Great Britain, there had been many points when the succession to the throne was in dispute. Compared to the Wars of the Roses or the great Civil War, the transition from Queen Anne of the House of Stuart to King George of the House of Hanover was scarcely worth mentioning. Nor was it surprising that there should have been some dispute. After all, King James II had had a legitimate son. Admittedly, James II had been dethroned years ago by the nobles of Britain, with the help of his daughters, Mary and Anne. But he had been king, and he had had a son, and that son, James Edward Stuart, was alive. When Queen Anne died without a living child to her name, it might have been readily assumed that James Stuart would be recalled to ascend the throne as James III.

Yet there remained the tiny matter of religion. Officially, England is a Protestant nation. Queen Anne was a Protestant queen. James Stuart remained stubbornly Roman Catholic.

So, the queen and lords were forced by various carefully written laws to find some Protestant relative to take the throne. The nearest such person was George Louis of Hanover, now King George of Great Britain.

That was meant to be the last word upon the subject. But James Stuart, now called the Pretender, was not prepared to let the matter rest. He'd tried to forcibly change the succession decision in '08 and again just last winter. Naturally, where there is rebellion, there are spies. And a spy, one supposed, should be such a person as could pass easily in a variety of company without being suspected. A pleasant, witty lady of good birth, for instance.

Could it possibly be true that the mother who had sung me to sleep and taught me my letters and taken me on walks was a *spy*? It would explain what my uncle saw that caused him to say my mother was "going about with men." She was gathering information. It was exciting. It was dramatic. It was also ridiculous beyond imagining, because it meant that the beribboned, fluttery figure who had just left the room was himself a spy, possibly even a spy master.

What would such a man want with *me*?

I looked to the maid, still busy at her mending.

"Have you worked here long?" I asked. She did not even raise her head. I repeated my question. This time she did glance up. She also smiled and shrugged and returned to her needle and thread.

So much for gaining information from the servant. I took a deep breath. I looked toward the door and the window. If I meant to flee, now was the time. But where would I go? And how? I had no cloak to keep off the rain I could hear drumming against the windowpanes and no money to pay my way. I could pawn my pins and kerchief again, and my earrings, and my ribbons, but there was a limit to how far what I wore on my back would take me.

As fleeing did not seem the most practical option yet, I settled for lifting the poker off its stand and laying it on the floor behind my heels so my skirts would hide it from immediate view. The maid did not once look up from her needlework, and I began to wonder whether she was deaf or just well practiced at not noticing what the masters of the house did. Neither possibility made me feel any easier.

The door opened again. I rose reflexively as Mr. Tinderflint entered, followed by two much thinner, much more soberly dressed persons.

"My dear miss, my very dear Miss Margaret Fitzroy . . . allow me to present my partner, Mr. Peele. And this is Mrs. Abbott."

Mr. Peele had evidently taken the view that as his friend wore enough ornamentation for the entire district, he need not trouble himself with any at all. His coat and breeches were unrelieved black velvet, and his shirt a plain and perfect white. The only colors about him anywhere were the silver buckles on his shoes and knees and the startling scarlet ribbon tying the short queue of his wig. Mr. Peele's eyes were dark and deeply shadowed by his overhanging brow. His general build was an angular one with a square jaw, square shoulders, and sharp elbows. By way of contrast, his hands were long, narrow, and immaculately kept.

Mrs. Abbott was taller than either of the men, though not by much. She also seemed to feel that severity was in order on this day. Her black dress was so plain, and her white cap tied so tightly under her chin, all I could think was that she was either a highly proper upper servant, or an adherent to some strict Calvinist sect. Her hair, what showed of it from under the sharp edge of her starched cap, was iron gray streaked with black. Although her face was deeply lined and its skin drawn tight, one could see that she had been a beauty. Her eyes stood out large and bright above her cheekbones, but they were red-rimmed and deeply shadowed, as if she had not slept in far too long. I wondered if that accounted for the measure of anger and distaste which seasoned the way in which she looked down her long nose at me.

Mr. Peele folded his immaculate hands behind his back and began walking around me in a circle, as if I was but recently come on the market and he did not quite trust the seller.

My heart tried to squeeze itself far enough to hide behind my spine.

"Parlez-vous français?" inquired Mr. Peele. Do you speak French?

"Sprechen sie Deutsch?" added Mr. Tinderflint. Do you speak German?

"And Latin," I told them both, in that most ancient language. The last thing I had expected to feel today was gratitude toward Uncle Pierpont. But my uncle had a particular distaste for "empty-headed females," so Olivia had been educated with a rigor my aunt feared would spoil her looks. While not an official pupil, I'd sat in at her lessons, where I turned out to be hopeless at drawing and composition, but much better at mathematics and languages. For good measure, and perhaps to hide my nerves, I switched over to the tongue of the Athenians: "But the tutor of my cousin says my Greek requires much work."

Mr. Peele raised his heavy eyebrows toward Mr. Tinderflint, and the two men shared a look full of Meaning and Import. He said nothing, however, and merely resumed his thoughtful orbiting and ogling of my person.

"Perhaps you wish to inspect my soundness of wind?" I muttered. "I can produce a certificate swearing my teeth are my own."

To my surprise, Mr. Peele let out a bark of laughter. "Very good, miss!"

"Yes, very good, very good!" Mr. Tinderflint clapped his hands. "And her appearance, you see, Peele, is quite perfect."

"Yes, and who will look for her?" Mrs. Abbott still had not moved from the doorway. Her voice was taut around a heavy French accent. "She is clearly of quality. When she disappears, who comes asking questions?"

Disappears? My body stiffened, and I nudged my heel back against the poker. If I swung for Mr. Peele first, I could probably catch Mr. Tinderflint second. But that left Mrs.

Abbott blocking the door. Perhaps I ought to try smashing the window first? Oh, why wasn't Olivia here? She'd seen more dramas than I had. She'd know what to do.

"Well, Miss Fitzroy?" Mr. Peele smiled as if he enjoyed my discomfort. "It is an excellent question."

But it was Mr. Tinderflint who answered. "Surely Miss Fitzroy deserves to hear the proposition in full first. Then she can provide whatever additional information we might require."

Mr. Peele shrugged, as if it was of no matter to him, but Mrs. Abbott responded with a stream of French so rapid I caught only one word in three. Mr. Tinderflint stood his ground at this sudden Gallic bombardment with admirable, and wholly unexpected, courage.

"She is exactly the one we need," he answered, also in French. "Exactly."

It was very clear Mrs. Abbott did not agree. The look she leveled against Messrs. Tinderflint and Peele would have done murder even without a poker's assistance. Mr. Peele responded by walking her out into the dim hallway, where they stood whispering and casting glances through the doorway in my direction. I felt suddenly quite cold, despite the pleasant fire flickering in its tidy hearth.

Mr. Tinderflint sidled up to me and opened his mouth.

"Sir," I said, "if you intend to tell me she is not as bad as she seems—"

"Oh, no, oh, no. She is at least that bad," replied Mr.

Tinderflint. "I wished only to ask if you'd care to take a little wine to refresh you after your trying day?"

"Yes, thank you."

He said a few words I didn't understand to the servant girl, who laid by her needlework, curtsied, and hurried out.

"Dutch," he said when he saw my surprise. "All servants here are Dutch. No English among 'em. No English at all."

"Very well, Mr. Peele." From the hallway, Mrs. Abbott raised her voice. "But only for my lady's sake. You understand me?"

"You've made your point, Mrs. Abbott," replied Mr. Peele firmly. "As I have made mine."

Mrs. Abbott gave him another withering glower, turned her back, and stalked away.

Mr. Tinderflint let out a gusty sigh, and I realized he'd been holding his breath. "Oh, do let us sit. Yes, my good Peele, sit, sit." He availed himself of one of the room's arm-chairs while Mr. Peele took the other. I lowered myself slowly back onto my own seat.

"Now, Miss Fitzroy," said Mr. Peele, "you will forgive me for being blunt, but our time is short, and our business urgent. My colleague and I have been searching for a young woman of good breeding to take on our most exceptional com-mission. She must be in possession of wit, sense, nerve, and complete discretion." He dipped his chin to better look out at me from under that great shelf of a brow. "Would you be willing to produce a certificate swearing to these attributes?"

"That would depend," I answered.

"On what?"

"On who was asking and to what use they intended to put . . . my attributes. Mr. Tinderflint said something about a post . . . ?"

Mr. Tinderflint fluffed the lace at his throat nervously. "As maid of honor to Her Royal Highness Caroline, Princess of Wales."

There was a long moment of silence. I took Mr. Tinderflint's words into my mind and turned them over, trying in vain to fit them into a narrative that bore any semblance to objective reality.

"I understand how mad it sounds," said Mr. Peele. "This whole business has involved far more madness than any of us could have foreseen. I will be as plain as I can. Last year, Mr. Tinderflint's ward, Lady Francesca Wallingham, was named one of the maids of honor to Caroline, our new Princess of Wales. But Lady Francesca was struck by sudden illness while she was visiting home and died of the fever." Mr. Tinderflint shook his head slowly, his round eyes having turned quite moist. "It is our intent that you should take up the post in her stead," Mr. Peele continued.

"Because the Princess of Wales's prerogative no longer extends to choosing her own maids?" I inquired with a mildness that surprised even me.

Mr. Tinderflint adjusted the angle of several buttons on his left sleeve. "We do not mean for anyone to know you are a replacement, no, no." He switched his attention to the right sleeve. "You will assume the name as well as the place. You will become, yes, become, Lady Francesca."

Become Lady Francesca. They had brought me to this house to ask me to assume the place of someone I'd never met, in a station to which I was untrained and unsuited. I looked from one man to the other. Neither betrayed any hint of being other than perfectly serious.

Heaven help me, I had gone down into London and come up in Bedlam.

"And when I've stormed the palace in the guise of Lady Francesca, what then?" I inquired. "Shall I marry King George and become Queen of England? Or just bring Pretender James back from over the water to take his father's throne?"

"Oh, you mustn't joke about *that*, Miss Fitzroy, you mustn't." Mr. Tinderflint fluttered his lace and looked about as if I might be hiding a Jacobite behind my skirts rather than a fireplace implement.

Mr. Peele waved one long, white hand, dismissing us both. "All that will be required of you is that you smile and charm, wait on Her Royal Highness, and generally be an ornament to the court. You're pretty enough; the rest should follow with practice. For this service, you will be granted by the Crown a salary of two hundred pounds sterling per annum, which you will turn over to your beloved guardian." Mr. Peele nodded to Mr. Tinderflint, who bowed nervously from his seat.

I smoothed my skirts and tried not to look as if I was searching for additional weaponry. "What you intend is that I risk my neck by committing a patent fraud against the King of England, for which you are to reap the reward?"

Mr. Peele's patient smile took on an edge, as if he had honed it against some mental whetstone. "A maid of honor is a person of influence. She has the ear of her royal mistress. She is regularly in the company of important ministers, the Prince of Wales, and even the king, when he's not gallivanting off to Hanover." Mr. Tinderflint winced at this. Mr. Peele ignored him. "Such a person is much flattered. Gifts come into her hands from all quarters: clothes, jewels, money. Sometimes the value of these gifts amounts to much more than her salary, especially if she is clever and witty. Such gifts would be entirely yours. Mr. Tinderflint would receive only the salary."

Mr. Tinderflint fluttered again.

"Why?" I addressed myself to Mr. Peele, as he was clearly the more efficient speaker of the two.

The edge of Mr. Peele's smile was refined several degrees further. "Mr. Tinderflint finds himself in . . . delicate circumstances, from which Lady Francesca's position—and her salary—would have given him relief. Without her . . ." Mr. Peele waved his so very eloquent hand, indicating we need not say anything further on that score.

Disappointment dug oddly deep. Mr. Tinderflint had lured me here with mention of my mother and a post at court simply for money. Perhaps I should have guessed. Many a

gentleman in our troubled times found himself with a distressing shortage of funds and had to make shift to supply the
lack. Make shift or flee the country.

I could only assume it was Mr. Peele that Mr. Tinderflint owed. With those soft, unmarked hands, Mr. Peele
could easily be a financier. Or possibly a tailor. Given Mr.
Tinderflint's evident passion for lace and ribbons, he could
have amassed a substantial debt to London's various stitching
men.

I covered my mouth, because I was coming dangerously close to hysterical laughter. I had to remain serious.
The scheme was mad. It was also dangerous, and the threat
to my neck quite real. Our Hanoverian-born sovereign lord,
George, by Grace of God King of Great Britain and Ireland,
was not reported to have much sense of humor. Or any at all.
I could not picture an ordinary man—let alone a king—taking kindly to discovering a fraudulent upstart in his home.
But how could I refuse? The way back from this house led to
repentance, obedience, and Sebastian Sandford.

It occurred to me that I might have a third option. I
could play the game just long enough to find out what Mr.
Tinderflint knew about my parents or any surviving family.
Then, once Kitty Shaw came back to town or Honoria Dumont recovered from her measles, I could flee. I'd already gotten away once. I could do it again.

True, it might not be easy to discover information about
my friends while I lived under an assumed name in a strange

house, but that was a problem that could be solved in its own time.

Perhaps it appears I tripped rather lightly across this marsh. The truth of the matter is, I could not think about my situation too deeply. Otherwise, what remained of my senses would sink into sheer terror. I had to hold tightly to the belief that I could escape as soon as I truly tried.

"Very well, Mr. Peele," I said. "Mr. Tinderflint. I accept."

CHAPTER NINE

IN WHICH MANY SORTS OF LESSONS
ARE LEARNED, CONSEQUENCES INTENDED
AND UNINTENDED ARE FACED, AND REALITY
COMES UNCOMFORTABLY CLOSE.

Thus began my time as lady-in-training. Had I any conception of what lay before me, I would have used that poker and made my escape, rain or no rain.

I cannot in honesty say my situation in the house was cruel. I had an airy and well-appointed chamber, a comfortable bed, and the use of all Lady Francesca's clothing and jewels, which were as plentiful as one might expect for a girl who had lived at court. What I did not have was even a modicum of freedom.

Had I found my time in my uncle Pierpont's house dull and confining? Oh, the follies of youth! That life was a whirlwind of social gaiety compared to the one I now led. There, I had Olivia as friend, my aunt as a silly but affectionate chaperone. I had but one master, and him I saw only on select occasions. Now I had no friends at all and a total of three taskmasters, who seemed determined not to leave me a moment to myself.

Mrs. Abbot was my mistress of the robes. Not that she dressed me—oh, no. She had a whole infantry of little Dutch maids for that. Mrs. Abbott quizzed me. I must memorize all aspects of a lady's dress: all fabrics, all trimmings, all furbelows and gewgaws, and all their gradations. I must be able to identify the difference between Egyptian cotton and Irish linen on sight. I must be able to tell which lace was Belgian and which Parisian. Nor was it simply clothing. It was cosmetics, the styles of patch, jewel, and fan, and all the ways hair might be dressed and wigged. I knew some of this, of course, but the extent of all I was now expected to recognize was bewildering.

When my head was dull and aching from this delightful tutelage, I was permitted the luxury of a midmorning snack: cold ham and lobster salad, perhaps, or oyster pie and spring greens accompanied by small beer or a light wine. Then it was Mr. Tinderflint's turn. He was my master of dancing and deportment. As a woman of the court, I must move with perfect poise and grace, and without disturbing a false hair on my wigged head. "The true lady treats the whole world as her dance floor," he said, and being Mr. Tinderflint, he said it two and three times. "Concealment is her highest art. You are an ornament to the company. Such a decoration must show only decorum. A misstep would be disastrous. Disastrous."

Which remark invariably made me stumble.

But Mr. Tinderflint was not only a master of deport-ment. Despite his mild eyes and stuttering speech, he proved to have a prodigious memory. He could recall without effort the names, ranks, and genealogy of all the members of court. I must learn precedence, politics, alliances and enmities, and I must demonstrate what I knew in conversation, usually while being led through the steps of yet another variation of the minuet.

After I'd worn myself out by dancing and deporting, I was given a sumptuous nuncheon, served by Mrs. Abbott's infantry and supervised by Mr. Tinderflint so that I would not neglect the intricacies of soup spoons and fish forks. I had been taught all my life that ladies ate sparingly in public, but Mr. Tinderflint evidently had not received this bit of news. Nothing would do but that I taste everything presented to me and come back for seconds, until I felt my stomach press tight against my stays, which, I suspected, were being let out little by little. During these meals, in addition to prac-ticing my skills with the entire range of superfluous cutlery, I must practice all my languages in conversation, including the Latin and the Greek, where Mr. Tinderflint matched me eas-ily enough to set me wondering about the true depths of this round, overdecorated man. But my attempts to draw him out failed. He had nothing to say about himself, let alone about my mother or my father.

"I understand, my dear, I do," he twittered. "And one day we will have a good talk. For now, we must focus on the task at hand. It would not do for you to get your stories confused, it would not."

After this, Mr. Tinderflint launched again into the life and history of me, that is, Lady Francesca.

Lady Francesca was born in Dover, daughter of Francis Wallingham, second Duke of Kingsbroke, and the Countess Sophia Frederica von Hausen, a Hanoverian born lady. "Which makes your ability to speak German so very fortunate, my dear," he told me cozily. "So fortunate!"

I did confess I had never been to Dover, which might have been a mistake, because for three solid weeks after that, I was permitted to read nothing but descriptions of Dover, its famed cliffs, its principal towns, its imports and exports, all of which were added to my quizzes, in three languages.

I was further informed that Francesca's parents and her only surviving brother had all died of the smallpox when it had swept through London three summers ago. It was her mother's last act to write to Princess Caroline. The von Hausens had apparently known the princess's family back in Hanover, and Countess Sophia had begged that her daughter, Francesca, be given some post at court when King George came to take possession of the kingdom.

"Also terribly fortuitous for us, you see. Francesca was — you were — raised in England. Prior to her arrival in '14, Princess Caroline never actually met Fr—you. Her Royal Highness, therefore, will not be overly familiar with the tiny details of your past life."

"But I was at court," I argued. It had ceased to feel odd to talk of my alternate past this way, and I found that disquieting in and of itself. "I formed friendships, shared intimacies. They'll notice when I contradict myself."

"But you've been ill. Deeply ill. Severely ill," Mr. Tinderflint reminded me, in French, which was the court language, so we used it frequently. "Such long and serious illness disorders one's memories. Besides . . ." He paused here, and I thought I saw something underneath Mr. Tinderflint, a hint of something hard and unforgiving. "No one at court remembers anything for long. Unless it be to disgrace an enemy. Then they never forget."

This tidbit dropped so cold and serious from him that I started and my napkin slid from my lap. I bent to retrieve it, but a waiting member of the Dutch infantry was there before my fingers touched the linen.

"*Merci*," I murmured on reflex.

"*De rie —*" she began, but clamped her lips shut tight around the end of the word and backed swiftly away.

I dropped my gaze, to cover my fresh surprise. Mr. Tinderflint had already turned the conversation back to names, genealogies, and politics. He'd missed it, but I'd marked her. The middle-sized girl with the spotty chin and unruly reddish hair under her cap had understood my French, and she had returned to her place, pretending nothing had happened. There was a chink in the fence erected by the firm of Tinderflint, Peele, and Abbott.

After nuncheon, it was on to what was rapidly becoming

my least favorite activity. I must sit down and play Mr. Peele at cards.

"Cards are the chief activity of the ladies of the royal household, including Her Royal Highness," that gentleman explained to me. "They play deep, and they play constantly. If you cannot match them there, all the rest of this practice is for naught."

And so it was cards, for hours upon end: lottery, basset, piquet, cribbage, and particularly and dreadfully, ombre. This last, my tutor assured me, was the game most favored by the denizens of the court. I must learn all its variations: two-handed, three-handed, four, and five. For these last, Mrs. Abbott was drafted to join the game. I may say without fear of contradiction that the only thing worse than being quizzed by Mrs. Abbott was sitting across the card table from her. She was a grim and terrible player, and she hated to lose. My stays, earrings, and ribbons all got tighter if I had the nerve to take even a single trick.

On Sundays, I was allowed some measure of rest. There were no card games, at least. I could sit in my room and read. Mr. Tinderflint provided a selection of newspapers and gossip sheets, and even some new plays and poems. Without these, I would have perished from a dread surfeit of boredom and loneliness, because one thing I was not permitted to do was leave the house. I could not even walk in the kitchen garden. Lady Francesca was supposed to be in the country recuperating from her fever. She could not be so much as glimpsed at the window, so the curtains were always kept drawn in my rooms. I had begged Mr. Tinderflint to let me send a note to my cousin to let her know I was safe and well, but he only shook his head and repeated how much he understood, but their plan required strict secrecy, yes, strict.

I missed Olivia cruelly. I wanted to tell her what was happening to me. I wanted to hear what she made of it all, especially Mrs. Abbott, who dressed and acted like an upper servant, but who addressed the men who should have been her employers as equals, if not inferiors. Or her opinion on the fact that my room, which I was told belonged to the original Lady Francesca, bore no trace of her personal existence, excepting a workbasket so tidy I could not believe it was much used.

Now my chance to communicate with Olivia had appeared in the form of the redheaded maid, and it was on a Sunday that I was able to seize that chance.

I'd finished my breakfast and conversation with Mr. Tinderflint, and the gentleman had excused himself to go about his business. Outside, the church bells rang across the city, each calling to the other, reminding the faithful it was time to pray. I seldom enjoyed church. It was too stuffy in the summer, freezing cold in the winter, and endlessly dull, no matter what the season. Now I missed it, because it would have meant a change of scene and new faces about me. I sighed and tried to find something in my stack of papers and books that I had not read a dozen times.

Then there was a knock. The door opened, and there she

was, my red-haired, linguistically talented maid. She bobbed a curtsy and scuttled over to the hearth, wielding a dust rag to polish the mantel and its ornaments.

I watched her. It was a good thing her back was turned at that moment, or she might have gotten the impression I wished to devour her whole, possibly with mustard.

I gathered my French together and whispered, "What is your name?"

The maid hesitated the tiniest amount and then began rubbing the mantel with renewed energy.

"Keep about your work," I went on, softly, so softly. I focused my eyes on the door the whole time. I strained my ears for the scrape of a bolt or the tread of a foot. "I will make no disturbance. I ask only a favor. I leave a letter on the table. I beg that it be taken to the direction written there. That is all. To any person who does this thing, I will be most grateful." I had been permitted to retain the earrings I'd worn the day I came, and I'd kept them ready against this moment. I drew them out now and laid them on the table with the letter I'd composed to Olivia. Then I sat down in my chair by the hearth and held up the *Female Tattler* gossip sheet in front of my face. I heard the girl rustling and shuffling about the room. I did not lower the paper. I heard her breath wheezing in her nose and the sound of ornaments being slid back and forth on the mantel. I crumpled the pages as I tried to keep my hands from lowering so much as one corner of my paper. I heard the door open and shut. The gossip sheet fell from my bloodless fingers.

The letter was gone. So were the earrings. I closed my eyes and whispered a prayer of thanks. It was a slender thread, and I knew it. It was very possible that my nameless maid might pocket the jewelry and throw the letter away. But there was a chance now. That letter might just reach Olivia. If anyone could work out how to get word back to me with news of friends who could take me in, it was my cousin.

CHAPTER TEN

The great day arrives,
and brings a reprieve.

After this, my confinement rested easier on me. I had something of my own to look forward to now, something that belonged to Peggy Fitzroy, not Lady Francesca. More important, however, I had found a way around the firm of Tinderflint, Peele, and Abbott. I was not locked absolutely into this very strange prison.

There remained, of course, the possibility I might be found out, and I did not forget this. I watched the Messrs. and the Abbott so closely for signs and portents that I fumbled my forks and forgot the alliances of the Walpoles and the Cowpers, and who still reported to the venomous Duchess of Marlborough, making Mr. Tinderflint cough and repeat himself more than usual.

All that watchfulness produced an unexpected revelation. I was sitting at the card table with Mr. Peele that
Wednesday, suffering through yet another round of ombre,
when I saw something new. Something in the way his dexterous fingers held the pack and dealt the cards.

"You cheated!"

To those of you who live in more virtuous climes where
the tyranny of the card pack is unknown, let me explain that
a charge of cheating is most serious. Between gentlemen, it is
in fact casus belli, and might result in having to face swords
or pistols at an inconveniently early hour. I was expecting at
least a shout of denial.

But this was Mr. Peele I addressed, and he simply pursed
his pale lips. "I? Cheat?"

"Yes! You pulled this"—I brandished the offending five
of clubs at him—"from the bottom of the pack!"

"Well, well, my lady." Mr. Peele plucked the card from
my fingers and slipped it back among the others as he began
to shuffle the cards again. "You finally saw it."

I goggled. I gaped like a fish. Mr. Peele gathered up the
cards I'd let fall and shuffled them into the pack as well.

"You . . . you've been cheating me all this while?"

"Sometimes. Sometimes not." He cut the cards and cut
them again. "I told you, these games are deadly earnest. People
do cheat. They cheat to gain money and advantage, and they
will not be deterred because you are a female or bear a title.
You need to know who cheats, and when it is happening, and

how to adjust your own play to your advantage. That, my lady, is the real game."

He spoke of more than the truth of cards, and I knew it. There was a whole world beneath those words waiting for me to look more closely. "It is in fact so important that I will be expecting regular reports from you while you are in the princess's train." He paused here, laying the pack in front of him and signing that I should cut the cards. "You will write to me about your games and the company you keep at the tables, most particularly about who is playing with whom, and for how much, and how honestly."

I meant to ask him why. Of all the strange commands I had received so far, a requirement that I deliver a recitation of card games seemed very strange indeed.

But any potential remark on my part was interrupted by the door opening, and the Abbott sailing into the room.

"If you please, sir," said Mrs. Abbott, who did not curtsy to anyone, ever. "I would like a word. Now."

"You've had many words in the past weeks, Mrs. Abbott." Mr. Peele collected the cards and began shuffling them yet again. "What might this one be?"

Mrs. Abbott reached into her apron pocket. She laid my letter on the table. Mr. Peele's hands stilled.

"Against express orders," Mrs. Abbott said. "Against all reason, *she* wrote this letter and bribed a maid to have it delivered."

Carefully, Mr. Peele set the pack down so its edges

aligned exactly square with the table. With equal care, he picked up my letter and read the direction. "How did you find this out, Mrs. Abbott?"

"Anneke was arguing with a porter over the cost of delivery. It seems she understands rather more French than she admitted to."

I fell as far back in my chair as my corset would allow. I must be cursed. It was the only explanation. Only a lady cursed could find the one maid in the whole of London town who did not know how to effectively sneak around her employer.

"I have dismissed her," Mrs. Abbott was saying.

"I wish you had not." Mr. Peele turned my letter over in his long fingers.

Mrs. Abbott was not to be distracted, however. "Do you still believe this plan can move forward? That this girl can be in the least trusted?"

"Well, mademoiselle?" Mr. Peele lifted his gaze to me. "Mrs. Abbott says you cannot be trusted. What is your answer?"

I was ready to strangle on my own breath. I'd been afraid of getting caught, but I hadn't concocted any lie to cover my actions. That was not just a mistake, it was an error of gargantuan proportions. My mother surely never was so careless in her intrigues. Here I was the spy's daughter, and I could not smuggle out a simple letter. What would she say when I joined her in Heaven? I might not have to wonder long, because judging from the way Mr. Peele leveled his slitted gaze at me, he meant to accomplish that reunion sooner rather than later.

"It is a letter to my cousin." Speaking the truth had to be better than being caught in hasty lie. "I wished to let her know I am safe. As I could not send it openly, I tried other means."

"Very reasonable, of course. The sort of action I feel I should expect from you." Mr. Peele broke open the letter and scanned it. "And just as you say. To your cousin, and you are safe and well, and will write when you can. By the same messenger, I presume?" He lifted one brow.

"Evidently not." I kept my voice even and my eyes on Mrs. Abbott. Her lip quivered in its most dangerous fashion, holding some tirade in check. Mr. Peele, on the other hand, refolded my letter and sat back, tapping the edge of the paper against his hand.

"We had an agreement, my lady. You have violated it."

"As I told you she would," announced the Abbott.

"As Mrs. Abbott did indeed prophesy you would." Mr. Peele inclined his head.

"It was a letter to my cousin," I told them both once more. "You see for yourself it had no return direction or other information in it."

"That is not the point, my lady. The point is whether you can be trusted. Whether you will obey." Mr. Peele kept his dark gaze on me and slowly tore my letter in half. "Because if you will not obey, you are of no use to me. You become, in fact, a risk." His subtle, beautiful fingers tore the letter again and again. "And I will not tolerate a risk."

The door opened then. "Peele . . ." Mr. Tinderflint bus-tled in. When he saw our tableau, he drew his protruding stomach in tight, as if a blow had been aimed at it. "Peele, there's been a message. From the palace. It's time, Peele." He was looking at the paper scraps on the table as he spoke, waiting to be told what had happened here.

I waited for Mr. Peele to say there'd been a letter from this house too, or an attempt at one. I waited for him to order me packed out into the street once more. I had thrown away my only chance—however strange and strained—at life and livelihood, and with it, the chance of learning some truth of my parents, especially my slandered mother.

But Mr. Peele simply reached out to take the new mis-sive from Mr. Tinderflint. He read it carefully and slowly, which did nothing for my composure.

"It would seem that His Majesty King George will be leaving to visit Hanover in less than a month." Mr. Peele looked over the edge of the paper at me. "It is Her Royal Highness's express wish that Lady Francesca join the court in its summer residence at Hampton Court Palace in time to see His Majesty safely on his journey." Mr. Peele paused. "That does not leave us enough time to locate or tutor an acceptable substitute. It seems we need you, my lady."

Hope swelled in me. If I was needed, I had some power. I might be able to make some negotiation.

Mr. Peele's lips twitched. "You are painfully obvious, my girl. Do not be tiresome and attempt to make use of our necessity. You have already disappeared without anyone bothering to search for you." He paused to be certain I compassed the full import of these words. "Perhaps you think that kind Mr. Tinderflint will save you before we reach any extreme?" Mr. Peele said. "Tell her, Tinderflint."

Mr. Tinderflint fluttered and fidgeted, obviously trying to divine what had occurred before he entered the room. "I'm so sorry," he stammered. "Truly. Necessity, circumstance could impel, yes, impel us all to regrettable measures . . ." The words trailed off miserably.

"Take her to her room, Mrs. Abbott," said Mr. Peele. That good lady drew herself up to her full height, but Mr. Peele raised his hand. "I must confer with Mr. Tinderflint. I will speak with you afterward."

And that, it seemed, was that. Mrs. Abbott followed me up to my pleasant, airy chamber and waited while I walked inside. With the feeling of having nothing left to lose, I turned to face her.

"Why do you detest me, Mrs. Abbott? What have I done to you?"

For a moment, Mrs. Abbott stood stone still. I was sure she was going to berate me in her colorful French, as she had so many times before. Instead, she reached beneath the collar of her black dress and brought out a miniature on a gold chain. She held it out, and hesitantly, I stepped forward to look. The miniature was an oval of ivory bearing the delicately rendered portrait of a dark-haired girl. She was a beauty, with round cheeks and an artful smile, posed so she seemed to be just turning to greet the viewer. There was only one person this could be. And it was true—she and I could have been related. Our dark eyes and the color of our skin were quite close. Her hair had been arranged in long curls to lie across one shoulder, and it was at least as black as mine. Her brows were arched, as if she were questioning . . . something. It was a lively expression, maybe even a little mischievous. Lady Francesca knew something, and she might just tell.

But I was not the only person she resembled. I stared at Mrs. Abbott, taking in afresh that woman's large, dark eyes and the shape of her face, which still showed the beauty she had once been. Mrs. Abbott said not one word but slipped the miniature back in its hiding place, and closed the door between us.

Why hadn't I guessed it? Mrs. Abbott's devotion to her former mistress had shown itself to me in a thousand ways as she constantly compared me to her, and always un-favorably. Why hadn't I seen that she was Lady Francesca's mother? Aside from the fact that Mr. Tinderflint had told me Lady Francesca's entire family was dead of the smallpox, of course.

My breath came short enough to set my head spinning. I'd thought Mr. Tinderflint at least was my friend, but he'd just refused to defend me to Mr. Peele. Now I found he had lied to me about Francesca's mother. So how could I believe what he said about mine? What other lies had he told?

I still couldn't breathe. I needed air. I must open the window, whether my jailers permitted it or not. I crossed to the window and grasped the edges of the curtains. I glanced over my shoulder. The door remained shut. I clutched the velvet tighter, ready to draw it aside.

The velvet crinkled sharply.

I stopped. I fingered the fabric once more. Once more, it crinkled, with a sound like dry leaves. Or paper.

I looked to the door. It was still closed. I brought the curtain up close to my face and ran my fingers across it until I discerned the faint edges of a rectangle. Something had been sewn inside. Something the size and shape of a letter.

The door was going to open at any minute. I was sure of it. The Abbott and Peele were going to mince me up for pies. I ran to Francesca's workbasket and fished out her delicate scissors. The door was going to open right now. It would open this second, while I was very, very carefully snipping the stitches between the curtain lining and the velvet. The only thing in the room louder than the ticking of the clock was the banging of my heart. I eased two fingers into the hole I'd made until their tips touched the rough edge of a piece of paper.

I held my breath and drew the paper out. It had been folded flat like a letter but had no seal or ribbon, let alone any direction written on it. I opened the folds as quickly as

I dared and angled it toward the thin strip of sunlight that showed between the curtains.

It was not a letter, but a drawing: a lively pencil sketch. There were men in loose cloth draperies and a winged woman in a classical Grecian gown standing amid a landscape of fluffy clouds. Below them, a similarly dressed couple lay on a rocky outcropping with ocean waves crashing into it. Some cherubs had been thrown in among the clouds for good measure. A frame of flowers and curlicues surrounded the entire picture, graced by two oval medallions. One medallion held a woman's face, the other a man's.

The door stayed shut. I squinted at the sketch, trying to make the faces out clearly, but they were strangers to me. What I did see was two tiny letters written in the bottom corner of the sketch—FW.

Francesca Wallingham. My predecessor and double had drawn this, and someone—Francesca herself, probably—had hidden it. Who was she afraid would find it? The threatening Mr. Peele? Or the false Mr. Tinderflint? I squinted harder, trying to make out more details, but those details stubbornly refused to add to my understanding. It remained a classical grouping of old gods and a goddess, pointing and declaiming, with a mortal couple down on the rocky earth. The portraits in their medallions smiled enigmatically.

I did not want more mystery. I had trouble and to spare. The urge to throw the paper into the fire took strong hold, but I resisted. This sketch, whatever its meaning, seemed to be the only artifact Francesca had left in this so-very-tidy room. It just might assist me in finding out who the firm of Tinderflint, Peele, and Abbott were, and what they were truly doing.

In fact, as I turned back toward my room, I was already wondering if there might be others.

CHAPTER ELEVEN

THE GRAND MASQUERADE BEGINS.

It was decided I should arrive at Hampton Court by water. Mr. Tinderflint hired a river taxi to take me and himself up the colorful and crowded highway that is the Thames. The day was beautiful, with the summer sun so bright it struck sparks even from the Thames's dull and fragrant waters. I had to remain shaded by the small black and silver boat's greasy canopy to avoid the possibility of browning my features. As our two oarsmen steered us deftly around the wide river bend, the sunset lit Hampton Court's square towers, white crenellations, and infinite number of windows with scarlet and gold fire.

And I was so terrified, I could not enjoy any of it. There was no way on earth I could do this. No matter what reassurances Mr. Tinderflint offered, I knew all was doomed to failure. It didn't matter that Mrs. Abbott was already at the palace, unpacking my truly astounding array of boxes and trunks. Neither did it matter that I'd been able to fashion a hiding place for the three mysterious sketches I had unearthed in my previous room. No one could succeed in such a deception. I would be found out the moment I set foot onshore.

I reminded myself of my resolve and my daring plans for the future a hundred times over. With each repetition, I added to my determination to discover the truth of these circumstances in which I had placed myself. These private recitations, however, always ended with me looking over the taxi's low gunwale and wondering how far I could swim before the weight of my clothes dragged me under.

"What could be worth all this?" I murmured.

"You mustn't talk to yourself so, really you mustn't," said Mr. Tinderflint from his seat beside me. "You never know who might be listening."

"I meant . . . I was just —"

"I know, my dear." My pretended guardian patted my hand. "I do know."

I wished the knot in my throat had not eased at this small gesture. I did not want to like this fussy, spherical man. Since his display of subordination to Mr. Peele, I strove to marshal as much ire toward him as toward Peele and the Abbott. But of them all, Mr. Tinderflint was the only one who remained kind to me, and I could not help but take comfort in that kindness.

"Now, there are a few details to take care of before we

arrive. Just a few, I assure you." Mr. Tinderflint pulled a leather purse from an inner pocket of his heavily embroidered coat and handed it to me. "Some pin money for you. Also, you should know, when we are in company, you may hear people referring to me as Lord Tierney."

"Lord Tierney? You're . . . you're . . . a m'lord?"

He shrugged and fluttered at my outburst and entirely failed to address it. "One day I'll tell you the full tale that brought us here. But today . . . today we brazen it out."

"We?" I asked with a feigned casual air as I looped the purse strings around my wrist. The contents were heavy and clinked. Whatever else he might be, this man was not a mean soul.

"Oh, yes, we. Very much we. For if you are caught in your masquerade, how long do you think I will remain at liberty, hmm?" Mr. Tinderflint's head wagged heavily. "No, no, no, we are in this together, you and I, my dear. We must be bold. Timidity will yield us nothing."

"And what of Mrs. Abbott? Is she in this with us?" Mr. Tinderflint nodded. "And Mr. Peele?"

"Never underestimate Mr. Peele," Mr. Tinderflint murmured. "He is as committed to his ends as the rest of us." This last he spoke to the passing riverbank, and I could not help but notice the choice of words: Mr. Tinderflint said "his ends." Not "our ends." I wished I had not noticed, because in doing so, I threw away any comfort I might have otherwise derived from those words.

Mr. Kersey's *New English Dictionary* assures us that the word *palace* means "a king's court or prince's mansion." I would at this time like to say his definition does nothing to adequately prepare one for the first sight of such a place. Hampton Court was not a mere mansion. It was a city's worth of red-brick buildings crammed together around three great courtyards and sequestered behind a county's worth of park, meadow, forest, and garden.

The yard we entered was as lively and bustling as any London street at midday. Richly dressed persons in silk and velvet and every other appurtenance of wealth milled about the cobbles. Some got out of chairs, and others from coaches. They rubbed shoulders with servants in livery and workmen out of it. Grooms led horses about; boys with bare feet cleaned up after them. Women and girls in starched caps with their strings fluttering huffed and puffed in every direction from dozens of doorways. Some carried wood and water; others, bundles and baskets, or even babies. Guards in scarlet and blue uniforms leaned on their pole arms and looked on this great crowd with mild interest. Distant music underscored the babble of voices, human and animal, and the air was filled with an incredible odor distilled from smoke, hot kitchen, perfumed parlor, and horse.

"Steady, steady now, my dear," murmured Mr. Tinderflint as if I had turned into a horse myself. "Almost there. You'll be allowed a rest as soon as—"

"*Fran!*"

The voice cut across the echoing noise of the cobbled

yard. The next thing I knew, a dainty girl running at top speed plowed into me, knocking me back against the nearest passing footman, who muttered several rude words and pushed us both away.

"Oh, Fran!" cried the girl again. "Oh, I'm so glad to see you! Let me look at you!" She stood at arm's length, the better to suit deed to word. "So thin! So pale! Everyone will quite envy the change! Oh, dear. I probably shouldn't say such a thing, as you've been so ill, but it only goes to show it's truly an ill wind that blows no one any good. Goodness, is that a pun? I must remember it for the drawing room. I am so glad you're back! It's been unendingly dull since you've been gone. Even Mary's said so. But now we're the Sparkling Three again!" Another embrace punctuated this realization. For the first time in my life, I felt glad of my stays. Without them, my ribs surely would have given way. "But how you stare, Fran! You've forgotten poor little Molly, quite, I'm sure."

"No, no, of course not, Molly. How could I ever?" I felt Mr. Tinderflint fluttering beside me, and I managed a smile. This dainty, exuberant person must be Molly Lepell, one of Lady Francesca's—one of my—sister maids of honor. The scandal sheets considered Molly to be the prettiest of the maids and reported that the court had given her the pet name "the Schatz," meaning "the treasure" in German. "It's just, it's been a long journey . . ." I went on feebly.

"And you're tired, of course." Molly tucked her arm into mine and dragged me close. It was fortunate she had such a small stature. If she'd been of a more sturdy build, she'd have done someone an injury years ago. "I'm taking you straight up to your room. You should know I took charge of the whole situation personally as soon as your maid arrived." Her voice dropped—"Merciful heavens, Fran, where did you acquire that dragon?"—and rose again before I could improvise any answer. "Everything has been laid out *just* as you like it. You'll excuse us, won't you, sir?"

I expected Mr. Tinderflint to protest at my abrupt removal. In fact, I hoped he would. But instead, he sketched as grand a bow as his round form could support, which earned him a giggle and a toss of the head from the sparkling Molly "Treasure" Lepell.

Molly dragged me effortlessly up the nearest staircase and through a bewildering array of gilt and painted galleries and chambers. Fewer than half of them were lit, so we were constantly plunging from light to shadow to light again, and none seemed to be heated at all, which was just as well, because between my fear and Molly's speed, I had already begun perspiring in a most unladylike manner.

The brief flashes of light, however, did give me a chance to gain a clearer impression of my fellow maid. She certainly was a beauty. It was difficult to tell whether that beauty was natural or cultivated, which I suppose is part of the point. As we weren't in the sort of company where women must don their wigs, I could see she had rich, dark hair. She also had a white neck that many swans, or at least Lady Clarenda Newbank, would envy. Her heart-shaped face was ornamented with a tiny pointed nose, tiny pointed chin, and a cupid's bow of a mouth, which was emphasized with a single heart-shaped patch on the left side. Her brows had been plucked down to narrow lines, and her eyes were exceptionally large and lustrous in that tiny, pointed face. So much so, in fact, that it was actually difficult to discern their true color. Probably most of her figure was provided by her corset and hoops, but as such, it was very much the fashionable form and size.

After an indeterminate number of rooms had flashed past, Molly finally broke stride and threw open a door.

"There!" she announced as she propelled me inside. "Have I not done a fine job?"

Living in a palace was clearly not going to be an altogether unpleasant experience. The chamber Molly ushered me into was narrow and, I suppose, by the standards of a palace, small. Yet it still held a canopied bed hung with sky blue velvet. The walls were painted a midnight blue to contrast with the bed curtains, and the ceiling had been painted to represent a perfect summer's day, provided that day had a flock of pudgy pink and peach cherubs in the middle of it. In addition to the fire in the fireplace and the armchair beside it, there was a sofa and several tables and a footstool. A silver carriage clock took pride of place on the mantel among the porcelain ornaments. One side door led to what I assumed must be the maid's chamber. Another opened onto the closet with its chests and dressers and vanity table, and all the dresses already hung out for airing and brushing.

I was looking for something quite different, and to my immense relief, I soon saw it. My wicker workbasket sat serenely next to the armchair. I'd concealed the sketches I'd discovered in Francesca's other room inside. I itched to have a moment to myself, so I could make sure they'd arrived safely. But it was not just Molly Lepell who was a bar to this activity. Mrs. Abbott stood beside the fireplace, not a full yard from my precious basket, her eyes modestly and most uncharacteristically downcast. As Molly dragged me farther inside, the Abbott dipped a minute curtsy. Which was terribly thoughtless of her, because this additional shock came close to sending me into a dead faint.

"Thank you, Abbott," said Molly in an offhand manner that sent a bolt of fear through me. "Are the refreshments ready?"

"I was just going to see to them, miss," Mrs. Abbott murmured in a soft, humble tone I would never have suspected her capable of. But as she turned to leave, from beneath her lowered lashes, I caught the deadly glitter that I knew all too well. The world righted itself, and I could breathe again.

Molly shut the door firmly behind Mrs. Abbott and dragged me to sit next to her on the sofa.

"Now, quickly," she said in a voice more serious than the breathless, girlish one she'd used in the courtyard, "tell me how you left things with Sophy."

"Sophy?" I repeated, mostly to give myself time to remember that Sophy must be Sophy Howe, one of the two remaining maids of honor, along with Mary Bellenden. "I . . . really, Molly, there's nothing to tell."

"Fran, this is no joking matter. When it was announced

you were returning to court, she almost fainted. I overheard her later . . ." I would not have believed that heart-shaped face could take such a serious cast as Molly shook her pretty head at me.

"She's . . . still very angry, then?" I ventured.

"Angry? Sophy's fortunate it was I who overheard her, and not Her Royal Highness, because I don't think either one of them would have survived the scorching from her language. So tell me, what happened? Was it over Robert?"

Robert? *Robert*? I ran my mind down the long list of names I had been forced to memorize over the past weeks, searching for the most likely Robert.

Fortunately for me, Molly misinterpreted my hesitation and rolled her eyes. "Honestly, Fran, did you think I didn't know? Don't worry. I've said nothing . . ."

Surely, I have at some time done good with my life, for it pleased Heaven at that moment to open the door and send in an angel in the unexpected form of Mrs. Abbott. Behind her trailed a new procession, this one of footmen in an array of sizes bearing an array of covered dishes.

"Hush. Not now," I said urgently to Molly.

Molly looked mulish but gave a small nod as Mrs. Abbott directed her followers to spread the cloth and lay a table. The dishes proved to contain a lovely dinner of boiled fowl, pease pudding, and two tarts (one of onion and one of plum), as well as a gooseberry fool and a fine golden cheese.

"Well, you'd best eat that, and I'll tell you all the news." With these words, Molly launched into a speech that was a marvel of endurance. The girl seemed to have no need for breath as long as she had words to fill her. Names I recognized from Mr. Tinderflint's lectures galloped past at such breakneck speed that I soon gave up trying to keep pace. Instead, I concentrated on nodding at reasonable intervals and taking enough small bites of whatever was set in front of me to keep Molly from saying "reallyyoumusteatsomethingFran" every few minutes.

Mrs. Abbott had apparently attempted to wait for Molly to take a breath, but after a full hour, gave it up as a bad job and simply interposed herself into the flood of words.

"If you please, miss. My lady must be got ready to attend Her Royal Highness."

"Oh! Yes, of course. I'm such a ninny. I'll see you there, Fran. It's so wonderful to have you back again!"

I readied myself for another alarming hug, but this time received nothing more than a bracing kiss on the cheek before Molly dashed from the room.

When the latch snapped firmly shut, I let myself fall back on the sofa. "I survived," I whispered.

"One foolish girl," replied Mrs. Abbott in her usual encouraging manner. "On your feet."

"Yes, but we . . . they . . . were good friends," I said weakly as I stood and followed her into the dressing room. "Surely if she's convinced, then others will be."

"Pah!" This was followed by a string of French deprecations and a great deal of pulling and tugging at my person while I was stripped of my traveling clothes. "It is plain that

Mademoiselle the Treasure cannot see an inch beyond her own so-adorable nose."

I contemplated these words as I assumed my dressing position; stock-still, with arms out to the sides. Was it possible Mrs. Abbott missed the intelligence that remained steady in Molly's eye, despite the rapid shifts of her manner? It was clear from the way Molly spoke that the Abbott was not a well-known figure here. Could she be as new to the palace as I was, and gaining her first impressions alongside mine? Or was she trying to make me doubt myself? I came back again to the idea that Mrs. Abbott did not merely believe that I would fail — she might actually be hoping for that event and doing what she could to urge it along.

What, I wondered, as she yanked back my hair to ready it for my wig, would the Messrs. T and P think of that?

~~~~~~◆~~~~~~

CHAPTER TWELVE

IN WHICH OUR HEROINE MEETS SEVERAL PERSONS
OF AN AUGUST OR MYSTERIOUS NATURE.

It took an hour to complete the process, but eventually I was successfully stuffed into the full plumage of Lady Francesca's best mantua: a pink watered-silk overdress with the ruffled petticoat of cream Brussels lace and Prussian blue trimmings. A split train of pink figured damask trailed behind me. If I had been laced any more tightly, I would have dropped dead of asphyxiation. As it was, I believe the only thing that kept me standing was a desire to rob Mrs. Abbott of the satisfaction of watching me expire.

My fan was more creamy Belgian lace with gilded staves, and my silk gloves had been embroidered over with lilies of the valley, which probably signaled something important or provocative. I couldn't think what, my mind being fully occupied with preventing my hands from clawing at my itching face. Mrs. Abbott had painted my visage into a pure white mask livened only by pink paint to indicate where my cheeks ought to be and adorned with no fewer than three stiff black patches: a diamond at the corner of my eye, a heart on my right cheek, and a circle by the left corner of my mouth. I suppose I should have been thankful that Mrs. Abbott preferred white talc rather than the mix of white lead and rice powder Olivia's mother considered the most estimable cosmetic for young ladies, because in the quantities my attendant lavished on me, I think it would have pulled the skin clean off my face.

I was about to present myself to royalty, and I felt like a cross between a piece of lady's china and a high street mountebank. My hands were shaking yet again. I clenched every muscle tight against my bones to stop the tremors. I could do this. I must do this.

All this while, the Abbott circled me slowly, searching for a flaw or signs of weakness. Much to my surprise, she nodded.

"*C'est bon.*" Did I see the tiniest glimmer of approval in her eyes? I dismissed that as a figment of my terrified imagination. "Her Royal Highness is expecting you in her private apartments. You know the way, of course?"

"Of course." The words were still warm on my breath when I regretted them, but I could not take them back any more than I could fail to sense the blade of Mrs. Abbott's smile as I attempted to sail past her out the door.

She closed that door behind me, and I was alone in the gallery.

Did I mention that palaces are poorly lit places? Or that they are cold? It was the height of summer outside, but as I moved, my skin prickled with goose bumps. Where had all the people gone? Hampton Court had seemed full to bursting with life and motion when I entered it. Now I walked through shadowed galleries without encountering a soul to keep me company or, more important, point the way to the princess's private apartment. I struggled to call up the floor plans of Hampton Court that Mr. Tinderflint had so diligently tutored me in. Why, oh, why had I spent so much time wishing to be elsewhere when I should have been committing every line and notation of that map to memory?

In the midst of these bitter reflections, I heard a new sound, a ferocious and suppressed hissing and grunting, like someone cursing through clenched teeth. I froze in place, my heart hammering, but only until I heard a violent ripping, as if someone was tearing cloth. Visions of Sebastian's attack in the greenhouse propelled me to action. I snatched up the poker from the hearth that stood nearby. I meant to charge forward, but swaying hoops and suffocating stays permitted only a quick waddle.

Despite this, I rounded the corner into the darkened chamber, brandishing my weapon before me. Ahead, I could just make out a man's form wrestling with something unseen. Suppressed curses and groans sounded in the cool, still palace air.

"Stop!" I shouted.

Somewhat to my surprise, the shadow did stop. Buoyed by this success, I ventured a further utterance. "What are you doing?"

Slowly, the shadow turned. I stood my ground, lace fan in one hand, poker in the other. As my eyes adjusted to that deeper darkness, I saw the shadow was a young man. He wore a plain linen smock covered with stains in a variety of shades and thicknesses. Crumpled lumps of paper lay scattered all about him. Both his hands clutched yet more paper that he had plainly been in the act of tearing in half. He stared at me. I stared back. Understanding came late and reluctantly to my fevered mind and, I realized, to his.

The shadow bowed. In return, I curtsied. He looked down at the scattered, ruined papers. I looked at those same papers. I nudged one with the tip of my poker.

"I do not believe they present any further threat," I said.

"I would tend to agree." The shadow had a light, cultured voice, although the burr of the north country hung about the *r*'s and *e*'s. Something in it made me want to see him more clearly, but I stayed where I was.

"Perhaps they were not quite so dangerous as originally supposed?" I suggested.

"There you are wrong, mademoiselle," the shadow replied gravely. "They were far worse. Veritable demons from the seventh circle."

"Then you have saved us all. I thank you, sir." I curtsied once more.

"It was the least I could do." The shadow bowed with becoming modesty. Our eyes met, and I thought I saw that shadow smile. A blush crept up my throat, and I became acutely conscious of the poker. I am not proud of what I did next, but in the interests of laying down a faithful memoir, I will report: I hid it behind my skirts and scooted backwards.

"Wait," said the shadow. "If I might . . . perhaps escort mademoiselle to her destination? The streets are not safe at this time of night."

"Demons?" I suggested.

"Just so." He aimed a swift kick at the nearest paper lump. "And that for your impudence, sirrah!"

I laughed. Now that he had come closer, I was able to gain a clearer impression of this young blade. He was tall. I'm far from petite, but my eyes were only level with his chin. That chin, I can report, had a cleft in it that lent a jaunty air to a face that might otherwise have been too sharp and lean. The stains on his smock appeared to be paint, and more stains covered his hands and wrists. Several locks of his unpowdered hair had escaped his queue, and there was just enough light for me to see they were a dramatic dark copper color. I could not make out the shade of his eyes, and I realized this disappointed me. That realization, in its turn, brought on the rapid and most unwelcome return of my blush, and I wished I had some way to retreat without trip-ping over my train.

"But we've not been introduced," I said, my voice oddly tight.

"A thousand apologies. Matthew Reade, at your service." He bowed again.

"M—" I caught myself just in time. "Lady Francesca Wallingham."

"*Lady Francesca?*" Matthew Reade stiffened. "Ah. Yes. I should have seen. Well, Lady Francesca, if you're prepared to bear a shabby cavalier company, where might he escort you?"

"To Her Royal Highness, my good cavalier," I said loftily. "Before the miscreants recover themselves." I jabbed my poker at a crumpled page.

"Then if I may?" He took the poker. He wasn't wearing gloves, and his fingertips brushed mine. A thrill ran up my arm, only to collide with memory. I'd been touched like this before in the dark. By Sebastian. I didn't know whether to laugh or curse. What a wonderful thing a fan is. I snapped it open and peeked over the edge of that most welcome shield. Mr. Reade, oblivious to the warring impressions he had set off in me, shouldered the poker like a musket, positioned himself in front of me, and set off at the march.

I picked up the nearest lump of paper and tucked it hastily into my décolletage before I followed.

Matthew Reade moved more slowly than Molly Lepell but still had a good stride, as a man who has never had to contend with stays and light-soled slippers will. Still, he navigated the chambers and galleries with certainty, and I was grateful to follow his lead, even though I struggled to keep up. At last he turned us down a broad flight of stairs and descended to the first landing. There he stopped and bowed yet again. "Your door, my lady."

The corridor below was brightly lit from sconces and chandeliers that flickered in the drafts and lent the illusion of motion to the many paintings decorating the red walls. A pair of carved and gilded doors was flanked by two footmen, one of whom had his eyes rigidly fixed ahead of him, and the other of whom was staring directly up at me in a way that made me want to pat my wig to make sure it was on straight.

Instead, I curtsied to Matthew Reade. "I thank you, sir." Feeling greatly daring, I added, "I hope we may meet again. Perhaps without the demons?"

Mr. Reade took longer to answer than was strictly comfortable, as if he were considering whether to answer at all. "I will look forward to it, my lady," he said at last, in a tone of utter neutrality. He took my hand and bowed over it, turned, and vanished up the stairs.

I faced the doors below and snapped open my fan. It was time. I would either succeed now, or I would fail. I wished there were some third option, but none occurred to me in the all too brief time it took me to descend the remaining stairs.

The portly footman on the left cleared his throat, reminding his compatriot they were on duty. How the right-hand man could have forgotten, I don't know, because his eyes were fixed on my approach. The footman on the right was twenty years or so younger than the one on the left, much trimmer, and might have been handsome if his face hadn't been so pale and sickly-looking at that moment. Together, this mismatched pair heaved open the gilded doors. Light and heat rolled over me, and I stood blinking like a mooncalf in the flood.

This was no simple chamber such as I was accustomed to. The apartment of a princess was a vast series of rooms leading one into the other. Every light blazed. Every surface glittered. And now I knew what had happened to all the people I had seen previously. The entire population of Hampton Court was crammed into these rooms. The myriad shimmering colors of coats and mantuas made it look as if a rainbow had met some terrible accident and been scattered across the room. Some pieces of it stood in knots or sprawled in armchairs. Other bits sat at small tables, cards in hand. Others clustered around a table decorated with an array of bottles and decanters, while still others helped themselves to dainties heaped upon little round tables.

And as the doors opened, every wigged and powdered head of that rainbow gathering turned toward me.

Mr. Tinderflint stood at the edge of the silken mob, near the vast fireplace. He was a splendid orb of emerald green and sapphire blue all done up with chartreuse and silver stitchery. He excused himself from his companions and began to edge his way through the crowd. Before he could reach me, however, one of the young women at the nearest card table turned her head, slowly and ostentatiously late, to stare at me. As if to make up for lost time, she now made a great show of looking long and hard, from my wig down to my ruffled hemline and back up again.

"Well. Look what the wind blew in," she said. "Roughly, and from a distant country."

That great room full of people began to laugh. Mr. Tinderflint froze in place, startled and trapped. Nor was he the only one. It would not be too much to say that if there'd been a parapet to hand, I would have gladly hurled myself off it. But absent any convenient cliff, I found my sustaining strength. It came not from Mr. Tinderflint's advice, but from surviving Lady Clarenda's parties. This time I was not simple Peggy Fitzroy, poor relation. I was Lady Francesca, if you please. I had rank and money, and I could sweep into that room with the finest of them, having been severely drilled in the art of the sweep, and look that card-playing wit in her bright green eyes.

"And I can't tell you how very dull it was in the country," I said, fluttering my fan and pitching my voice to be overheard. "Not one word of pleasant conversation to be had, either. How very kind of you to make me feel at home once again." I smiled and bent to kiss her cheek and took a risk. "Hello, Sophy." I saw by her tight little smile I'd guessed correctly. As I straightened, I also glanced down at her cards, which I could see perfectly from this angle. Then I shook my head and murmured to her partner, "Oh, dear. Are you sure you should wager *that* much?"

A trail of soft chuckles followed me as I walked on, and I felt the painted cherubs overhead sing choruses of triumph. Mr. Tinderflint finally edged himself free of the crowd to offer me his arm.

"Well played, well played," he breathed as he laid his gloved hand on mine. "Now for it. The princess is waving you over."

My mouth, which had been dry before, was now positively desertlike. But Mr. Tinderflint's grip on my hand did not allow for retreat. We crossed through the crowd. It took a long time, and I gained an appreciation for the grand scale on which Her Royal Highness lived and entertained. We passed thresholds that led to at least three other chambers, each of which opened onto side chambers of its own. This main room that we now crossed had its own recesses and alcoves, increasing the size while giving the illusion of including some snug comfort. The people of the splintered rainbow smiled and nodded, or murmured behind their fans, but I saw no suspicion in their eyes.

"Is this really happening?" I whispered to him. "Do they actually believe—"

Mr. Tinderflint's grip grew hard. "People see what they expect, my dear. You wear the clothes, you bear the name. Who on earth would dream of substitution?"

I hadn't stopped to consider that. The audaciousness of the plan bolstered its chance of success. Because, really, who would envision such a scheme? But I had no time to think on that now, because I faced the woman who would one day be my queen.

My first thought upon seeing Her Royal Highness Caroline, Princess of Wales, was that the tattling papers had gotten their facts more than usually correct. She was a large, plump woman. She had the famed fair Germanic complexion, and her blue eyes popped out slightly on either side of her straight, narrow nose. On another person, this might have made her look foolish, but those eyes were quick and clear. They combined with an expressive mouth and an alert bearing. The impression produced by all these features was quite at odds with the studied languor I had been told ladies were supposed to cultivate. I decided I could like this woman, which was as well, because she was my mistress now. But those clear, clever eyes worried me.

I lowered myself into the deepest curtsy my mantua allowed, my own eyes carefully directed at the floor and my heart rattling against my ribs.

"Oh, do stand up and come here, Francesca," said Her Highness, in perfect French without any trace of Prussia flavoring her words. "Let me look at you."

I did not want to get any closer to this alert, intelligent woman, but I had no choice. I couldn't even put up my fan to hide any part of my face, because this was the princess and that would have been unforgivably rude. Her Royal Highness leveled her calm, clever eyes at me, drinking in every detail. I was lost. She turned in her chair, ready to summon the footmen from their duties carrying in fresh bottles or decorating the doors to throw me in the Tower. Mrs. Abbott was somewhere pulling out her knives, getting ready to feast on my failure.

"But, Lord Tierney, she's so thin!" said Her Royal Highness to Mr. Tinderflint. "Did no one feed her during her convalescence?"

Mr. Tinderflint, Lord Tierney, bowed to the princess, perfectly calm and apparently very much at home. "If I had had my way, ma'am, she would have rested another month, but she was so eager to return to her place . . ." He waved his hand, indicating a general helplessness.

"As tractable and obedient as ever, I see." Her Highness smiled at me. "Surely a sign she has made a full recovery. Well, we are glad to have you back among us, Francesca. You are well enough to come walk with me tomorrow, yes?"

"Thank you, Your Highness," I murmured to the gold-embroidered tips of the royal slippers. "I would be honored."

The Princess of Wales nodded. Mr. Tinderflint bowed. I curtsied. Mindful of my train, I let him help me back away into the rainbow, while another pair of courtiers came up to speak with the princess.

"Don't let go," I whispered. "I'm going to faint."

"Of course you're not," replied Mr. Tinderflint. "You're perfection itself. Ah, there's Sir Everett!" He hailed a tall, saturnine man. "Now, Francesca, what was it that you were saying I must remind Sir Everett of, now, what? Ah, yes, I have it."

And so it went. Far from letting go of me, my guardian steered me deftly through the hot and crowded rooms, subtly introducing me to an array of people I was already supposed to know. All the while, I was conscious of Sophy Howe shooting me sharp little glances over her gilt-edged cards, and despite the crushing heat of the room, I shivered.

A full five hours of hot air, chilled punch, bright gossip, and lingering introductions later, Mr. Tinderflint informed the room at large that I must be excused on account of my still delicate health, and Her Royal Highness gave us permission to back into the blessed, blessed dark and cool of the galleries.

"You were splendid, my dear!" My guardian all but bounced on his toes as we climbed the stairs. It was strange to see this ebullient manner matched with sotto voce praise. "Splendid! All I could have hoped for and more."

I reminded myself sternly that this man was a liar and perhaps the reason Francesca had been forced to conceal those mysterious sketches. But it didn't matter. I flushed at his praise and felt the ring of my success in every nerve. When we reached my door, Mr. Tinderflint took my hand and bowed deeply over it. That strange gravity I had glimpsed on the riverboat came over him. "I am aware this is a difficult circumstance, my dear. Truly. And I am grateful to you."

"Do you . . . do you think my mother would have approved?" I asked him.

When Mr. Tinderflint lifted his head, his eyes were shining brightly in the gallery's dim light. "I think she would have been enormously proud. Yes, enormously. And I tell you, she could have done no better on such a day than her brave and clever daughter." With that, he opened my door and bowed me through.

I glided into my beautiful new chamber, carried by a creditable amount of deportment and effervescent relief. I had done it. I was accepted by the court, the maids, Her Royal Highness, and one paint-stained mystery man. Mr. Tinderflint had said my mother would be proud. I could do this after all. I could do anything.

So full of this pleasant contemplation was I, that I completely failed to see the man standing behind the door.

CHAPTER THIRTEEN

WHEREIN THE IDENTITY OF
THE MYSTERIOUS ROBERT IS REVEALED.

Fran! It is you! I can't believe it!"

Wiry arms wrapped tight around me, and a rough cheek scraped mine as I was enthusiastically and repeatedly kissed on every portion of my face. How he could endure the taste of the talc was beyond me.

"What! No! Stop! Are you mad?" This was the final blow. I was resolved. I was going to make it the fashion for women to wear an iron poker at their side to fend off all over-enthusiastic suitors. It would become the mission of my life.

In answer to this singularly disjointed protest, the man did stop, but it was only to pull away so he could stare down at me, while his hands splayed across my cheeks and temples to hold my face tipped up toward his.

"God in Heaven, Fran, I was so afraid — oh, never mind, just let me look at you."

I had no intention of standing still for that. "I . . . but . . . where's Mrs. Abbott?" I shoved his hands off my cheeks, backed away, tripped hard over my train, and backed away some more.

My intruder was a young man, perhaps a few years older than I. He wore a footman's scarlet coat with gold braid on his shoulders, white lace on his cuffs, and a tightly curled, short-queue white wig. This was as much as I was able to take in. My head was spinning. This was bad, as bad as it could possibly be. I had no idea who stood in front of me. Was this the mysterious Robert whom Molly had talked about? Or another paramour entirely?

Oh, Francesca, why, why, WHY didn't you hide a diary instead of those useless sketches!

Not that it mattered. I was sunk. Especially as he wanted to have such an intimate look at me. I was not a twin to Francesca. Even in wig and face paint, someone on kissing terms with her was going to notice the differences.

"I sent your maid on an errand . . ." The footman gestured vaguely toward the door. "Fran, why didn't you write? I've been waiting to hear from you. Did you . . . are you angry with me, Fran? No, no, don't answer. I'm sorry." He took both my hands in his, contemplating them as his thumbs rubbed my gloved fingertips. "I'm just being a fool. Of course I couldn't expect you to write when you were ill and being watched so closely. But . . . Fran . . . was it so very bad?

They said . . . they said you . . . died almost. Is that true? Please, tell me."

His concern seemed genuine, as did the fear that lent a tremor to his voice. I took a deep breath, attempting to gather my wits from all the corners to which they had been so rudely scattered.

"It was very bad," I said in what I hoped was the tone of someone admitting a confidence. I also took the opportunity to step away again, this time putting a table between me and him, in order to deter further sudden lunges. "I believe the doctors were quite concerned."

The footman swallowed hard, and his face took on a most unhealthy pallor. So shaken was he, he turned to face the fireplace, clearly trying to collect himself.

"Robert?" I murmured. He turned his head, and I had to struggle not to melt with relief. I mustered a smile for Robert. His distress was real. He had felt something genuine for Lady Francesca, and now I felt a genuine guilt at deceiving him. This was not anything I had been led to expect. To hear Mrs. Abbott talk, Francesca had been next to a nun during her time at court. "It is all right," I said to Robert. "I am quite well."

Now that I had a little distance, I could take him in more fully. He had a long face with a strong nose and eyes the color of dark amber. Despite his current pallor, his face and cheeks had the ruddy bronze of someone who spent time out of doors. There was breadth to the shoulders under his coat, a good shape to the legs under his breeches, as well as some gentleness to his gloved hands. The relief in his expression was so great that my guilt twisted hard within me, but it had to contend with my uneasiness for space. Despite my efforts, Robert still seemed too close. He was looking at me much too hard. My wig and now smeared cosmetics were not anything like concealment enough. He was raising his hand again, as if he meant to reach across and wipe away my concealing powder.

"Fran." He hesitated, his fingertips less than an inch from my cheeks. "Fran," he said again. Then he backed away, slowly. Footmen do not apply cosmetics, and I could see his face flushing with deep emotion.

Get him away, get him away, gibbered a voice in the depths of my mind. *He'll notice any minute. He'll see your face isn't right, your eyes, your shape. How can he not see?*

At the same time, the small part of me that remained calm remembered Molly Lepell's remark about Fran having a falling out with Sophy Howe over this Robert. I wondered at it. I couldn't see the haughty Sophy Howe being put out with Francesca over a *footman.* A viscount possibly or a poet, perhaps, but a servant? Surely not.

"What is the matter, Robert?" I asked, and hoped he would think it was any emotion other than fear that set my voice wobbling.

"I just . . . for a moment thought . . ." He shook himself. "No. I truly am being a fool. Seeing a ghost in your eyes like a frightened child. But as you say, you *are* well, and you *are* here, and I thank God for it." He grasped my hands again, kissing them both. "Oh, Fran . . ." Robert moved forward, and I was quite sure he meant to resume his attentions to my face and person. I pulled my hands away hastily and slid sideways to avoid both him and my treacherous train.

"What's the matter, Fran?" Robert frowned. "We don't have much time. That dragon of a maid will be back any minute. Where in Heaven's name did you find her?"

"She was put in place by my guardian," I said, honestly enough.

Robert turned an entirely fresh shade of white at this. Now I recognized him. He had been the right-hand footman guarding Her Royal Highness's door, the one who had stared at me when I came down the stairs with Matthew Reade.

Ah! How fate laughs at us. Here I was discovering Francesca had a secret gallant, and he had already seen me smiling at another man. Fortunately, at this moment Robert seemed more concerned with my guardian than any potential rivals. "He doesn't know anything, does he? About us, and about . . . our other business? You didn't . . . you didn't give anything away, did you?"

"Of course not." *Other business?* I let myself hesitate while those words echoed in my thoughts. "At least, I said nothing while I was myself. I was feverish for a very long time. I don't know all I may have said then."

The footman rubbed his mouth hard and bit on the tip of one gloved finger. "This could be very bad. But we mustn't worry too much. Anything you said then will be put down to simple delirium."

It was a slender opening, but I jumped at it. "I'm sure you're right. Still, we should perhaps be careful for a while. Just until we—"

The doorknob turned. Robert, with impressive agility, jumped backwards so he was hidden when the door opened and Mrs. Abbott entered. For my part, I staggered back, tripped once again on my train, bumped against the sofa, and sat down abruptly. Robert lit out the door behind the now staring Abbott's back.

But not fast enough. She heard his step, whirled around, and caught sight of the flapping skirts of his scarlet coat vanishing into the gallery shadows. The door slammed, and she turned on me, swollen to twice her normal size with righteous triumph.

"Well, well." She smiled, and it was a sharp, bright, vicious smile. "You could not wait one night to sample the delights of court, could you? Not one hour. This will be of great interest to your guardian."

Which was more than enough. I had been manhandled, abused, and badly frightened, and I was not going sit in my unbearably tight bodice and endure her defamations. "Why didn't you tell me? Why didn't any of you tell me?"

That at least wiped the smile from her face. "Keep your voice down! Tell you what?"

I was in no mood to take orders either. "She had a lover!"

"What? Impossible!"

"*That*"—I pointed my fan at the door—"was your lady's

paramour come to find her! It was none of my doing! He just . . . he was . . ." Shaking with fury and fear, I plunged blindly ahead. "I'll tell Tinderflint! You deliberately kept this from me!"

The words were out of my mouth, and there was no retrieving them. For a moment, I thought the Abbott was going to strike me. Instead, she ran to the door and peered out into the gallery. From there, she checked all the other doors in the apartment. Only when she was satisfied we were alone did she return, speaking low and rapidly, and in English.

"Tell me again of this man. Leave out nothing. Describe him. Tall or short? Thin? Everything you can remember."

I'm not certain how I managed it, but I swallowed my outrage and did as I was bidden.

"A *footman!* She would never," murmured Abbott. "It's a lie. You're lying. You must be."

The breaths I took then were far closer to sobs than I would have wished. I had to think. I had to be clear. "Mrs. Abbott, I am risking my neck by standing here. Do you honestly believe I am so very stupid that I'd spend my first night intriguing with a *servant?*"

Slowly, Mrs. Abbott backed away. Her lip quivered. Her cheeks quivered. For a moment, it seemed as if her hand groped behind her for support. "But . . . she can't have . . . she would never. She would have *told* me." Mrs. Abbott spoke this last with a terrible ferocity, willing herself to believe it was true. "How is it you come to this before me?"

"Molly Lepell let slip about it when she was here, and young Robert was very upset at not having heard from Francesca in so long, so he took a risk to come see her." *And got you out of his way very neatly.* I might have pointed that out, but for once in my life, I obeyed my finer instincts and kept my mouth shut.

Mrs. Abbott had one hand on the mantelpiece. She passed the other over her perspiring brow, her reddened eyes, and her mouth. For the first time since I'd seen her, she seemed to diminish in size, as if the weight of this discovery pressed her whole self slowly down. I thought of the miniature she wore beneath her dress and how it was her dead daughter we spoke of now.

"You could have trusted me," Mrs. Abbott murmured behind her hand. "Why did you not trust me?"

"I'm sorry," I whispered, my voice hoarse with regret and the tiniest bit of wondering whether Francesca knew this woman was her mother. If she'd been illegitimate, Mrs. Abbott might not ever have told her. She might have posed as nothing more than the faithful servant, even to Francesca herself.

How sad that was, that Francesca should have a devoted, if frightening, mother and not ever know it. How very sad and very strange.

"I shouldn't have said it. I was afraid . . . I . . ." I stumbled about amidst these thoughts searching for a way to apologize, but Mrs. Abbott turned toward me with a look of such sorrow and rage, I would have drawn away, if I'd had anyplace to go.

"Why are you doing this?" I asked her. "What is any of this to you?" Because it couldn't be about the money, not to this iron-souled woman. I would never believe that.

For a moment, Mrs. Abbott seemed about to speak. Her fingers knotted in her collar and the hidden chain underneath. But she shook her head. "No more. The maid will be here any moment."

"But, Mrs. Abbott "

I got no further. She clamped her slit of a mouth shut and quivered at me, fully in control of herself again. That brief moment when we might have shared some communion or confidence had vanished. There was nothing left for me to do but stand still for Mrs. Abbott and her assistant so I could be stripped of my maid of honor disguise and put into bed while the lights were snuffed and the fire banked. Fortunately, while they were both turned away fetching boxes or towels, I was able to retrieve my stolen scrap of Matthew Reade's demon paper from where I'd stuffed it into my bosom and stuff it instead underneath my pillow.

When I was finally left alone, I stared into the darkness for a very long time. My scalp felt tight, as if my skull had swollen from being crammed too full by all I had learned that day. It wasn't enough that I had finally begun my masquerade; I had learned that others had been wearing their masks for much longer. Did Tinderflint and Peele even know Mrs.

Abbott was Francesca's mother? And to whom was Mr. Tinderflint lying about his name? I had assumed it was me, but why could it not be the princess? He was bold enough to fob off a counterfeit maid on royalty; why would he stick at claiming a counterfeit title for himself? Much less at offering counterfeit praise to an anxious daughter about her departed mother?

Biting my lip, I slipped out of bed and, after some little difficulty, lit a candle from the fireplace embers. By its flickering glow, I retrieved the crumpled paper from beneath my pillow.

It was a pastel drawing, a detailed study of geometric patterns. Each panel was a tiny world of flowers and birds. I ran my finger across it, just to be sure it was still a flat piece of paper. In that dim light, the illusion that I was looking at raised panels was truly amazing. I'd known from the paint and the smock that Matthew Reade must be an artist, but this was a work of extreme skill. Why was he destroying it?

Another puzzle I didn't want. I liked Mr. Reade. I didn't want him to be complex and mysterious too. After a moment's hesitation, I retrieved the workbasket from its place by the chair. I emptied it of its silks and threads, and lifted up the padded bottom I'd installed during my last days at the Tinderflint house, and the layer of tissue I'd put underneath that, finally revealing Francesca's sketches. I pulled them out and laid them on the table.

First there was the tableau of robed figures and cherubs with its portraits in their medallions. It had a partner, which I had found stitched into the bed curtain. This one showed an old woman lying in a huge bed, a white staff in her withered right hand. Clearly, she was dying. A crowd of well-dressed men surrounded her, and they all seemed to be arguing with one another. It reminded me of engravings I'd seen in the papers depicting the death of Queen Anne. But this drawing had a major difference from those. In Francesca's sketch, there was a pathetic-looking little monkey in a braided coat crouched on the corner of the mantelpiece. A man patted the creature with one hand, while he pocketed a letter with the other. There was a rectangular hole in the fireplace. Was that some sort of little priest's hole? Perhaps the man was not, after all, pocketing the letter. Perhaps he was hiding it.

If I hadn't spent so much time staring at the plan of Hampton Court Palace with Mr. Tinderflint, I might not have known the third sketch was a floor plan. Here, Francesca's drawing skills had all but failed her. All I could tell was that this was the plan of a large house with large grounds, but it wasn't Hampton Court. Indeed, the lines were so faint and crooked that I could barely make out which marks were meant to indicate a staircase and which showed a doorway.

I replaced the drawings, with Matthew Reade's pastel rendering on top, and set the basket back beside the chair.

I stayed up for a long time after that, watching my candle burn. I thought of the question I'd asked Mr. Tinderflint about my mother, although I believed him to be a liar. I thought about my mother herself. I remembered how many nights I'd climbed out of my bed, which was strictly forbidden. I'd creep to the nursery door and open it just a crack, hoping against hope that I might see her climb the stairs, so shining and beautiful in her velvets and lace. After she died, I woke every night I remained in that house. I stood at the door and stared into the dark, silent hallway. I was sure if I waited long enough, I'd see her climbing the stairs once more.

My nurse had had to pick me up bodily when it was time to move out of our house. She held me down while I kicked and screamed in the coach. I knew once I left our home, I'd lose all possibility of seeing Mama again. That was the day when, for me, my mother truly died.

Was that what brought me here? Was I still that trembling little girl, alone in the dark, willing to dare the worst her child's mind could conceive on the chance of receiving a glimpse of her mother's ghost? Did I think that by taking up her calling as a spy of sorts, I'd somehow be close to her again?

But it wasn't any ghost I'd found here. Robert said Francesca and he had other business, beyond their affair. What could that business be? His manner indicated it was serious indeed. Did the sketches have anything to do with it?

If Francesca had been hiding her sketches from Robert, why also take such care to hide them from her guardian and attendant? Surely if she was in trouble, they were the ones she'd turn to. This led my thoughts right back to the Messrs. Peele and Tinderflint and how I could no longer be certain they had told me the truth about anything regarding Lady Francesca.

And what about Mr. Peele's insistence that I report to him regarding the card games and their players? How did that figure into the firm's many lies and intrigues, political and otherwise?

This brought another idea from the dark and the cold. I'd been lied to about so much by my three overseers, it was surprising I hadn't considered it before. What if they'd lied to me about Lady Francesca's death? There was no reason for it to have really been a fever, when it just as easily could have been another sort of misadventure that took her life. It could have been an accident, for example.

Or it could have been murder.

CHAPTER FOURTEEN

IN WHICH OUR HEROINE PERFECTS
HER ROLE, RENEWS ACQUAINTANCES,
AND UNFOLDS FRESH MYSTERIES.

That initial fortnight at Hampton Court Palace passed without much additional trouble, a fact for which I was profoundly grateful. I remain convinced that any further sudden revelations would have struck me dead on the spot. I had more than enough to do settling into my life as Lady Francesca, maid of honor.

Among the readers of these annals there may be those who believe life at court is all pampered luxury. I beg you should disabuse yourselves of this notion as quickly as may be, and spare some pity for a maid of honor.

The poet Milton tells us, "They also serve who only stand and wait." Well, that was the vast portion of my business in the train of Her Royal Highness; to wait and to stand while doing it. Whole afternoons were spent in the private apartments where the princess received formal visits from assorted gentlemen. There were ladies too, but fewer of these. Most gentlemen ushered into the royal presence were either learned or political, although from what I could determine, they were seldom both. During this time, due to our rank and station relative to Her Highness, we maids of honor were not permitted to sit down. The gentlemen, being invited guests, could sit, and I began to hate them all for this privilege. Like Molly Lepell, pert Mary Bellenden, and Sophy Howe, I stood in my pretty dress, with my face perfectly painted and my hair perfectly arranged, becoming more of an ornament in the literal sense than I ever would have imagined. On occasion, our mistress would address a remark to one of us or make a request. In such an eventuality, that one might answer or move. But otherwise, I waited.

The experience was agonizing in more ways than producing aching feet and a sore back. Preachers and wits might rail about the shallowness of women, but Princess Caroline brought to her side the likes of Sir Isaac Newton and Dean Jonathan Swift. She kept Frideric Handel as music master for her daughters and consulted with him frequently about concerts and entertainments for the court. She cheerfully, and at length, argued with both laymen and divines on all subjects, and spent so much time in deep conversation with Robert Walpole, I was beginning to wonder if it was not the two of them who guided the ship of state, rather than the king.

These conversations were diverting, fascinating, and raised many questions on many subjects. And I could not join in, because I did not have permission to speak. Agony!

Of His Royal Highness, the Prince of Wales, I saw little in those first days. Usually, he stopped at his wife's room briefly on his way to or from riding through the park with a parcel of gentlemen in waiting. The heir to the British throne was a man of middling height, and his fair Germanic complexion had gone ruddy from all the time he spent out of doors. I suspected he would become stout as he aged, but he carried himself with a martial bearing that sorted well with his public nickname of Young Hanover Brave. I can report his English was very good, although he would lapse into French or German if the conversation carried on for more than a moment or two.

The prince seldom stayed long among the learned men, preferring the company of bluff and hearty sportsmen. To these, from what I saw, he was very amiable. But there was in his Prussian blue eyes a restlessness. Sometimes I thought I glimpsed an anger being suppressed, especially when he looked on his wife and the political men.

On the day the king left for Hanover, I learned I glimpsed correctly.

The preparation for this royal departure had been a current running just below the rest of the palace activity since my arrival. After all, a king does not travel like a private person. There are a thousand details to be arranged, a thousand persons to be prepared, and a thousand trunks and boxes to be packed for each of them. Who was chosen to go (such as Frau Melusine von der Schulenburg, the royal mistress), who was left behind (such as the three illegitimate daughters of La Schulenburg, and the three legitimate daughters of Their Royal Highnesses) was the subject of much gossip. My ability to speak German was suddenly much in demand as courtiers whispered half-overheard and badly remembered bits of argument between the Prince and Princess of Wales and asked me for translations. I fear I put some highly improbable words into the royal mouths.

The morning of the departure dawned fair and clear, which was a blessing, as the entire population of Hampton Court was required to assemble in front of the great gatehouse to bid our sovereign farewell. The king preferred to travel by road rather than by river, so there was a train of massive coaches filling the lane, pulled by teams of Belgian horses so huge, I felt sure they had at some point been bred with elephants. They were flanked by red-coated soldiers and royal marines on somewhat smaller horses. The royal carriage was brightly polished and heavily gilded, with the coat of arms on the door and a whole cavalcade of footmen, postilions, and outriders standing at strict attention around it.

As an attendant to Her Royal Highness, I had a good place standing at her right hand, just behind the two royal children old enough to be allowed to bid their grandfather farewell. I would have been able to see everything, except, as soon as the horns blasted and the shouts declaring "The king! The king!" began, I had to bend into my deepest curtsy and lower my gaze.

Feet trod loudly on gravel. A pair of polished black shoes with elaborate golden buckles appeared at the upper edge of my vision. The shoes paused.

The king was standing directly in front of me. A trickle of sweat ran from under my wig and traced a line down my temple.

"This is the girl who was so long sick?" he asked, in German. He had a soft, hesitant voice, not at all imposing or kingly. I held my pose, knees bent and gaze lowered. I hadn't been given permission to stand, and anyway, he wasn't talking to me. He addressed the Princess of Wales.

"Lady Francesca Wallingham, Your Majesty," murmured Her Royal Highness, also in German.

"Ach, yes. She is well now?"

"Yes, Your Majesty."

"It is good. It is good."

"A damned girl he remembers," muttered the prince in low, furious English. "His son he forgets."

The world went suddenly and completely silent, except for the rush of dozens of breaths being sucked in perfect unison. The king had created a council of regency to manage affairs of state while he was away. Everyone knew the Prince of Wales was not one of those named to it. He might be our future king, but the prince was not to have any authority while his father was out of the country. It seemed His Royal Highness was not taking this well.

It also seemed that, despite rumors to the contrary, our German-born king did indeed speak English. The polished black shoes walked slowly to the left, to where the Prince of Wales was standing. "What do you say, sir? You will speak up like a gentleman."

"What can I say but may God bless my king and father?" replied the prince. I wished I could see their faces. I didn't dare look up. I strained my eyes sideways as far as they would go, but couldn't see past my own hemlines. "And may He hear my fervent prayers to return him safe to his throne, and soon."

"You may be very sure I will return, and soon." The acid in the king's voice could have corroded iron. "And I trust I will find the ministers I have left in charge have governed well and properly and not in any way been interfered with by any man—or woman." His Majesty spoke the last two words with great deliberation. I thought again about the princess's time with the political men, and my jesting consideration as to who really held the tiller of the state. It seemed I was not the only one who'd meditated on that subject.

"Of c—" began His Royal Highness, but the heels of the royal shoes ground on the gravel as the king turned his back and moved on, without waiting for his son or daughter-in-law to kiss his hand or say a formal farewell. He climbed into the carriage, and the door was closed.

Well, I thought with an odd resignation. *I know what I'll be*

repeating a dozen times every evening for the next month of Sundays. Because the whole court was going to want to know what had
just passed between father and son, and why the king had cut
the prince dead in front of the entire court. Molly Lepell had
already elbowed me in a highly significant fashion. I wondered what Mr. Tinderflint would have made of this scene,
had he been here. Then I wondered why he wasn't.

Evenings at court brought some measure of relief, even the
ones during which I was in special demand for multiple gos-
sips after the leave-taking of the king. Although we were
required to change into our most elaborate and confining mantuas, complete with trains and layers of paint that would put
a fresco to shame, the gatherings were often of a less formal
nature. We were, in short, finally allowed to sit.

Mr. Peele had been correct when he informed me that
the most frequent entertainment during the evening was
cards. What he had neglected to mention was that we maids
were expected to partner with the gentlemen of the court
or the guests of the prince. We were to smile and laugh and
play in an entertaining fashion. Once the bottles of port and
claret had made their rounds and been emptied several times
over, these gentlemen made jesting wagers for kisses and little tokens such as handkerchiefs and ribbons.

When I wrote my letters to Mr. Peele describing the card
games, I reported with accuracy and vehemence that those
gentlemen cheated. They cheated badly, and they cheated

worse when their partners were pretty, so they could win their little "love tokens," as they called them.

What I did not report was that these games were the time when I began to take the true measure of my sister maids. Molly Lepell was a particularly fine player. She knew what she was doing with both cards and gentlemen, and could gauge her wins and losses to an astounding nicety. From watching her, I learned which of the court gentlemen might be judged relatively harmless, because those she would consent to lose to, and then would flirt with them shamelessly. The ones who were turned away with a cheerful laugh and a smile or a witty quip were the men of whom a maid should be wary.

Mary Bellenden, the third member of our Splendid Three, did not play the silly maid. She *was* a silly maid. She did not care whether she won or lost and laughed equally at all the men who claimed their little wagers from her. If she noticed her playmates were cheating to get closer, she did not care.

Sophy Howe, on the other hand, not only cared, but cared a great deal. Whenever cards were proposed, she moved swiftly to engage the wealthiest or most highly titled man in the room as her partner. She had the impressive ability to watch each hand closely and yet miss nothing that happened in the room around her. I had observed my uncle at his accounts enough to be able to tell when someone was keeping a mental running tally, and Sophy Howe did so constantly.

Hers, however, was not of income and expenditure. Sophy tallied the court, and I was sure the ledgers of her mind were scrupulously kept, down to the smallest detail. This worried me, because Sophy might just make use of those mental ledgers to compare the Francesca she knew with the Francesca in front of her now. What would she do if those columns did not add up?

Nothing got easier on those rare nights when visitors were scarce and we maids sat down to a game with the more senior ladies of the bedchamber. These ladies were a sharp-eyed crew, and to play with them was to be scrupulously honest, because they were not playing for flirtation, but for honor and for hard coin. When I was partnered with Molly at a table across from Lady Cowper or Lady Montague, I needed all my wits about me, or I might easily have lost my entire stock of pin money in a single hand. As it was, I managed to increase my stores by a comfortable margin and became a sought-after partner. Even Her Royal Highness requested that I join her more than once.

I began to live for these moments. During those informal evenings, I could distract myself from my constant worries about my position as an impostor and the fate of my predecessor. I could talk of books and music and ask the questions I had stored up over the day while overhearing the learned gentlemen. Her Royal Highness watched me over the edges of the cards and seemed pleased, which made my spirits soar. I also found I lost rather more frequently to my royal mistress than to any of the other ladies, and not because either one of us was cheating. But I didn't care. Here was I, the poor relation whom Sir Oliver Trowbridge Preston Pierpont took in out of Christian charity, and yet I could make the Princess of Wales laugh or consider a question I posed.

My pleasure in these moments was not at all diminished by the fact that the more animated my conversation with Her Royal Highness, the more tightly Sophy Howe screwed on her spiteful smile. I swear, if I could have carried all her sharp-edged glances about in my pocket, it would have burst at the seams.

Neither was it only Sophy who noted my mistress's preferences. After the first few evenings, the drunken and flirtatious gentlemen sought me out. With them came titled and calculating statesmen paying me compliments, seeking my better acquaintance, and even soliciting my opinions on small things they had read, a new piece of music, or a play. I was no longer at the edges of the party, searching for a way not to look like a fool. How I wished Lady Clarenda could see me now.

The first gift arrived just two weeks after my presentation to Her Royal Highness. It was a garnet and pearl pin shaped like a heart pierced by an arrow. It was swiftly followed by a gold and amethyst bracelet, and another of pearl. I did not wear any of these. To do so would have been to suggest I favored the givers above other gentlemen, and I was already juggling enough without adding another heartsick man to my cascade.

The gentleman I did not see at these triumphant

gatherings was Mr. Tinderflint, Lord Tierney. Given my uncertainties about my predecessor's fate, this left me distinctly uneasy. If there were wasps in the room I inhabited, I preferred to keep them in view. But, contradictory soul that I was, his absence also left me a little bereft. Trustworthy or not, apart from Mrs. Abbott, he was the one person who knew who I truly was.

It seemed Mrs. Abbott was not much interested in keeping me company either. Since my discovery of Robert and Francesca's amour, I saw her for only the briefest of moments, and always in the company of other working maids. Consequently, I had no opportunity to ask her about my guardian's whereabouts.

Robert also seemed to be keeping his distance, but for this my gratitude was unalloyed with other emotion. I admit it: I was afraid, not just of this mysterious business he'd mentioned, but of finding out exactly what sort of favors he had enjoyed from Francesca. As with Mrs. Abbott, I did continue to see him frequently. Robert stood in attendance on the princess's door and watched me as I was bowed through with the others. Sometimes we passed in the galleries or the grounds as he was on some errand and I was on my way to stand in one place or the other. Those were odd, strained moments when we would glance at each other and I would remember his hands holding my face as he drank in the sight of me.

Thus did the routine of court continue smoothly and without hint of undue intrigue or duplicity, until the morning the Princess of Wales took us all out to see her husband hunt.

The king had been gone for two weeks. Their Royal Highnesses, denied official political power, seemed determined to hold open house in Hampton Court, inviting huge parties of noble ladies and gentlemen to all manner of social activities, such as a hunt through the palace woodlands.

"Well, this should be a rare treat indeed," muttered Molly as she looked up at the clouds that had lowered themselves to make a gray lid for the courtyard. She'd come to fetch me so we could walk out together, with Mary Bellenden at her other side. Mary, as usual, just smiled.

While the gentlemen were all on horseback, a string of white carriages waited for the ladies, or most of us anyway. Lady Montague perched in her sidesaddle among the hunters, dark skirts fluttering in the freshening wind. She laughed and chatted with the gentlemen, one of whom might even have been her husband. Less adventurous, the princess and Lady Cowper occupied a gold-trimmed carriage. Sophy Howe had already been installed in the somewhat plainer vehicle directly behind.

"Think how the gentlemen will gape when we're all soaked, with our dresses clinging," Mary Bellenden giggled.

"Think how they'll gape when our eyes are streaming and our noses are swelled because we've all caught cold," I muttered back, adjusting my blond straw country bonnet and wishing I could change it for one of the newfangled umbrella sticks some city gentlemen were beginning to carry.

"Oh, not me. I'm never sick. Oh, look, Molly . . ." Mary nudged Molly in the ribs, but I was no longer attending to either of them. I was watching Sophy Howe.

In addition to the huntsmen, a goodly crowd of servants milled about. Maids of all degrees handed their ladies baskets, shawls, and gloves. Footmen passed between the horses, carrying trays laden with steaming mugs. The mulled wine added the scents of spices and oranges to those of horse, perfume, and approaching rain. I was not surprised to see Robert among this red-clad cohort, nor to have him walk by me without any sign of recognition. I don't believe I was surprised either to see him stop by the carriage that held Sophy and raise up a tray so she could take the cup from it.

"Oh, thank you, Robert," said Sophy, loudly. "Do you know, this hat is impossible. Where is my maid? You must go fetch her." Sophy settled back as Robert bowed. She smiled and raised her cup to me before taking a delicate sip.

"Someone's satisfied with herself this morning," said Mary cheerfully as she continued her favorite occupation of casting her eyes at each and every man on horseback, as if sizing them up for a meal. "I wonder who she's thrown over this time? Was it you, Fran?"

"You can ask her yourself, Mary," said Molly before I could muster any reply. "I'm sure we'll all profit from the knowledge."

"Oh, there you are, Fran!" cried Sophy as if she'd just seen us. "Where did you find that treasure of a lady's maid? She made me up the most wonderful cream for my hands. You must take very good care of her; otherwise, someone will steal her from you."

"My maid?" I said before thought could catch up with my tongue. I had been ready for her to make some remark about Robert. There was no possibility that this flaunting of her ability to command him was accidental. "Mrs. Abbott?"

Sophy smiled and showed all her pretty teeth in doing it. "Yes, Abbott. Clearly, you don't appreciate what you have."

"Look, Fran," said Molly, just as loudly, turning me forcibly away. "Her Royal Highness wants you."

Our mistress was indeed waving to me from her carriage.

"You'll join us, Lady Francesca," said Her Royal Highness as we approached and curtsied. "I'm sure Molly and Mary will do very well keeping Sophy company."

I was less certain on this point. Nor did I particularly relish the honor my royal mistress did me, so taken up was I with wondering what Sophy meant when she threatened to steal Mrs. Abbott. But lacking any choice in this matter, I let the nearest footman help me into the carriage as Lady Cowper drew aside her skirts to make room for mine. I was not sure I liked Lady Cowper. She was tall and proud, and always seemed to be talking up some business of her husband's, who was the Lord Treasurer. She was also a demon for cards, and when play grew deep, she went in all the way. Despite all this, if I'd had my guess, I would have said she genuinely cared for Her Royal Highness.

"Oh, Robert, there you are," Sophy was saying from her carriage as I settled in with the lady and the princess. "Help Molly in beside me. Oh and, poor Mary, you're quite blue with cold. Fetch her a rug, Robert."

"Mr. Russell and Lord Blakeney were quite full of your praises last night," said Her Royal Highness to me. "You are going to have the ladies in jealous fits if you keep stealing all their gentlemen in this way." Did the royal gaze flicker toward Sophy, who was fussing over how Robert arranged the rug on Mary's lap, or was it just my eyes that could not help turning in that direction?

"Some young ladies need to learn to be satisfied with what they have," remarked Lady Cowper. "Or they'll be chasing swains like our gentlemen chase the deer, and no one comes out the better for it."

"Except for those who would rather feast upon gossip than good venison," agreed the princess. Lady Cowper laughed at this royal quip, but Her Royal Highness was regarding me too steadily for my own laugh to be anything but forced. Fortunately, I was saved from further bon mots by one of the host of liveried footmen approaching the carriage and bowing deeply. It was Robert, and he held a silver tray bearing a single cup and a single letter.

"I was instructed to bring this to you, Your Highness."
He handed across the letter. "And a cup for my lady."

He held out the tray and the cup, and as I took it, he was
joggled, it seemed, and caught my hand to steady himself.

"I do beg your pardon, my lady!" Robert let go almost
instantly. Almost, for he took time enough to press a scrap of
paper into my hand.

I drew back sharply and wrapped my hands around the
warming cup.

"Who gave this to you?" demanded the princess suddenly, clutching the open letter in her gloved hands. A flush
of anger glowed underneath her face powder. "Where are
they?"

Robert fell back, bowing hastily. "I . . . Carter passed it
to me, madame, since I was coming with the cup. I didn't see
who gave it to him —"

"Is there a problem, my sweet?" called a voice in German. The prince brought his great roan gelding alongside Her
Highness's carriage. He looked down on her with grave concern.

By dint of heroic and visible effort, the princess swallowed her anger all in a lump. She then answered her husband easily, and in French, so all listeners might more readily
comprehend. "No, no. I wanted another shawl, that is the
only matter. But we've already delayed enough, do you not
think? Is it my husband's pleasure to sound the horn?"

The prince saw the missive clenched in her fist, and their

eyes met. Whatever they shared between them in that moment, it surely included the understanding that at times silence is best, because His Royal Highness bowed his head.

"Of course." He signaled to his men, and the first among them blew three long, looping notes from his curved brass horn. The courtyard gates were opened by a team of men to allow the hounds and their masters, the prince and his huntsmen, and finally our carriages, to pass out into the lane through the gardens that led to the hunting field. I took advantage of the general distraction to stuff the scrap Robert had given me into my sleeve.

"Burn this." The princess shoved her letter at Lady Cowper, but snatched it back at the last moment. "No. I reconsider. Lady Francesca, you shall take care of this for me."

Slowly, and with the feeling of entering into a new trap, I took this new paper from the royal fingertips.

"You may as well read it," she said. "You have become such a quick study of late, I will be most interested to hear your opinion."

I opened the paper and read.

Dear Madame,

It is well known that you are a God-fearing and Christian woman. As such, I do urge that for the benefit of your immortal soul you shall consider the great error and falsity of the position of your husband, George Augustus, called Prince of Wales. For it is well known to all that the prince is no legitimate son of the house of Hanover, but rather the bastard child of Sophia

Dorothea of Celle, and her lover, Philipp von Königsmark, who
was most foully and unnaturally murdered to silence him before
he could confess the paternity of their child.

It is for you to consult God and your conscience and pro-
claim that the only right and true heir to the throne of Britain is
James Edward Stuart, called by some the Pretender. For he is as
surely the legitimate son of James II of England as your husband
is the bastard of Königsmark.

God Save the True King!

The letter was, not surprisingly, entirely lacking in the
matter of a signature.

"So? What do you think of it, Lady Francesca? Have I
not charming correspondents?"

I swallowed and looked up at my royal mistress. Her
clear eyes had gone hard as sapphires. "I have heard this
story before." In fact, I'd read it in the papers, around about
the time last autumn when I read of the men and arms being
amassed in the North. "I also heard that the baby who grew
into James Edward Stuart was carried to his mother's bed in
a warming pan to substitute for her stillborn child. The one
seems to me as likely as the other."

The corner of the princess's mouth twitched. "Promptly
spoken."

"It is not worth dwelling upon, Your Highness," said
Lady Cowper stoutly. "It is malice and madness. Let it be
destroyed and forgotten."

"Such malice and madness have already cost hundreds

of lives, not to mention thousands of pounds the treasury can ill afford," said the princess. She was still speaking to me. "And there are too many ready to spread slander if it might persuade others to their cause. Is that not so, Francesca?"

I folded the letter back up and took my time about it.

"I think there are those who would dare anything for gain," I said. In the other carriage, Sophy was leaning forward, tapping Mary on the knee and laughing about something. "And they cannot see how small that gain will truly be or how much pain it causes."

"Our Lady Francesca has turned quite the philosopher," said Lady Cowper. "I advise you to send her to Herr Liebniz to study, Your Highness. Who knows what heights she could reach?"

"Who knows?" replied the princess thoughtfully as our carriage rattled down the lane. "Who knows indeed?"

CHAPTER FIFTEEN

IN WHICH A BRIEF ACQUAINTANCE IS
EVEN MORE BRIEFLY RENEWED
AND AN ORIGINAL IS DISCOVERED.

My own little missive, when I was finally able to pull it gingerly from my soaking sleeve, was only moderately less distressing than that handed to Her Royal Highness. The running ink read *I will find us a place.*

At least I think it did. Despite my best efforts, it tore in two between my cold fingers.

The rain had begun before we were a half hour out the gate, and it proved to be a heavy, soaking downpour that left us with our dresses clinging to our skin, as Mary had predicted, and our noses swollen and streaming, as I had predicted. For once I was grateful for Mrs. Abbott's brusque efficiency as she stripped me down to my skin, wrestled me into dry clothing and a warm wrapper, and stuffed me into the armchair in front of the fire with my feet in a mustard bath. The result of this was that my nose and eyes dried up in time for the evening's gathering, although I felt my feet, having been so thoroughly stewed in hot mustard, were now good for nothing but to be served up with a boat of gravy and furnishings of boiled greens.

While I steamed, however, I could not but wonder about the letter the princess had received. Perhaps when Robert found a place for a tête-à-tête, I could question him more closely about who gave it to him and where it came from. I could then make sure that information got to Lady Cowper or Lady Montague—quietly, of course. The idea pleased me and did much to alleviate my overstewed feelings.

But either Robert was not in as much of a hurry to see his lady again as might be thought, or the weather thwarted him. It certainly thwarted the rest of us. The rain continued through that night and into the next morning. We played so many hands of cards that my letters to Mr. Peele about the games and the players filled multiple sheets, and I actually began to wish he would write me back, just once, so I would have something new to read.

The princess was unable to indulge in her habit of an early walk on these dreary mornings, and the conversation in her salon grew listless. The gentlemen in attendance that day were of the political breed, and although I tried to follow their reasoning regarding the virtue of reforming the banking system to more fully acquire for the Crown the benefits and profits to be brought in by easier investment in the ships of the merchant navy, I was in grave danger of fidgeting. Even

Molly Lepell, that paragon of maids, had shifted her weight from foot to foot twice in the last half hour, causing the Howe to roll her eyes, ever so delicately, which in turn caused Mary to snort, and the princess to frown, although Mary, being Mary, immediately put on an elaborate show of insouciance.

The princess turned to her guests. "My Lord Owens, my Lord Dalton, I don't believe you have yet had a chance to view the Great Work."

Lord Owens, a tall, austere gentleman in an impeccable green coat, looked taken aback, as if he could not understand why anyone would introduce a new topic when he had barely begun to warm to his financial theme. He and my uncle Pierpont would have gotten on extremely well. Lord Dalton, however, looked relieved.

"And how does Mr. Thornhill, madame?" Lord Dalton was the older of the two, dressed in blue and black. His face was as wrinkled as last year's apple, but he possessed a surprisingly cheerful eye for a banker.

"You shall ask him directly." The princess got to her feet, which required the gentlemen to do the same and bow as she passed. They fell into step behind her, and we maids formed ourselves into a train behind them.

"Well, well," murmured Sophy. "This should be most amusing."

"Oh, why?" fussed Mary. "We've seen the wretched ceiling a hundred times."

"You'd know if you paid any attention at all."

I looked to Molly, who tipped me a sly nod. Everybody

knew what was so interesting, except me—a phenomenon I was growing both used to and increasingly tired of.

But I knew what they were on about as soon as we walked into the new rooms. This grand apartment was constructed on noble lines. Despite that, it appeared more closely related to a lumber room than a royal chamber. There were no curtains on the windows, and the watery daylight filled the room. There were also dozens of candles lit, and the air was heavy with the scents of fresh paint, plaster, and strong oil. The reason for this was clearly the partially completed mural decorating the high ceiling. It appeared to be another arrangement of ancient gods and modern cherubs. Doubtlessly, it was some new and significant allegory to join the others that graced the walls and ceilings of the palace. But I scarcely noticed the painting. The first thing I saw among the drapings of canvas drop cloth and the forest of scaffolding was Matthew Reade. He was bowing too deeply to the princess for me to see his face, but I knew him by the dark copper of his hair and also by his form and motion, even though it had been weeks since I last glimpsed him. This was not a realization that made for calm reflection.

"Mr. Thornhill," said Her Royal Highness brightly as she gestured for the lean man in front of her to straighten up. "A tour of your great works, if you would be so kind. My guests were pining to see what progress you make."

"I am most honored, as always, Your Highness, and I think you will be pleased with what we have accomplished." Mr. Thornhill was a pleasant-looking man of middling height, with an oval face and a long nose. His hands were bare, and the skin was strangely mottled-looking, stained, I supposed, by the colors of his work. He dressed in plain breeches and a plain smock but carried himself with an air of consequence.

He also turned to me and flashed a broad courtier's smile. "And you have brought me Lady Francesca! How delightful to see you again, my lady."

By this time, I had some experience with greeting people who knew me far better than I knew them, and I made a shallow but polite curtsy. "Thank you, Mr. Thornhill. I trust you are well?"

"Very well, thank you. But I will have words with you later, my lady. I understand you have been ill, but you have not my leave to permanently neglect your studies." He turned to the princess. "Your maid, madame, has a wonderfully deft hand at sketching. And a quick eye. It is a shame she is not a boy. I would have taken her on to 'prentice immediately. I'm sure she'd profit from the office more than some . . ." His voice trailed away, and I could not help but notice his gaze trailed away too, until it was pointed straight at Matthew Reade. Mr. Reade was not looking at his master. He was instead hunched over a crowded worktable, laboring busily with mortar and pestle. I had the distinct feeling he'd been through similar scenes before, and I wondered what he had done to earn so much disdain from Mr. Thornhill.

"Well, Lady Francesca," said Her Royal Highness, bringing my attention back where it belonged, "you did not tell me this was what you were doing with your free days."

"Oh, I did not want to bore Your Highness with a recita-tion of my little hobbies." Modesty, I had found, made for an excellent distraction, and was almost always an acceptable excuse for neglecting to mention some point later found sig-nificant.

"Nonsense." Her Highness spoke lightly, but I felt the regard of her clever eyes like a fingertip laid against my arm. "I wish more of my ladies would decide to spend their time engaged in such improving activities."

Why do our mistresses say such things? Now all the maids were looking at me; Molly thoughtfully, Mary mock-ingly, and Sophy Howe as if she heartily wished I were the one being ground to powder by Mr. Reade.

"Now, Mr. Thornhill," the princess went on briskly, "let us hear your report."

"Of course, Your Highness. Tobias, Ezikial, bring the plans here."

The two young men bustled forward, laying out great sheets of paper for the princess and her guests. Everyone clus-tered around to hear Mr. Thornhill expound on the composi-tion of his ceiling decoration, drawing our attention now to the plan, and now to the partially completed painting over our heads. He sent Tobias and Ezikial scurrying about the room, fetching other sketches and plans to further explain what he had done in regard to other ceilings, and how that decoration compared to this. Not once did he call on Mat-thew to perform any function.

All the party obligingly clustered at the center of the

room and looked up or down as directed. I will freely acknowledge it was a splendidly rendered scene. The illusion of sunlight and open sky created to surround the old gods was indeed impressive. Yet my eyes kept straying to Matthew Reade. His table was apart from the bustle and clutter. It was covered with wooden boxes and jars of glass and clay. For a long moment, he seemed aware of nothing but his hands and their work. But then he raised his eyes, just a bit, to see me looking at him. One corner of his mouth turned up, and I saw he knew me, as I knew him.

"And here, of course, we have the figure of Leucothoe attempting to restrain Apollo from entering his chariot, and . . ."

As everyone again lifted their eyes to the sun god facing the defiant woman, I slowly faded backwards toward Mr. Reade's table, keeping my eyes dutifully pointed upward. It was against all protocol to turn one's back on royalty, so walking backwards without tripping over my hems was something I'd been able to practice with great regularity of late. I prided myself that I was getting rather good at it.

"You have not encountered any more demons, I hope, Mr. Reade?" I asked, keeping my back to him and my gaze toward the ceiling.

"I have done my best to avoid them, Lady Francesca. I trust you have not been troubled?"

"Knowing you are on watch, how could I possibly be?" I risked a glance back and saw that a small smile had appeared on Mr. Reade's face.

"So this is your occupation?" I gestured at the table.

"As you see." The smile vanished, replaced by a much more bitter expression. In addition to the mortar, there were delicate trowels and knives, brushes and palettes arranged neatly around him. There were also scoops and scales and vials of viscous liquid enough for any alchemist to begin work at once on his philosopher's stone. "Mr. Thornhill regards it as fit work for the son of a London apothecary. Sometimes I am permitted to trace a fresh line on a plan or tie a new brush."

"You have my sympathies."

"And this is your occupation?" He cocked his head toward the maids and lords. Mr. Thornhill was leading his guests about in a small circle, describing the various shades of blue and the allegorical significance of the robed figures. Something about the ceiling bothered me, but I could not say what.

"Today we are permitted motion. It is a wonder and a delight."

"You have my sympathies." He grimaced and looked down at the bright yellow compound he had been grinding. "I'm sorry. This is done. If I work it any more, the consistency will be wrong and then . . ." He glanced significantly at Mr. Thornhill, who was tracing sweeping arcs with his arm to illustrate some progression among the images. I contemplated them, aware that Matthew Reade was contemplating me.

"Lady Fra—"

Why my mind chose this exact moment to realize I'd been a blind imbecile, I will never know. But it did, and I was, because I knew these figures and this mural. I clapped my hand over my mouth to muffle an undignified squeak.

I owned a copy of this work, drawn in pencil on a page that I had stared at as often as I could contrive to do so. It had taken me so long to recognize this because the penciled copies, it seemed, were not exact. In fact, they were quite poor. Francesca's rendering of the portraits of the Prince and Princess of Wales in their medallions, for instance, was nothing like what I now saw overhead. Her sad and desperate version of the figure of the winged Leucothoe attempting to pull Apollo back from his chariot was quite different from Mr. Thornhill's decorously determined lady. In fact, the only figures she seemed to have taken a good likeness of were the cherubs.

I became conscious of a slow, terrible sinking sensation within. I had pored over those sketches. I had spent hours wondering what great and wonderful clue they might hold to the mystery of my predecessor's life. Was it possible they were simply a shy artist's attempt to hide sloppy work?

"What's the matter?" murmured Mr. Reade. "Don't tell me you've found an incorrect proportion with your quick eye?"

He was trying to raise a tart response, but it was all I could do to remember where I was just then. "No, not here. It's just . . . another drawing."

"Another drawing? Of this work? For Heaven's sake, don't tell Thornhill. He doesn't let anyone copy his paintings before their debut."

"No. No. Not this one." Several inelegant and descriptive curses rang through my head. All the trouble I had taken to keep those sketches safe, all the time I had wasted attempting to fathom their secret meanings, and here it seemed they meant nothing, except that the other Lady Fran was not so accomplished an artist as she first appeared.

I could tell from his tone that Mr. Thornhill was reaching the end of his lecture. I glanced at Mr. Reade in sympathy and guilty apology and moved closer to the royal party. Molly noted my return with a quizzical and somewhat worried look. Mary gave me that particular cheerful sideways glance of hers that always meant "Caught you."

I shrugged at them both, but what pleasure I'd felt in seeing Matthew Reade again was now entirely gone. Because not only did it appear that I had been an overly dramatic ninny regarding Francesca's sketches, I had made an error in deportment in sidling away from the flock to speak with a mere apprentice. I told myself it was nothing serious. We were all supposed to be flirts. It hardly mattered that one or another might be seen talking with any man. If Molly or, more likely, Mary, mentioned it, there would be gossip and a few jokes tossed about the card table, along with professions of jealousy by the gentlemen who wanted their feelings soothed, and that would be that.

At least, that's what I tried to convince myself of. I

might even have succeeded, had Sophy Howe's sparkling eyes not also been fixed upon me. She lifted her fan to her temple and tipped me a sly salute.

My room was empty when I returned to change for the evening's gathering, but a silver tray with a sealed letter waited on the table. When I picked it up, there proved to be another missive underneath, with only the letter F written on its face.

I broke open the forest green sealing wax on the first letter and found that it had been written in a tiny, tidy hand, and entirely in Latin.

> *My dear,*
>
> *I can only hope you will forgive my most inconsiderate absence. Business has kept me away from court, but I assure you I will return the instant I am able. I urge you to be mindful of your part and behave just as you should. I know you will heed your guardian and give him no cause for concern. If any little thing arises, you may write to me care of Lloyd's Coffee House on Tower Street.*
>
> *Yours, etc.,*
>
> *Mr. T*

And that was all.

While I was relieved he'd thought enough of my situation to give me some way to reach him, I missed any sign of friendship. I should not have been left disappointed by this. We were, after all, only partners in a most peculiar crime at best. At worst, he was another danger to me and my hopes for a future, and I should be glad he was keeping well away.

But I also could not help noting that I was to write him care of a coffee house, not the house where I'd been hidden during my ladyship lessons. I thought about the austere and very much absent Mr. Peele, with his delicate hands that belonged to someone so adept at cheating at cards. I thought how Mr. Tinderflint quailed before his anger. I thought about how many lies Mr. Tinderflint had told me, and Mr. Peele's interest in the people I met during the games at court evenings. Was it possible Mr. Tinderflint didn't want Mr. Peele to know it when I did communicate with him?

I glanced at the door and tucked Mr. Tinderflint's letter beneath the sofa cushion. If I had time, I'd hide it in my workbasket. Trepidation fluttered through me as I picked up the second note. This one was much shorter and told me in its few words that my interlude of relative calm was at an end.

The Wilderness. NE corner. Tomorrow. Noon.
    R.

CHAPTER SIXTEEN

In which Our Heroine attempts

the taming of a dragon.

In all dramas featuring heroines of a romantic nature, there is one constant character: the trusty lady's maid. She may prove false or true, but she is always present at her mistress's side, fully involved in whatever travails the playwright has seen fit to lay upon her. It was only during my time as maid of honor that I came to I understand why this was.

As a lady, I could not do for myself what the youngest farm hand could: I could not get dressed.

The keen observer of fashion will note that the laces that are so very necessary to securing a lady's garments all tie at the back. As a result, we frail flowers of gentle English womanhood are rendered helpless by our own clothing. We become dependent entirely on the goodwill of others to escape the necessity of parading about in our night things.

But my assistant was of more dubious character and temperament than any maid in any drama. If I rang for the Abbott, she would want to know where I was going and why, and I remained at a loss as to what to tell her. Surely not the truth. All I knew for certain about Mrs. Abbott was that she remained devoted to her lost and secret daughter. She had assigned herself the part of avenging angel in our particular drama, but exactly what she was avenging and how she intended to carry out her role were still a mystery to me.

As I meditated irritably on this, it occurred to me that I might not need the answer to this mystery yet. I might, in fact, have what I needed to persuade Mrs. Abbott to play along with my plans. I kicked my way out from under the quilts and rang the bell.

Mrs. Abbott entered my rooms under full sail, the glare in her dark gaze lit and well stoked. But I was ready for this. I kept my back straight, my chin up, and my visage calm as I faced her grand displeasure. That my heart was attempting to beat its way out from under my ribs was my own affair.

"I need to get dressed, Mrs. Abbott, if you would be so kind."

"It is too early," she snapped back. "You will be remarked on."

"I intend to walk in the gardens. If anyone remarks, I will say that I am following the example of Her Royal Highness as to the importance of fresh air and exercise."

"They will think you are currying favor."

It was with great self-control that I refrained from rolling my eyes. "And in what way will this be out of character for a courtier? A light morning dress, if you please, and my half boots." With luck, she would not feel the immediate need to send for an undermaid to assist with this task.

Mrs. Abbott clearly did not like any of this, but for now, at least, she failed to find new objections. Instead, she indicated with a curt gesture that I should precede her into the dressing room. I stood beside the table with its oval mirror while she opened the various drawers and boxes. She was not looking at me, and so did not see me take a deep breath and attempt to gather my courage.

"Mrs. Abbott. Have you learned anything new about the footman Robert and Lady Francesca?" *Possibly while you were making up a hand cream for Sophy Howe?* But this last I kept to myself.

She did not even bother to straighten up. "That is nothing you need to know."

"I'm afraid it is. Robert has asked me to meet him in the Wilderness."

"This is why you call me?" The heat of the glare she now turned on me had increased to the point where I was in danger of becoming a charred cinder, rather than simply well-toasted. "You want me to help you to an assignation with that man?"

"I want you to tell me what you've found out about him and how things stood with him and Lady Francesca, so I do not give myself away."

"You do not need to know," she repeated as she held

open the closet door, clearly indicating that she expected me to exit now. "You will not meet him. That will end the difficulty."

This was no less than I had expected. I stood up as tall as I could in my bare feet and nightgown. "Mrs. Abbott, if we are to continue here, I must play the whole part. Robert can expose us as well as anyone with a title. Maybe even better, because no one will know where the gossip comes from if a servant starts to spread it. I know this is painful for you—"

I faltered. Her steady and powerful gaze did not in any way mask her hard mind full of calculations, anger, and grief. It also showed how she disdained any display of pity from such a creature as me.

"I understand that I am not Francesca, and I never will be, and you have every reason to be bitter about my assuming her name and station. But Francesca was keeping secrets, Mrs. Abbott, and you and I both need to know what they were. Yes, I have my own reasons for what I do. Believe it to be the money, if you will. We can help each other in this, and I am ready to pledge that help to you. Which is, I think, more than Messrs. Tinderflint and Peele have done."

That last was a shot in the dark, brought on by Mr. Tinderflint's sudden departure from court and the belated letter that contained so little explanation. I held my breath and prayed to the departed soul of my own mother, wherever she might be, for steadiness and luck.

Slowly, Mrs. Abbott closed the door to the outer chamber. Her gaze slid over me without pause as she turned back to the business of my clothing. Our only light now was the candle, protected by its glass chimney and reflected in the mirror. Mrs. Abbott considered possibilities with regard to petticoats and brought out my yellow morning dress to inspect the folds and lace ruffles for damage before pronouncing it fit to wear.

As she worked, Mrs. Abbott began to speak. Against her habit of keeping to English with me, she fell into French. Her words were smooth, but there was a lilt and an edge to them, an accent I did not recognize.

"She came home suddenly. She had not written—she just appeared at the door in a hired coach. She was already not well. She did not sleep. She did not eat. It should have been no wonder she fell into fever. But she was not despairing. No. She was all but giddy with some excitement. I begged her to confide in me, but she would not say what nourished such feeling. That was why I agreed to this mad scheme when Monsieur—Mr. Tinderflint—proposed it. So I could come here and find out who had driven her to her illness, and to be certain they would pay for what they did."

Giddy. I rolled the word about in my mind several times, trying to grow accustomed to the feel of it. It was not what I had expected to hear. Frightened, possibly. Depressed, or even despairing, most definitely. But giddy? That spoke to happiness and the expectation of good fortune, not the sort of trouble that would drive a maid from court.

"When was this?" I asked. "When did she come home?"

"She came home for the Christmastide. She had before

this told me she would be spending the season with the court, but then"—Mrs. Abbott shrugged—"she did not. And no, before you ask, she did not say why she changed her mind on this point either. I questioned her about it and received no answer."

There was a deep sorrow under those words, and a very old one. I thought of how vehemently Mrs. Abbott had defended her daughter's character and actions, and the myriad secrets she was uncovering. I wondered at the heart within her, and how many more secrets it would be able to bear before it broke.

"Why were you not here with her?" I asked.

Mrs. Abbott bit her lip, and for a moment, I thought she would cry. "I had a commission from Mr. Tinderflint," she croaked at last. "Letters that needed to be carried. It took longer than expected. When I at last returned, I myself was ill with fatigue for a time and then . . . and then . . ." She did not go any further, and I did not ask her to. Indeed, I determined now would be a good time to change the subject.

"How did you meet Mr. Tinderflint?"

"Tinderflint." Mrs. Abbott smirked as she laid the petticoat she'd selected over the back of the chair and gestured that I should assume the position to be dressed. "The man has more masks than a whole troupe of Italian players." She loosened the ribbons on my nightgown and pulled it off over my head. "When I met him, his name was Taggart. He had come to the Court of Saint-Germaine. You know of what I speak?"

Of course I knew. Saint-Germaine was the palace that

King Louis of France had deeded over to James the Pretender. Saint-Germaine was the inmost heart of a recurring series of plots to dethrone the Hanoverians and return the Crown of England to the Stuarts. This last winter, they had come closer than usual to succeeding. In addition to the fighting in the North, there had been Jacobite riots in the streets of London. Aunt Pierpont had locked Olivia and me into our bedrooms and had the male servants stand guard with staves and carving knives. Uncle Pierpont had been away from home at the time, and when he returned, he was not at all pleased with his wife's dramatics.

"Five years ago, Tinderflint had come to Saint-Germaine to speak with some English exiles," Mrs. Abbott was saying as she tightened the laces on my stays and held out the petticoat for me to step into. "And Francesca and I . . ." She shrugged in that so-eloquent French fashion. "I was able to do some favors for him, to make sure some letters reached certain parties and others did not. It was the beginning of our . . . association. In payment, he promised to bring Francesca and myself to London, to furnish her with education. He had turned her head with his stories, I think. After we met Tinderflint, she begged me to let her go to England. If it would help her become the lady I knew that she could be, I was ready to make the attempt." Mrs. Abbott smiled wanly. "Blood will out, you understand, and my Francesca had the blood, but also the quickness and the beauty. All she lacked was a chance."

A chance, and a father who would acknowledge her, I

suspected. But given my own uncertainties in that regard, I was not going to cast aspersions.

"Let me help, Mrs. Abbott," I said. "Let me find out what part Robert played in what happened to Francesca."

"Why would you care?" she demanded.

"Because I know what it is to be alone and to have no choices." The words came to me slowly, so weighted down with truth were they. "Because I'd be sorry to help anyone who hurt such a girl."

I could not reveal my whole reason, but this was the foundation of all. It was not, however, anything like enough to please Mrs. Abbott. Her rigid stance and her grim expression told me as much. She was determined I should be nothing more than an adventuress without conscience, while her daughter, who had worn this same disguise, was a sweet and clever girl lacking only opportunity. Although how any girl of dubious birth raised among a court made up of the ambitious and disappointed of three different nations could remain as sweet as Lady Francesca was purported to be was surely one of nature's great mysteries.

Still, Mrs. Abbott also wanted to know what had driven Francesca from the court, exhausted but giddy, and that was the desire that won.

"This footman Robert's family name is Ballantyne. They have been in service to the kings of England for three generations." She moved about me, knotting the laces of my overdress and straightening the bows at my elbows and waist.

"Robert is the last son of the family. His father died waiting at the door of old Queen Anne, at the same moment she
herself died, or so they say." Mrs. Abbott shrugged again,
indicating what she thought of the probable veracity of this
detail. "Robert Ballantyne is not much liked among his fellows. They say he is ambitious, which is acceptable, but he
thinks himself better than they, which is not. He is not the
only servant who willingly consorts with the quality, but it
is said he is not careful enough and that he will one day bring
trouble to himself because of it."

"Do you think that he was looking to Francesca as a way
to fulfill his ambitions?"

"I think it is possible." She pushed me into the dressing table chair with her customary roughness and set about
brushing and pinning my hair. Alliance was evidently not
reason enough to grow soft with me. "Men are known to do
such things."

"Did Francesca care for him?" I asked.

Mrs. Abbott knotted a hank of my hair in her fist. "He
bragged that she did."

After that, Mrs. Abbott's mouth shut like the lid of a
box. I let her have her silence. For now, it was the only favor
I could return her for her pain and her honesty. At least she
had helped allay one fear. Francesca had met her end at home.
The story I had gotten from Messrs. Tinderflint and Peele
about her fever matched what Mrs. Abbott now told me,
and that was something. At least I hoped it was. This little

conversation with Mrs. Abbott raised yet more questions, though. Why had Francesca so suddenly changed her mind about where to spend Christmastide? And what had made her so happy?

When Mrs. Abbott had finished with my hair and pinned my dainty cap in place, we faced each other. She still did not like me, and she probably never would. That was fair, as I would probably never like her. But we needed each other. I believed that as long as I was of use, she would help me, and in so far as I was doing her work, I could trust her.

It was not much, but it would do for now.

CHAPTER SEVENTEEN

WHEREIN WE OBSERVE THE
ALCHEMICAL FORMATION OF CERTAIN
DANGEROUS ENTANGLEMENTS.

Among her many other pursuits, the Princess of
Wales was much addicted to fresh air and vigorous exercise.
On fine days, she rose early to walk through Hampton Court's
parks and gardens for two or three hours. This was done at
a clip that left all of us poor maids and ladies breathless, except Lady Montague, who I had begun to believe could have
outstripped the king's best hunting horse if she had a mind
to. It also meant that I was at least as well acquainted with
the grounds surrounding the palace as I was with the galleries inside it.

We maids were permitted some occasional days for our
private use, as long as at least two of us were in waiting at
any time. I had been allotted today as one of mine, a fact
that Robert had surely discovered when he decided on this

rendezvous. We were fortunate in our timing. The morning that bloomed around me was beautiful. The rain had abated at last, leaving the air cool and fresh. Dew and cobwebs made a silver fairyland of the lawns. I picked my way gingerly along the damp, sloping bank where the reeds and flags nodded in the breeze. This was not a place Her Highness generally chose for her walks—I did not want to risk coming across the royal party. I needed time to bring some discipline to my deeply disordered thoughts before I kept my rendezvous.

What Mrs. Abbott had said about Robert Ballantyne was important to me, but nothing like as important as what she said about Mr. Tinderflint. Mr. Tinderflint had been in the Pretender's court and had been involved in intrigues there. How had my mother figured into those intrigues? He'd said she had written him letters with pieces of news. Was she keeping him abreast of comings and goings in London while he traveled? I tried to imagine Mama sitting at a card table as I did. I tried to imagine her making conversation with the great lords, teasing out bits of information that might lead to conclusions of loyalties and alliances. The visions made me oddly queasy. On the one hand, I liked the idea that Mama was clever and daring. On the other hand, what did one do with a mother who was not only daring but duplicitous, perhaps even dangerous?

What if it was worse than that? What if Mama had been in the pay of Mr. Tinderflint not because she was clever and dangerous, but because she was foolish or desperate? Mr. Tinderflint, I realized as I stared across the river, surrounded himself with women he found useful. With my father gone, Mama could have easily been in need of money. There certainly had been none for me to inherit. I had no idea how we had lived, at least I hadn't until now. There was more than one form of blackmail in this world.

So what use did Tinderflint ultimately intend for me? I did not even know which side he stood on. Was it possible he was a Jacobite and that I was a Jacobite's daughter? Surely my fat, beribboned, fluttery guardian did not mean to call on his purported acquaintance with my mother to try to persuade me to do . . . something. Some Jacobite thing involving plots and gunpowder.

Except Mr. Tinderflint had already succeeded in convincing me to follow him this far, and he'd been very much helped along because I wanted to stay close enough to him to find out what else he knew about my mother.

I berated myself bitterly and at length for not asking Mrs. Abbott the vital question of which side Mr. Tinderflint had intrigued for. Given the boldness of the scheme in which he had embroiled me, he could be for anything or anybody. It might be that my initial supposition that this business was about money was not wholly wrong. Tinderflint and Peele might simply be working for whosoever paid the best.

I again thought over Mr. Tinderflint's badly explained absence and how it coincided with the arrival of the anonymous letter that had so angered Her Royal Highness. Could he have sent it?

And what on God's good green earth did any of this

have to do with the mysterious business between Francesca and Robert? Was Robert in Tinderflint's pay as well? Or was he on the other side, whichever side that might be? Such things happened in plays and epic poems. It would be horribly romantic, two spies from opposite sides falling in love. Olivia would devour such a tale in a single sitting.

But what of Mr. Peele? Was he another useful person? Did he pore over the letters I sent, looking for coded messages in the fall of the cards and the arrangement of the tables? On the other hand, if Mr. Tinderflint, Lord Tierney, Mr. Taggart, was a secret Jacobite, this might explain the hold Mr. Peele seemed to have on him. Jacobites, even titled ones, had been marched through the streets and beheaded as recently as five months ago. They had had their estates taken away and were forced into exile. Some were transported to wildernesses like Virginia.

The end result of all this profound and deeply uncomfortable pondering was that I did not immediately see Matthew Reade standing in the shade of one of the Thames's many willow groves. It is a further tribute to his own introspection at the time that he did not see me, even as I pulled up short to stare.

Mr. Reade stood on the bank, clutching a portfolio tied with black ribbon. He looked down at the sluggish waters, his fine-boned face drawn tight by both fury and despair. He hadn't even bothered to tie his hair back, and the dramatic dark red locks tumbled around his shoulders, getting caught by the freshening breeze and whipping across his tightly clenched jaw.

I could have turned away. I had plenty of worries of my own, but there was something in his stance, alone at the riverbank, that would not let me leave.

"Good morning," I called, unable to think of anything more original.

He jumped and whirled, and for a moment, I saw the whole of his anger plain on his face. The force and heat of it were enough to make me draw back a step.

"It's . . . Lady Francesca." Then I added feebly, "Not contemplating a dramatic ending, I hope?"

He recognized me then and managed a rueful grin. "Not seriously," he said. "But maybe I should be." This last he said to the portfolio in his hands, which—I could see as I drew closer—was filled with stacked pages.

"Last time you were wrestling papers. Now you're going to drown them. I think, sir, you've picked the wrong apprenticeship."

"How odd. I was just thinking the same thing."

His tone was soft and bitter, and something twisted in me to hear it. The sketch I'd taken from the other papers was truly lovely. I couldn't believe these would be less so.

"May I see?" I asked.

Mr. Reade looked at me for a long, quiet space, his sharp face drawn and grave. I don't know what answer he saw in my own expression, but he did pass me the portfolio.

It was, naturally enough for an artist's 'prentice, filled with sketches. They were landscapes mostly, or fragments of them—a single tree or flower might be rendered from multiple angles on the page. There were bits and pieces of rooms as well: a window latch, the inside of a clock, a barred door. But most remarkable were the portraits. I had never seen drawings where the people seemed so alive, and so very true to their originals. Here were Molly Lepell and Sophy Howe, the one laughing, the other peering out from behind a fan. Another sketch portrayed Mary Bellenden kicking up her skirts as she descended the stairs. The study of Mr. Walpole had all his suavity—and showed no mercy for his girth. Another drawing showed the Prince of Wales looking down over his wife's shoulder as she played at cards. It was an intimate, human view of the pair, without the posed pomp I'd seen in the portraits of kings that hung in the palace galleries.

"Astonishing," I breathed. Mr. Reade was quiet, and it occurred to me he was trying to decide whether I meant this. "I've never seen anything like these."

"I have, and better." He closed the portfolio and lifted it out of my hands. "Much better."

"Where?"

"In pictures from Amsterdam," he said. "They have painters among them . . . Their art is in bringing things to life simply, elegantly. Showing the fall of sunlight, shadows against earth. People as they are, as the eye and the heart see them. Life as it truly exists. Not gods and artificial allegories."

"I take it you've had your fill of the cherubs?"

"Oh, I'm not permitted to touch the cherubs. I'm good only for grinding paints and making my bow. I make a very good bow, you know."

"I had noticed."

"Had you really?"

I wish to remark here that it is entirely unfair for any man to be able to put so much into a serious look as Matthew Reade did. My cheeks began to heat, and as we were in the shade, I had no hope he would attribute my coloring to the warming sun. But there was more to my sudden awkwardness than the warmth of his look. Something was not right here. Something recently seen or done was leaving me restless, but I could not think what.

"An apprenticeship is not forever," I said, by way of changing the subject. Apprentices signed on to serve a master for a set length of time. At the end of that, they were free to go their way as journeymen. I reflected it must be a fine thing to see where the door out of one's troubles waited.

"No, not forever." Matthew sighed. "I do thank the good lord for that."

"What will you do when your articles are fulfilled?"

"Travel. Study. I'll go to Amsterdam, of course, and Florence, and Rome if I can. I'll work with whoever will teach me. Learn the new styles and how to bring real life to the canvas."

"But art is supposed to enlighten, isn't it? Not just reflect? It's to show us the best of the present modeled in the best of the past."

He shot me a look of pure surprise and was silent again, again seeming to try to discern if my words were sincere. I fought back my impatience. I'd already seen enough of court life to understand such hesitations.

"That's not the past on that ceiling." He ran a thumb restlessly over the black ribbon of his portfolio. "It's not even true allegory. It's flattery dressed up in a lot of flowing robes and gilding."

"And cherubs," I added.

"Oh, God in Heaven, don't remind me of the cherubs."

He was so overtly despairing, I had to laugh. Not a co-quette's showy laugh, but my own. It felt wonderful. Espe-cially when Matthew smiled and returned a low chuckle. He glanced at me again, a thoughtful look this time. It occurred to me that there were many things I would forsake if I might be allowed a little more time to be contemplated by Mat-thew Reade. This was improper and indecorous, and I regret-ted it not one bit.

"Will my lady . . . would you care to sit awhile?" He gestured toward the riverbank.

I was fully aware I should say no. I had my own business to attend to. If I truly meant to unknot the riddle that was Lady Francesca, I needed to keep my rendezvous in the Wil-derness. At the same time, I wanted desperately to have just a moment of friendship and simple country sunlight. But even this presented its difficulties. I looked at the damp and muddy grass and thought of my pale muslin skirts.

Matthew saw my dilemma at once. With a great show, he doffed his plain coat, spread it out over the offending ground, and made a deep bow. I returned a solemn curtsy and arranged myself on the slope.

"So, what of you, Lady Francesca?" he asked as he settled down beside me.

"I'm sorry?"

"Have you picked out your husband yet?"

All my pleasant feelings went up in a single puff of smoke, and I turned on him. "What makes you think I'm hunting a husband?"

"Oh, don't." Matthew waved the heat in my words away as if it were nothing at all. "Of course you are husband hunting. It's the only reason to come to court as a young woman, unless—"

"Unless *what*?"

"Unless you're seeking influence."

"I'm not even going to dignify that with an answer." I faced the river. I should not stay here. I should leave at once. I had an assignation to keep. And I hoped I was sitting on his only good coat and that it was becoming stained beyond retrieval.

"I'm sorry," Matthew said, sounding genuinely surprised. "I'd thought you'd prefer honesty."

"You're not being honest. You're being contemptible."

The truth was, I had no idea why his words hurt so much. The assumptions were natural. In fact, they were the most obvious ones to make. Still, I did not want him to think so little of me.

"But you must be keeping an eye out for a husband," Matthew persisted.

"Why must I?"

"Because you have to get married. Otherwise—"

"I think you'd better stop now. You're not making yourself sound any better."

He did stop, and we sat together, silent and awkward, watching the dragonflies skimming over the waters. The sun had risen high enough that it touched the back of my neck with an uncomfortable warmth. I needed to go. I truly did have to meet Robert. I didn't move. I could not bear to leave this particular conversation in such a shambles.

"I do not have my eye on any man," I said to the reeds and the dragonflies. "I have my reasons to be here, but they don't involve looking for a rich husband, or any kind of husband at all. I just . . ."

"Just what?"

"I just want to survive," I whispered. "I just want to be free."

Matthew said nothing in answer to this. I ducked my head and wished for a fan. I wanted to be able to hide my blushing cheeks and my prickling eyes. I was being ridiculous, and I knew it. There was no call for so much drama over so small a thing. But my private remonstrance made no difference to my private feeling.

It was Matthew who broke the silence. "I owe you an apology, m'lady."

"For what?" I asked, attempting to force some levity into my voice, as befitted a flighty little maid of honor, the sort who might be out a-husband-hunting.

"For thinking you might be like the others. You're nothing of their kind."

"I'll choose to take that as a compliment."

"I meant it as one."

A fresh warmth, which had nothing to do with embarrassment or even the sun on my neck, blossomed slowly within me. I found myself able to smile. I kept my eyes fixed on the river, however. If I looked at Matthew Reade, I might say something I should not, although I had no idea what on earth that might be.

"How is it you come to be here, Mr. Reade?" I asked the river. "What is it you seek at court?"

"It wasn't the court I sought. Just training." He ran his fingers gently across the tall grass stems, studying the play of sun and shadow as they moved. "I worked in my father's apothecary shop when I was a boy. I learned to grind the herbs and make up the pills, but what I loved most was looking at the handbills that came in with the patent medicines. I learned to trace the capital letters and the fancy script. Father thought this a sign I was fitted out to be a scholar."

I heard his rueful tone, but I wasn't watching his face. I was fascinated by his broad hand passing back and forth. His nails were short and clean, his fingers blunt and stained with faint color. There was a sprinkling of fine hair up by his wrist that caught the light as his hand moved in and out of the sun.

"My schoolmaster urged Father to apprentice me to an artist. Probably it had something to do with how there were always more cartoons than letters on my slate." We both chuckled at this. "So I was with a man named Barber for a while, and then Thornhill bought my articles, and here I am."

"And yet he doesn't think much of you," I ventured, and he grimaced.

"I should be grateful for my luck, I know." He closed his fist above the grass stems. "Everyone knows Thornhill is the foremost artist of our day. And I would be grateful, if he were interested at all in teaching us."

"What does interest him?" I asked.

"His grand plans and making the most of the name of Thornhill. He also doesn't think much of the new styles. He insists that the classical subjects are the only ones fit for great works." He shook his head. "So we disagree, and I am relegated to grinding paints until I learn to keep my mouth shut."

I meant to make some witty and consoling reply. But as Matthew talked of his life, a gray cloud settled over me. I could share nothing in return for his confidence. Not a single story of my past. Not a wish, not a hope. Not even my real name.

I stood.

"M'lady, what's the matter?" asked Matthew, scrambling awkwardly to his feet

"Nothing. Everything. I . . . I shouldn't be here." The sun was almost at its zenith. I couldn't remember when I'd last heard the great clock above the palace gate strike. Had it gone past noon while I was sitting here on Matthew Reade's coat talking piffle? "I'll be missed. I should go."

"I'll walk with you." He retrieved his coat and papers. "I must get back anyway."

"No, no, please don't." I couldn't let him see what would happen next, especially since I had no idea what it would be. He was thinking well of me, and I hated the possibility that I might show myself up to him as just a scheming courtier.

But Matthew mistook the reason I turned so quickly away. "Wait." He caught my arm. "I understand we cannot be equals, but is there reason we cannot be friends?"

Yes. Yes, there is. Of course I could not say this. In fact, I was quite sure my mouth would refuse to shape the words.

"Even for just this little while?" We both looked down at his hand where he held my arm. I could feel the warmth of it through the light muslin of my sleeve. "Friends only. Nothing more, I promise. I . . ." He raised his eyes to mine. They were a deep, steel gray, and stunningly clear. I had no doubt he could see right through a lady with those eyes, and if I stood here any longer, he would see through me. "I think you do not have many friends, and I am sorry for it."

"It is hardly your fault," I mumbled. My gaze fell once more on his hand, a sight that provided no respite for my mind. I pulled reluctantly away. I felt awkward, heavy. I slumped like a peasant woman, all decorum and deportment gone. Mr. Tinderflint would be appalled.

"Just the same." Matthew ducked his head, trying to capture my gaze again. Trying and succeeding. "Can you think of me as a friend?"

"Yes. Easily."

"Then do so." His smile grew hopeful. "And if ever you have need of a chevalier, I can be found in the long workshop in the king's courtyard. You know the building?"

I could have said I did not. I could have said that I would never seek help from a man I knew so slightly. Oh, folly! Oh, how weak is maiden's resolve, that she should melt so easily before a pair of steel gray eyes and the smile that lights a lean face! I could only nod in acknowledgment, for I did know the building, and I did want to feel I had earned a chevalier. Matthew Reade smiled again, and made his excellent bow, and walked away.

It was a long time before I could do the same. But it was not admiration that rooted me to the spot. It was realization. I knew what was simmering beneath my thoughts as we sat together on the riverbank. It was Matthew's collection of court portraits. He had taken the likenesses of three of the maids of honor—Molly, Mary, and Sophy.

Where was the drawing of Lady Francesca?

CHAPTER EIGHTEEN

In which the scheduled meeting is concluded, but not with any expected party, and Our Heroine makes a rash promise to a small but important person.

The Wilderness is the name given to Hampton Court's great hedge maze, though for what reason I know not. There exists nothing less wild than its rigidly clipped hornbeam hedges and meticulously maintained pathways.

I was so certain I was late, I decided to cut through the maze itself rather than take the longer, straighter way along the broad lanes. It might seem odd to choose a labyrinth over an avenue, but the true secret of the Wilderness is that it is fairly easy to navigate. One cannot, I suppose, risk royalty becoming genuinely lost. I selected the curving paths, to better keep out of sight of any other idlers, and carefully counted my turnings. The day had begun to warm in earnest, and the Wilderness felt as stuffy as any interior room of the palace. My skin began to itch with perspiration under my arms and under my corset, and under my garters, and under my cap. Still, I did not permit myself to slow down. I was entirely certain I was late. I attempted to berate myself for being so long distracted by Matthew Reade, but the voice of my conscience failed to muster her usual force. Instead I found myself remembering Matthew's hand as it passed delicately over the grass stems and the way the sunlight caught his eyes.

He'd contemplated my face, and he liked what he saw. He smiled, and he offered me his friendship and his help. He did not pay me clumsy or salacious compliments. He did not paw my shoulder, my cheek, or my skirts. There was no innuendo or bribery. Matthew Reade wanted to talk with me and be my friend. How had so simple a thing come to seem so rare and so very precious? And yet—and yet there was that matter of the missing drawing. Why had he completed portraits of all the other maids, but not of Francesca?

Consumed as I was by these disparate thoughts, I did not hear the footsteps I should have, and rounded the final corner only to collide forcefully with a small girl in a blue silk dress running in the opposite direction. We both staggered backwards and stared at each other.

I spoke first. "What are you doing here?"

"The Portland says I'm not to have a puppy," she replied with the particular and implacable logic possessed by young children.

Portland. I knew that name but could not immediately call to mind which of the long lists of courtiers it belonged to. The girl herself looked to be six or seven years old, and she regarded me with two large, slightly protruding eyes. She'd pulled her cap off her blond curls, and it dangled by its strings from one white and pink fist. I looked at those eyes, and I looked at her blue dress with its white ruffles on sleeve and collar, and the quantity of lace on her miniature petticoats. Mrs. Abbott's training in assessing cost and material flooded through me, and I felt a deep and sudden chill run up my spine.

"Does the . . . Portland say why you're not to have a puppy?" I asked.

"She says dogs are filthy creatures," replied the girl. "And they'll spoil my dress and her nerves, and if God had meant princesses to live with dogs, He would not have given them palaces, and what do you think?"

Privately, I thought that I was late to my assignation and that I did not have the time to face one of the royal daughters.

"What do you *think*?" the princess repeated with a stamp of one small, gilt-buckled foot.

"I don't know. I haven't spoken with God on the subject. Or your nurse, who should be here somewhere, shouldn't she?" I tried desperately to see around the obstructing hedges.

The princess shrugged. "They're all busy scolding Amelia and cleaning up Caroline. It's not hard to get out."

"Especially if you've had practice." This must be Princess Anne, the oldest of the three legitimate royal daughters. I had seen her only once before, on the day of the king's departure, and that had been from the back.

"It's been the only good thing about moving here," she

said. "It's big, and there's the back stairs. Have you seen the back stairs?"

"It is big, and not yet." At that moment, what I most wanted to see was the miraculous arrival of one of those busy nurses, because otherwise I faced a duty. A strangely domestic duty, considering my surroundings and my recent plans. No nurse came to my rescue, however, and I could do nothing but sigh.

"Well, Your Highness. We'd better return you to your people." As Olivia had no younger siblings, my experience with children was limited. I thought I should probably like them, given the opportunity. My experience with princesses, however, was both recent and extensive, and I knew for a certainty they were not permitted to run freely about the meadows or the mazes. I suspected this rule was observed all the more strictly for the ones rendered in miniature.

"Why do I have to go back?" demanded Her Minuscule Highness. "The Portland's an old fuss face."

I bit my lip and attempted to approximate a frown. I had been known to utter similar sentiments at a similar age. Despite this sympathetic accord, I managed to muster at least some severity. "You have to go back because if I'm caught with you, I'll get in trouble for harboring a fugitive. In which case, neither one of us will get a puppy." I started down the nearest path, and as I suspected she might, the princess ran to catch up with me.

"Are you going to get a puppy? What color? May I come visit?"

"Not if I'm locked in the Tower for harboring a fugitive."

"Oh. All right." She trotted along obligingly for a moment, then another thought seemed to occur to the small royal mind. "If you're not locked in the Tower, may I come visit the puppy?"

"My word of honor."

Someone was coming around the hedge wall. I heard the rustle of cloth in the still summer air. I prayed fervently it was the nurse. I feared desperately it was Robert.

It was neither. It was Sophy Howe. What was more, she was moving slowly, with her skirts clutched close about her, while at the same time pressing her back against the hedge wall. She was going to snag her laces doing that. But I did not mention it. Neither did I mention the fact that her eyes being open so wide and her chin being drawn so far back in surprise rather emphasized that she had been caught in a position best described as mid-sneak.

"Why, Miss Howe!" I smiled my best drawing room smile. "I'm sure you know our Princess Anne?"

Sophy's eyes narrowed, but protocol held sway. She let go of her skirts so she could render the deep curtsy that proper manners required upon the meeting of a princess, be she ever so tiny. I seized the moment, and the princess's hand, and hurried us both out of the maze and down the broad lane toward the palace.

On the way, I realized two things. First, although the formal gardens and well-spaced trees provided excellent views all around, there was no sign of Robert Ballantyne.

Either he'd also been hiding among the hedges and had decided not to make an appearance, or the person who had penned the note that brought me here was not Robert at all. Rather, it was the only other adult I'd seen since I left Matthew Reade: the sneaking Sophy Howe.

CHAPTER NINETEEN

IN WHICH OUR HEROINE ENGAGES

IN GAMES BOTH NEW AND OLD.

After my abortive adventure in the Wilderness, I returned my royal charge to a fuming governess whom I had to agree merited the title of fuss face. I then returned myself to my room, where I remained under the excuse of a "slight indisposition." This could be only a temporary retreat, however.

I had been allowed the day off from waiting, but was still required to be in attendance during the evening gathering. I eventually did have to permit myself to be dressed and painted so I could sit at a gilt and marble card table, partnered with Molly, facing Mary and, of course, Sophy over yet another hand of ombre.

That evening was a trial for us both. There was the glint of knives in her eyes and in her play. She was bidding high, much higher than usual. Even Mary Bellenden was struggling to keep up, and I'd seen Mary toss a silver-gilt bracelet on the table once over a wager she knew was as good as throwing it away. Thanks to Mr. Peele's intensive training in the observation of play and players, I knew by now that Sophy normally played not to win, but to impress. With the titled gentlemen, for instance, or the more influential ladies of the bedchamber, Sophy played with what I can only describe as fierce insouciance. For this game, however, there was no one at our table she could have wished to impress, except me, and I had no idea what sort of impression she meant to make. My failure to comprehend her signals was clearly driving needle-points into her already aggravated temper. I am sorry to admit it, but there was some small, malicious comfort in this.

It was Thursday, and an informal evening, and there were not above three dozen or so gentlemen and their wives in attendance. The majority of the wives were scattered among the sofas and refreshment tables exchanging light news and gossip. Some played together at the lesser gaming tables, lingering companionably over piquet, lottery, and the like as they waited on one of the subtle invitations that pass back and forth in such gatherings, which would allow them to draw closer through the layers of influence and precedence around the royal person. The gentlemen clustered in their own thick company. They had not yet refreshed themselves sufficiently from the bottles, nor had they finished their argument over whether there had been some skullduggery at the Newmarket races. When both had been completed to their satisfaction, then they would scatter among us ladies, to talk or take up cards.

My mistress was already at play. Her Royal Highness had for this time claimed Lady Cowper and Lady Montague for a game of three-handed ombre, and they were all currently seated at the triangular table made of inlaid wood and designed solely for such games. Absorbed in their own careful calculations of points and bids, they were not paying Sophy, or myself, the least bit of attention.

Or so I thought.

I had just bid two hearts when Her Royal Highness raised her voice. "It seems, Lady Francesca, that I am much reduced."

The argument over the claret and Bordeaux had been growing heated, but the instant Her Royal Highness spoke, the men fell silent. The gossip and gasps over the gaming tables also ceased. All ears, and the majority of the eyes, turned to me.

One cannot remain seated or with one's back turned when addressed by royalty. I was obliged to lay down my cards and stand while the whole of the gathering watched. I had not been so much the center of attention since my first night at court, and I was not enjoying this encore performance as I turned and curtsied.

"Madame?" I croaked, and felt Sophy's smile like a knife on the back of my neck.

"I am become an errand runner." Her Highness nonchalantly played the five of clubs over Lady Cowper's two of diamonds. A princess, of course, need not face a courtier, even one she has summoned like a naughty pupil to the head of the class. "I am instructed, most firmly, may I add, to carry a message to you."

"That is most kind of Your Highness," remarked Sophy at my back. "To go so out of your way. You must be keeping very important company these days, Fran, to have a lover who will importune a princess."

"Oh, you're just annoyed because none of your lovers will importune Her Highness for your sake," piped up Mary.

Which raised a general wave of laughter from the company.

"As opposed to yours, Mary, who couldn't even reach up high enough to importune a rat catcher," muttered Sophy to her cards. This earned a rush of laughter and a long current of *ohs* as the men drank and elbowed each other. Tiffs between the maids were considered grand entertainments and much relished by our fine gentlemen. I felt like asking Molly to go to them and collect their ticket fees. If I was going to be set upon the stage, I should at least be able to charge admission.

Molly Lepell, however, had more useful things to do. I heard the snap of pasteboard as she laid down another card. "One might wonder who gave such a message to Her Royal Highness."

"Yes, one might, so we can find the blighter," remarked one of the gentlemen from the herd beside the wine decanters. He had on a shocking pink and rose coat. It matched the flush in his cheeks, and I could not remember his name. "I'll beard the fellow myself for his temerity in sending messages to my fairest." He winked at me.

The princess smiled. "Lady Francesca, my daughter Anne wishes to know if you have been sent to the Tower yet, and if not, she asks to be informed when she will be allowed to come visit the puppy."

This, of course, would have been the time for a poised and witty response. What I believe I said was, "Oh."

"She then begged me to let you know that if you were in fact confined to the Tower, she would undertake to ensure your puppy was well cared for."

"Oh."

"Lady Francesca?"

"Madame?"

The princess put her cards face-down on the table and folded her hands across them. "Are you expecting to be confined to the Tower at any time in the near future?"

"No, madame," I said, hoping no one could tell how dry my mouth had gone. Probably they could not. The general laughter permeating the room would cover any such nuance of speech.

Her Royal Highness, with that nicety of judgment that she owns, waited for the laughter to die away so the whole room could clearly hear her next question, and my response, of course. "And have you a puppy?"

"No, madame."

"Oh, dear," murmured Sophy. "That will be such a disappointment to our dear Princess Anne." She had a further witticism poised on her sharp little tongue, I could tell. I had already been made a laughingstock to enliven a dull evening, and she meant to have her full share of the fun. The room was ready for it, and the princess would allow it. What I didn't know was why. Even under the smothering embarrassment, I found myself wondering what I had done to so offend my mistress. Was all this just because I had spoken rashly to her rebellious daughter?

"Not yet, that is."

Her Royal Highness arched her brows, and she was not the only one. For a moment, I found myself wondering who had said those words and how I was going to tell that person to be quiet without being hopelessly rude in front of royalty. Belatedly, I realized that it was I who had spoken.

"Not yet?" said Sophy. "The creature is coming by the next stage, I suppose? Is it right that a puppy should travel by itself, or will it have a chaperone?"

"Some old bitch, presumably," said another of the gentlemen, and they all guffawed at this cunning repartee.

The weight of shame fell back, allowing a blind panic to take precedence. What was I to do? I knew there were hunting dogs in the palace kennels, but other than that the only dogs I had any experience of in London were Olivia's and —

Inspiration struck with force and speed, setting my thoughts into a mad gallop.

"That's exactly it, Sophy." I turned as much as I could without actually setting my back to Her Royal Highness and pasted on my finest and most insincere smile. "You are always so clever. I am having the puppy delivered."

"Delivered?" inquired the princess. "From where?"

"Stemhempfordshire."

A giggle rippled through the assembly, but not from Sophy. "What an exotic location," she remarked, with the distinct seasoning of wariness in her tone.

"Not so. It's a little northwest of Kent." I fully faced Her Royal Highness again. "Lady Hannah Applepuss breeds a most superior race of pure white miniature hounds, and has promised me one as soon as I desire. I can write to her immediately, if Your Highness permits." I made this declaration with what must be considered an astounding clarity and level of assurance for someone lying through her teeth to royalty while an audience of the wealthy, powerful, and overdressed looked on. I even remembered to add a neat curtsy to underscore the point.

"You will write to an imagined acquaintance in a county that does not exist?" Sophy filled her voice with the most acid variety of surprise. "Fran, that is a very odd thing to say. Are you certain your fever has not returned? Perhaps, Your Highness, Lady Francesca should be excused."

I felt my own smile forming. I had hoped she'd say something like that. "I promise you," I said to the princess, and the room at large, "that by writing to the person I have named, I will have a pure white pup delivered here by next . . . Friday." I told myself silently that eight days would be enough for what I was abruptly and dangerously setting in motion. More than enough.

"You promise, do you?" said Lady Montague, who sat at the princess's right hand. There was in her words something akin to the quiver in a cat's whisker when it scents the approach of the mouse. "What do you say to that, Miss Howe?"

Sophy decided to make a play at loftiness, an attitude with which she was on intimate terms. "I say that our Fran loves a little drama. It will be no great feat to write to some friend in the city and pretend she's complied with all this nonsense. I could do as much without making up nonexistent places or girls with ridiculous names."

"Not so ridiculous," said one of the gentlemen. "Ain't there some Applepusses in Lincoln?"

"Darbyshire," his friend corrected him. "Grover Applepuss. Not much a one for dogs, though."

The conversation threatened to drift to the bloodlines of dogs and men, and I could easily have let it go. But I did not. Instead, I lifted my voice. "If a letter will not suffice to prove what I say, I shall advertise."

"Advertise?" The word came awkwardly to Her Royal Highness's tongue. "Advertise where?"

"In the shipping news, of course, as I mean to have the pup delivered. The *Morning Gazetteer* should suffice."

"You'll have mongrels from all corners of London lined up in front of the gatehouse," remarked Lady Cowper, who was rearranging the cards in her hand and clearly wondering when the play would begin again.

"Certainly not," I declared. "No one will mistake a notice for Lady Hannah Applepuss."

"She's making fun, Your Highness," said Sophy. "Really, Fran, you always did have the most absurd sense of humor."

"Better absurd than none at all," murmured Molly. Only the two or three ladies at the table closest to us could have heard her words, but they were already putting their heads together so their whispers and smothered giggles rippled about the room.

I turned three-quarters toward the Howe. Sophy still held her cards fanned in front of her, as if she was waiting for me to make my play.

Which, I suppose, she was, and which I did. "Would you care to make a wager on it?"

If there had been anyone in that room who had not been paying attention, the word *wager* ended that indifference. Members of the court would bet astronomical sums on the strangest and smallest outcomes. I had myself witnessed two gentlemen placing fifty pounds on the question of whether a fly would light on a spill of brandy or a spill of claret first.

"I say I can acquire a pure white dog, bred, trained, groomed, and fit to accompany a princess, as the result of one advertisement addressed to Lady Hannah Applepuss, by Friday week."

This was dangerous. I should stop. There was too much that could go wrong, especially once Mrs. Abbott worked out what I'd done. Which she would, because I had more than thirty extremely amused and highly voluble witnesses to my folly. But if the finish to this was my finally getting a message to Olivia, it was worth any risk. Or so I prayed.

"Why would I enter into such a ridiculous wager?" inquired Sophy with an expert arch of her perfectly plucked brow.

"Because," I replied evenly. "You're the one who says I'm lying."

Liar was not one of those charges one made in public. What had been an air of amusement emanating from our audience grew distinctly more chilled and serious. In that same moment, Sophy's painted cheeks took on a deeper color. Had we been men, and not in the presence of Her Royal Highness, there would have been fists thrown and swords drawn. As it was, we were girls and could only smile daggers and danger at each other.

"Well, Sophy? What answer will you make to that?" Her Highness remained apparently unruffled by the change of atmosphere about us.

"Very well, Fran. I accept the wager." I saw wheels turning behind Sophy's eyes, each one winding her anger a little tighter. "Shall we say ten pounds?"

"Say twenty, if you like." With my losses so far tonight, that sum represented my entire remaining stock of pin money. But that was the least of it. If I failed in this, Sophy would have succeeded on two distinct points. First, I would have made a complete and public fool of myself. Second, I would have angered Her Royal Highness for causing a disruption in the royal nursery. With the loss of her preference, I would further lose the cachet that was bringing me to the notice of the powerful, which was in its turn supposed to keep me in gifts and money that I could squirrel away for that distant future when I was free again. I thought of the jewels that I had already received with a longing that surprised and chagrined me.

And for what was I risking this all? A chance to throw my cleverness into the face of Sophy Howe, because she disliked my predecessor and reminded me a little too much of Lady Clarenda. That, and the barest sliver of a chance that this time my message might get through to Olivia.

"Twenty pounds, then," Sophy replied, her voice as taut as any harp string. "But you write the advertisement now, and I choose the messenger to deliver it."

"As you like," I answered steadily.

The whole gathering was diverted, and I heard other wagers being contracted as fresh bottles were uncorked. Mr. Fortinbras, he of the shocking pink coat, and his friend Lord Blakeney detached themselves from the pack of claret drinkers to make a great show of escorting me to the delicate writing desk in one of the great room's alcoves. There they laid out paper, inspected the quill in the pen holder, and dipped it carefully in ink before handing it to me, so I could write.

To Lady H. Applepuss: for immediate delivery 1 white dog to the Thames bridge, Molesey. Will Friday night, eight of the clock, suit?

I sanded and blotted the missive and handed it to Mr. Fortinbras, who then carried it with all due solemnity to Her Royal Highness for inspection, and to read aloud to the assembly. I had to look around a moment to find Sophy. She had left the card table and now stood with her back to the great doors, a triumphant expression on her face.

"That would seem to meet the conditions of the wager," declared the princess. "Sophy, how will it be delivered?"

"By hand, of course." Sophy pushed open the door just a little, and Robert, resplendent in his footman's livery, walked in. He looked disconcerted for a moment to find every person in the room attending his modest entry, but he kept his aplomb and bowed very low.

I was not in any way surprised, although I could tell from the edge to Sophy's smile that she expected grave consternation to overtake me. For my part, I had expected her to summon Robert if she could. Whatever war she and Francesca had engaged in over this man, Sophy would not miss a chance to demonstrate her power over him.

"Lady Francesca has a message to be delivered, Robert," said Sophy, clearly and distinctly, in case my continued calm was an indication that I had failed to notice which footman she had summoned. "You're to take it at once to the offices of . . . now, where was it?"

"The Morning Gazetteer." I retrieved the notice from the princess with a curtsy and then took several coins from my stack at the card table. "This should pay for the advertisement and for having to wake up the house." I reached out to put them all in his hands. Robert's eyes narrowed, wary and confused. All of an instant, I decided there was time to add one more gambit to my game.

I let my hands slip to drop coins and paper onto the parquet floor in a loud shower.

"I do . . . I beg your pardon . . . I am so sorry." Robert scrambled to retrieve the coins amid laughter and exclamation. I grabbed up the advertisement again, and again handed it to him. For a single heartbeat, we were face-to-face and there was noise enough to cover any whisper.

"Princess's new apartment, after this," I breathed as I straightened. Understanding flashed in Robert's dark amber eyes before he bowed and withdrew.

I turned back to the gathering and Her Royal Highness and executed another curtsy, which earned me a spattering of applause, which clearly did not sit well with Sophy. She lifted her pert nose as if she hoped to find cleaner air closer to the ceiling.

With Robert's departure, the immediate prospect of continued drama dimmed. The rich and noble crowd dispersed to pick over the bones of older gossip, call for fresh bottles of wine and port, and, on our princess's part, summon several political gentlemen to consult with about her cards.

"I imagine you're quite proud of that performance, Fran," sniffed Sophy as we maids settled back to our seats and our game. "But I should be afraid of being made so ridiculous by such a promise."

"Oh, you should," said Molly to Sophy. "Especially if that dog arrives."

"On the contrary," I said. I pulled the nine of hearts from

my hand and laid it down. "I'm feeling quite grateful to you, Sophy. I believe you've done me a favor."

"Well, I'm glad to be of service." She crossed it with the queen of spades. "I assure you it was unintentional."

"Of that I have no doubt," I answered. "No doubt whatsoever."

CHAPTER TWENTY

IN WHICH SOME MOST UNWELCOME SUSPICIONS

ARE CONFIRMED AND A TEACUP

IS LEFT BEHIND IN DARKNESS.

Well. I expect you are most pleased with yourself for that night's work."

To that growing list of items about which I was not surprised, I might now add the following: By the time I returned to my rooms, Mrs. Abbott was already well informed about my wager with Sophy Howe. After the scene with Robert, I had let Sophy take all the tricks and escaped the royal presence the moment the princess permitted us to withdraw. But no mortal can move as swiftly as gossip.

"It was necessary, Mrs. Abbott." I sat carefully on the sofa, making sure I was not creasing my train or any bows. My head ached, both from the weight of my wig and the disquiet of my thoughts. I desperately wanted to climb into my bed. Or hide under it.

"In what way was making a spectacle of yourself in front of the court necessary?" Mrs. Abbott inquired with the coldest of all possible calms.

"Because if I am successful in obtaining the pup, I will have endeared myself to Her Young Highness Princess Anne, which will surely increase my credit with the Princess of Wales."

Mrs. Abbott stood, silent as any statue. I had surprised her, and for a moment, she let it show. Tired and worried as I was, I felt the thrill of triumph in my veins at that sight.

"Very good," Mrs. Abbott said, drawing the words out to three and four times their natural length. "Yes. It is very well played, this."

"Thank you." I gave her a theatrically gracious nod. "I also have managed a fresh assignation with Robert."

I expected this news would be less well received, so her stony silence did not disappoint. I steeled my nerve, ready for the quiver in her lip that signaled a storm to be unleashed. I tried to prepare myself to argue, or to, unthinkably, issue orders.

Then, against what I would have believed to be all the laws of nature, Mrs. Abbott nodded.

"Yes. Now. It will serve." She added something too soft for me to make out, but my relief at not having to take on yet another battle royale was such that I wouldn't have cared if she'd begun talking to the furniture.

"When is this assignation?" she asked me.

"At once."

"Then it must look natural. You will wait here."

She left by the door to the gallery. I sprang to my work-basket, unearthed Francesca's sketch of the ceiling in the princess's new apartments, and stuffed it into my sleeve.

Wherever Mrs. Abbott had gone, it was not far. I barely had time to kick my basket back under the chair before the door opened again.

She'd brought a teacup. Ignoring my glance of surprise, Mrs. Abbott poured a measure of sherry from the decanter on the side table into the cup. She handed it to me, along with a candle.

"If anyone asks, you will say you take this to one of your sister maids. That Molly the Treasure perhaps. She has a low stomach, and this is a special tisane for her."

"Thank you." I looked at Mrs. Abbott with new respect. These small details brought home to me that this was not her first intrigue. She might even be very good at this business of spying. Could we, I wondered, eventually become something of friends? Could she teach me to do as she did?

I saw nothing to that end in her dark eyes. But hope is a persistent creature, and I carried it with me as I stepped into the gallery.

It was the small hours of the morning, but almost no one was abed. Palace residents and guests clustered together in the various chambers to talk or drink, or both. Some passed me in the galleries on the way to assorted apartments, whether their own or someone else's. Servants also traveled to and fro, bringing wine, basins, or whatever else their masters might need. Even though I was still in my court dress with its bulky train, I was in no way especially remarked upon. If I was saluted, it was with a jest about the promised puppy and what I might do with any money I won.

The gallery that led to the apartments being improved for Her Royal Highness was blessedly empty. As I drew the door shut, I was engulfed in silence. Robert had not yet arrived. The light of the full moon streamed through the diamond-paned windows. I set the teacup on a worktable beside the door and moved carefully to the center of the room, taking my candle with me. Its circle of light felt pitifully small in that great, silent moonlit chamber. Under the influence of the silver beams, the tables, buckets, ladders, and easels turned into a dreamlike wilderness. The scaffolding and drop cloths sprouted strange shadows. It was cold as well, and I shivered.

I pulled out Francesca's sketch and shook it open. The angle of the moonlight left much of the ceiling's mural in shadow, but the central tableau remained fairly clear, though its colors were dim and difficult to discern. I did not dare light any of the lanterns I saw on the tables around me. I might need to return to darkness in a hurry.

My plan was that I could at least put this bit of my mystery to rest and then turn my attention to Robert and to trying to find out more about this business between him and Francesca. I was ready to see sloppy workmanship on Francesca's sketch, and to be once and for all able to dismiss these drawings from consideration. I told myself I carried nothing but a failed attempt at copying a master's work.

But sloppy workmanship was not what I found. Overhead, Thornhill's painting showed a complex scene: there was the god Apollo, his chariot, and its horses. There was the winged woman, Leucothoe, hanging on to his arm. There below on a rocky landscape were a man and woman, lying side by side, plainly asleep.

In the drawing in my hand, that pair had their limbs clumsily sprawled and their heads thrown back. Francesca had drawn them not in sleep, but in death. The face on the central figure that took Apollo's place was too young and too long to be the god of the painting overhead. It was handsome still, but its nose was prominent and curving, and its eyes heavily lidded. Neither was this penciled Apollo amused, like the painted one above. He was determined, almost martial in his aspect.

There was something wrong with winged Leucothoe as well. But as I craned my neck in a futile attempt to peer more closely at her, I heard the soft sound of the doorknob turning. I blew out the candle and ducked behind the nearest canvas draped ladder, hastily tucking my sketch back into my sleeve.

A shadow darted inside, and as the moonlight flashed on loops of braid, I recognized Robert. I moved into the nearest moonbeam. He saw me at once, but held up his hand, leaning back to listen at the door he'd just closed. When he was satisfied with the level of silence, he rushed forward and clasped both my hands. I braced myself to be kissed, but Robert was not in such a mood this time.

"Fran, what on earth are you up to?" he whispered harshly.

I drew myself up and frowned in my confusion. "What am I up to? What about you? Where were you this morning?" I had made up my mind to act as if I still believed the note leading me to the Wilderness had come from Robert. In part, this was to draw him out, but I admit I had another aim as well: to see how he would react when I spoke Sophy's name. She had chosen him to deliver my advertisement to the *Gazetteer*. There had to be a reason for that.

Robert's first reaction was simple confusion. "What do you mean?"

"I went into the Wilderness to meet you, as your note said. If you had been there, I wouldn't be in this mess!"

The moonlight made it difficult to fully judge an expression, but the confusion in Robert's voice lifted to pure incredulity. "You found a note in your *rooms*? And you followed it?"

"Of course I did. What—"

"It's the oldest trick in the world!" he snapped. "I would never leave a note just lying about where anyone could get a look at it! You should have burnt it and stayed away."

I turned away in a pretense of shame. "It was Sophy, wasn't it? Making trouble?"

"Of course it was Sophy! Who else would it be? And you had to go make this stupid bet with her!" Robert paced across the room, moving deeper into the shadows. I could just see the gleam of his eyes now as they shifted restlessly, glancing from the uncurtained windows to the door. He was worried. No, he was frightened.

"I didn't plan this, Robert," I answered honestly, and I told him how I happened across little Princess Anne in the Wilderness and promised her access to a puppy I didn't possess. "And then Her Royal Highness brought it up, and Sophy was so spiteful, I got carried away, I suppose." Which was true, as far as it went.

It did nothing, however, to soften Robert's anger. His hands repeatedly clenched the empty air, and I had the sudden idea he'd put distance between us so he would not be tempted to grab hold of me. "God in Heaven, Fran, we can't afford for you to get carried away! You know that. Why must you court trouble?"

"And what would you have done? Let yourself be scolded and mocked for lying to the princess's daughter?"

"Of course! It's not as if any of this"—here he flung his arms wide to encompass the palace and the court—"matters to me."

"It matters to me." This was also the truth, and perhaps I should have been more chastened by it than I was. I knew my situation to be mad and precarious, but I enjoyed mingling as an equal with peers of the realm. I liked receiving attention from the men and being included in the company of the women and girls. More than that, I liked that I had gained some measure of respect from the Princess of Wales. I very much wanted to keep it.

"Will the advertisement be delivered?" I asked him.

"How can you be worried about that?" Robert forced the words through clenched teeth. "If you can't stop acting like a silly little girl, you are going to get us killed!"

Despite the fact that we both spoke in whispers, that last word rang through the empty room. *Killed*. He was in fear for his life. Our lives. Slowly I shrank back. A wave of nausea swept over me, and I pressed my hand to my stays. It was true, then. The reassurance I'd taken from Mrs. Abbott's tale of Francesca's last days had been fool's gold. Lady Francesca had been murdered. And I now stood in her place.

But I was not the only one distressed by the outburst. "Oh, Fran. I'm sorry." Robert choked on the words, and for a moment I thought he'd cry. "I'm so, so, sorry. I didn't mean to frighten you. Yes, it will be delivered. Sophy tried to argue me out of it, but I pointed out that everyone in court will be reading the *Gazetteer* to make sure it's there. I will deliver it. On my honor, I will. Please don't look at me like that."

I swallowed and closed my eyes, making a great show of composing myself. "I'm doing my best, Robert."

"I know it. I do know." He rushed forward then and wound his arms around me, pulling me into a surprisingly gentle embrace. I tried not to stiffen, but it was so strange, to be held this intimately, yet not be known at all. I could feel his heart hammering under his red coat and hear him swallowing his sobs. He had almost lost his Francesca, and he feared he was about to lose her again, and it hurt him deeply. I hated myself in that moment, and the deception I had taken on, because one way or another, I had to betray the love this man had given that other Francesca.

Slowly, terribly uncertain whether this was the right thing to do, I put my arms around Robert and returned his embrace.

"It won't be for much longer." Robert ran his fingers across my brow, seeking to smooth away the creases there. "I promise, I'll find a way out for us. But you have to see how difficult this has become, Fran. Sophy is insisting I find a way to have the paper's offices watched to see if anyone comes to ask about the advertisement."

"Sophy, again." I did not have to force the bitterness in my voice. "Ordering you about."

"Yes, ordering me about, and I must obey." Robert tried to chuck me underneath my chin, but I pulled away. "We have no choice."

Why not? What hold did she have over him? Over us? I turned away, pulling myself out of the circle of his arms. I did not want him to see the confusion and calculation that tumbled through me just then.

"I've let you down, I know," said Robert behind me. He was taking a step forward, and another. I could hear his shoes on the bare floor. "But things in the North finished so much more quickly than anyone guessed — there was simply no time to get us to our friends. We had to stay in place."

"Our friends?" The words were out before I could bite my tongue, hard. *Our friends in the North?* The North, where the Jacobites had rallied in their rebellion last winter.

"Yes, Fran," murmured Robert. "*Our* friends."

Robert was a Jacobite. Robert was not a swooning gallant or a pawn in some game played by bored courtiers. In this dark empty room, I stood next to a traitor spy, one in touch with the rebels in the North. They had plans for him, and Francesca had known. Francesca had known enough, been close enough, that she had been ready to flee with her paramour to join the rebellion.

"I've been looking for a way to tell you they've been in touch." Hope and energy returned to Robert's words. "Our plans aren't dead, only shifted."

I took a breath, and another. My ribs strained hard against my stays. I could not show surprise. Francesca had known this. I could not slide into the panic opening at the brink of my thoughts. I had to find a safe question to ask, one that would not give me away.

"But what can we possibly do now?"

Robert moved close again, a tiny smile playing about his mouth. "Fran, you know better." He closed his hands about my shoulders and shook me gently. "I can't tell you exactly what's happening. You're quite safe, of course, but we can't be too careful. We mustn't risk you getting . . . carried away again in the wrong company." He wasn't going to tell me what was happening. I had betrayed myself as monumentally indiscreet. I could only hope the fact that I was silently cursing myself as eighteen different kinds of fool did not show in the expression I turned up toward him.

"When we're done and safely out of here, I'll tell you

everything, I swear it," Robert said earnestly. "You believe me, don't you?"

I pulled back, partly because I needed space to breathe and partly because I wanted to see him better. His long face had become drawn and haggard as he looked down at me and saw his Fran.

"I believe you mean every word you say to me," I told him. This was the absolute truth, and the smile that erased the fear from Robert's face told me he accepted it. He kissed my brow, and my cheek, and the kiss was warm and tender. I thought I could feel the sorrow and the yearning in it. For the briefest moment, the loneliness in me chimed in a sympathetic vibration, for he was lonely too and in a danger that might, just might, be too deep for him. A treacherous little voice whispered, If I let him kiss me on the mouth, would that be so harmful? If I yielded just a little, to a craving for someone to be close to, what would it hurt?

"Fran." His mouth glided toward mine.

I lifted my hand and pressed my fingers to his lips. "We mustn't, Robert. I can't stay. I'm being watched too closely. It took everything just to get here to you."

Reluctantly, Robert loosened his embrace and stepped back. "I miss you so much, Fran," he said. "You have no idea. When I thought . . . when I thought you had died, I was ready to kill myself. I had the knife to my throat, and it was only the thought that I'd be denying myself the chance to be with you in Heaven that stopped me."

It should have sounded like bad melodrama, but there in

the moonlight and shadow, with the warmth from his kiss still on my brow, it was heartbreaking. I was suddenly certain Robert was going to profess love and expect me to do the same. I had to turn this conversation at once. Of all the lies I must tell, I could not tell that one. Robert was not some dress or mask that I could don to play my part and then discard. He was a man of flesh and blood: Whatever his loyalties, he loved his lady, and he deserved better than a counterfeit hope.

"It's only for a little while." I laid my hand on his and hated myself for being able to tilt my chin up and gaze steadily into his eyes. When had I acquired such skill at falsehood? One learned so many new things at court. "You promised."

"Yes. And it is true. I'll have you safely away before the court moves back to St. James for autumn, even if I have to snatch you right out from under that dragon's nose." He jerked his chin toward the door, and I knew he was thinking of Mrs. Abbott. So was I, and of what she would say if I told her all this.

Which, I realized, I was by no means certain I would.

"My bold knight." I moved my hand to Robert's cheek, and he smiled, and kissed my gloved palm.

I glanced quickly toward the door, and he nodded, slipping back to listen again while I reclaimed my unlit candle.

"Remember, you wait, and then slip out. We can't risk anyone seeing us leave together."

I nodded, and he left me alone in the moonlight and shadows.

It was a long, slow, uncomfortable walk back to my room. The loiterers had dispersed, and the patches of light that remained were far enough apart that I was at times in complete darkness. I scarcely cared. I was busy giving myself a scolding that would have done credit to Mrs. Abbott at the height of her powers.

"Weak, feeble, *fickle*," I berated myself. This was entirely unacceptable. Entirely. A few sympathetic words, a smile, a touch. It meant nothing. Nothing. I did not trust Robert. I could not trust him. I certainly could not be cherishing a *tendre* for him while I felt one blooming for Matthew, could I?

I'd never exactly been deluged by followers. Was I truly the sort of girl who would tumble for not one but two men at once? And one of them a Jacobite spy?

"Fickle, fickle, *fickle*, idiot!" I muttered through clenched teeth. "Lord above, why did you choose now to reveal this flaw in my nature? Whatever I have done to deserve it, I am sorry." It occurred to me then that my recent conduct might have given Our Lord Most High one or two reasons to express His Divine Displeasure, and I winced.

Heaven, however, did not seem inclined to send me a direct answer, at least not immediately. I determined not to worry myself any further about it. It was not as if I could form an attachment to either Matthew or Robert. The one was going to leave for Italy and other points of artistic inter-est as soon as he was able. The other was a spy who mistook me for a dead woman. A lasting foundation for mutual respect and support, that was not.

Besides, I had more important things to worry about. Robert Ballantyne was a Jacobite. Francesca had loved him, or at least produced a highly convincing display of love. They had made plans to run away together during the uprising last winter. That was why Francesca had so suddenly gone home at Christmastide. But the uprising had been finished almost as soon as it had begun, and their elopement never happened. Francesca had hidden her sketches in her guardian's house. Then she had died.

Robert, for his part, had feared discovery, and feared for both of their lives. His protestation that Francesca was safe was an astoundingly clumsy attempt at reassurance. She had been in danger all the while.

I could no longer believe Francesca had died of fever. It must have been murder.

But for what reason? Did the Jacobites think she might betray them to the king's men? Did the Hanoverians think she had sold their interests to the Jacobites? Or was some person close to Francesca angry that she would throw away her life at court when his own plans depended on keeping her there?

God in Heaven. How many reasons to be killed could one girl be cursed with?

CHAPTER TWENTY-ONE

IN WHICH A NIGHT FULL OF
UNWELCOME REVELATION GIVES WAY TO
SEVERAL UNWISE RESOLUTIONS.

Mon Dieu. How is it you are still awake?"

The little silver carriage clock on the mantel had just finished chiming five when Mrs. Abbott returned. I had not, as she so quickly observed, rung for her or anyone else to help me undress. I'd been able to do nothing but sit before the fire and turn the scenes of my deception over in my mind. I wanted to see them all from this certain and terrible angle of Francesca's murder.

Since I had known from the first that I risked imprisonment, or even hanging, it might be supposed the confirmation of this new danger would not occasion much new discomfort. However, human beings are marvelously adept at reasoning their way out of their most sensible fears. When it came to the legal punishment, I could convince myself that as long as I was clever, I could prevail. But murder was an entirely differ-ent matter. There waited somewhere an assassin who either knew me for an impostor or who believed the first blow had missed its mark. Such understanding did not leave one in a hurry to douse the lights.

"Hanover or Stuart?" I asked.

"What are you talking about?" Mrs. Abbott, as was her habit, checked the dressing room and the door to her own little closet of a back room to make sure we were alone. Only then did she return to bolt the door to the gallery.

"Who did Mr. Tinderflint pass messages for when he was in France? Was it the house of Hanover or Stuart?"

"I never asked."

"You never *asked*?" I trust my readers will pardon me when they learn that those words came out closer to a shriek than was necessary.

"It mattered not to me." Mrs. Abbott strode across the room to the sherry decanter and poured a healthy measure into a glass. "I wanted to bring my daughter to court and give her the life she deserved. What difference would it make to know the politics of the man who could accomplish this? Here. Drink that and calm yourself. Then tell me all that hap-pened with your Robert."

"He's not my Robert. Don't call him my Robert." I was lightheaded and a little hysterical from contemplating my probable violent death. "If anything, he was your daughter's Robert."

"You will mind your tongue, young woman. I do not need you so much as you may think."

My exhaustion and the rock-hard certainty in the Abbott's words silenced me, and I did drink the wine. It burned in my stomach, but it also steadied my nerve. "Where have you been all this time?" I asked her.

"Did you think I would allow you to go to this meeting alone? I have been following . . . the footman to see what he was about."

I blinked at her, once more taken aback by the reminder that she was practiced in these matters.

"What did you find? Was he meeting someone else?" Visions of Sophy Howe tripped smiling and malicious through my mind.

"That is what I thought at first. He took a very long route to little purpose, but in the end, he arrived at the Queen's Chapel." Mrs. Abbott's eyes narrowed and she was plainly choosing her words with care. "I crept inside to look down on him from the gallery. But he did not meet anyone. Instead, he went to the altar, where he opened a small panel in the wall. A panel that was in no way easy to see, I may tell you. There, he knelt to pray."

"He was a long time about it," I muttered.

"A most devout young man. But much more to the purpose, he removed a packet of papers from the space behind that panel. He read one and placed the others in his coat pocket."

Of course he did. It was an entirely . . . spylike thing to do. To assure his paramour she was safe, then go to retrieve secret letters. I pressed my hand to my mouth to cover the laugh that threatened to escape. Mrs. Abbott was already eyeing me harshly and would surely disapprove of hysterics. Furthermore, any such display would delay her telling me the remainder of the story.

"When at last the footman left his prayers, I also found this panel and opened it. There inside was a crucifix and rosary. I had heard of this. The space was made for James II's Catholic wife, so she could follow her faith in private and not offend the Protestant sensibilities of the country her husband ruled."

So Robert was, along with everything else, a secret Catholic. That was no shock. Were we not told that the attempts to return the Stuarts to the throne were all part of an insidious Catholic plot? They meant to rob us good Protestants of our freedom, our possessions, and our lives, all for the greater glory of their pope. Probably daughters would be ravished as well. The experts were divided on that point.

But setting aside the opinions of so many learned divines, I realized that the fact of Robert's religion had implications for the currents around me. Whatever he did for his friends in the North, he probably did for genuine love of the cause rather than for pay or mischief. This made nothing easier. I already had ample proof that Robert Ballantyne was a man of strong feeling, a true gallant. I tried not to dwell on the declarations of regard that he had so recently made. What was important here was that we now knew the means by which he accomplished his communication with "our friends in the North." No wonder he was so very careful about leaving notes around. I thought again of Francesca's sketches and how many times I wished for a clearly written diary. Perhaps she had learned one or two things from her intriguing paramour.

"What did Ballantyne say to you?" Mrs. Abbott asked. "Did you learn anything useful?"

I did not answer at once. I rubbed my face, smearing my glove with talc and rouge. How much should I trust Mrs. Abbott? Francesca had hidden the sketches from her as well as from the Messrs. Tinderflint and Peele. In fact, I thought uneasily, Francesca had hidden both the sketches and Robert. Why had she done that?

"He made professions of love, mostly," I said to the fire. "He was angry about the wager I made with Sophy Howe."

"Was there nothing else?" Mrs. Abbot looked down her long Gallic nose at me, and her eyes glittered with all the things she was not saying. "No mention of plans he had made with my lady?"

I shook my head. "I will have to try again."

"I expect you will, yes. I expect nothing will induce you to stop trying." Hard calculations passed behind her eyes, but I could not read what a single one might be. "With this wager having created so much amusement from your fellow courtiers, you are going to be even more the center of attention. You must be ready to sparkle and entertain, or risk the wrong sort of scrutiny, which none of us can afford. You must get your rest."

She made excellent sense, and I was very tired. The mention of new scrutiny brought on by my wager with Sophy raised the by now familiar and still unwelcome fear of courtly misstep. Sleep would be relief and escape for a time.

"But I haven't written my letter for Mr. Peele yet . . ." I shook my head before Mrs. Abbott could answer. "I wouldn't make any sense now if I did. I will do it in the morning." *Later in the morning.* I rubbed my aching forehead again.

"That will be in plenty of time." Her lips trembled for a moment before bending themselves into what I am sure was meant to be a reassuring smile.

I did not remark upon it. For the moment, Mrs. Abbott was being helpful. I let myself be undressed, unwigged, and put to bed. I was assured that I would be woken in plenty of time to attend Her Royal Highness. I let exhaustion and assurance cover me and was asleep almost as soon as my head touched the pillow. Almost. In the last fleeting moment before my thoughts swam entirely away, I was aware of doors opening and closing. Too many doors and too many times. I should have roused myself. I should have opened my eyes to see what this meant.

But I did not. I slept.

CHAPTER TWENTY-TWO

IN WHICH A RATHER TAWDRY DISCOVERY IS MADE
AND A TRUNK HOLDS IMPORTANT REVELATIONS.

It was not Mrs. Abbott who woke me. It was one of
the palace maids, a tiny, dark girl called Nell Libby. She said
she had been instructed to feed me breakfast and otherwise
get me ready for my duties of the day. I was so grateful for
the cup of chocolate and warm roll that she brought with her
that I did not ask any questions, but stood docile as a lamb
while she laced me into a light muslin morning dress decorated with green ruffles and rather outsized pink and blue
flowers.

That day proved Mrs. Abbott correct in a number of
ways. I was very much the center of attention as I moved
about in the princess's wake. There was no escaping speculation on the nature and breed of the dog that would appear, or
the exact location of Stemhempfordshire. Some enterprising

soul even brought forth a map of England for us all to pore over after nuncheon. Fortunately, I was restored enough to myself by then that I was able to turn the absence of any such shire into a guessing game, which pleased Lady Montague at least, as she won ten shillings from our fellows with her knowledge of the names of obscure villages.

Equally fortunate was the fact that this was one of Sophy's free days, and I did not have to endure her presence as I went about my decorative duty, waiting on Her Royal Highness. All the things Robert had said the night before followed me closely. Sophy had hold of him and must be kept placated. I did not want to have to meet and match her edged conversation until I knew more about the battle I entered. A day's reprieve was better than none at all.

Unfortunately, I was not able to make any excuse to enter into further conversation with Robert. We passed each other several times in the galleries, but I did not dare do more than glance at him. Sophy might not be present, but Molly Lepell was, and she had her bright eyes turned toward me every time we passed any man in scarlet livery. Clearly, she guessed something was escalating between the three of us, but I could not tell whether that worried or amused her.

I might have been afraid that Sophy, wherever she was, was planning to intercept my advertisement before it could be published, were it not for one thing: I had the means to circumvent her. This time it was a solid and complete plan with the great advantage that it did not depend on anyone belonging to the life of the previous Lady Francesca.

But if that worry was put away from me, it was soon replaced by a fresh and sparkling concern. Mrs. Abbott still had not returned by the time I was ready to retire. I asked Libby where she might be, but Libby insisted she did not know. It was strange. I had spent much time during the past few months wishing desperately to escape the Abbott's scrutiny. Now that I had, her absence so worried me, I found it difficult to sit still for Libby's gentler and more tentative ministrations. I even considered putting off my plan, but I dismissed this. If anything, Mrs. Abbott's absence would render one portion of the dance easier to execute. My plan also involved being woken and dressed directly at sunrise, news Libby received without betraying the least sign of enthusiasm. For this, I cannot truly blame her.

Thankfully, she also asked no questions about this instruction, and received my delayed—and much edited and watered-down—dispatch for Mr. Peele with equanimity. I made certain a few extra coins slipped into her apron pocket for this consideration.

The Kings of England first took Hampton Court Palace to their collective royal bosom in the days of the much-married Henry VIII. They had, as near as I could tell, been driven to improve upon it ever since. As I emerged into the gray damp of Saturday's dawn, it was to find the gates flung open and workmen arriving in knots and clusters. I wove my way between builders and building materials to quieter precincts, heading toward the long, low brick building at the yard's western edge that had been given over to the use of James Thornhill and his 'prentices. Smoke from its chimney told me at least one inhabitant was awake within. Francesca's sketch of the Thornhill ceiling was tucked once more into my sleeve. I planned to show it to Matthew Reade and ask his opinion of it.

I meant to trust him. This was a grave risk, because I would have to tell him at least a portion of the truth about myself, something I found I was strangely reluctant to do. He had offered me friendship, and I wanted to keep it as long as possible. Neither did I forget that a drawing of Francesca was missing from his portfolio. Given my heightened suspicion of everything that had happened to me so far, I could not dismiss that as a small thing.

To compound my worries, I still had neither sign nor word from Mrs. Abbott, and I was at a complete loss as to how to gain information about my attendant. Should I write to Mr. Tinderflint? I might have to. But what on earth would I tell him?

So intent was I on all this worrying and maundering that I did not at first attend to the grunts I heard as I brushed past the corner of yet another timber pile. The yard was as filled with goats, geese, pigs, and their diverse attendants as it was with laborers. Such a noise could have been made by any of them. It was the flash of white and pink in the gloom on the far side of the head-high stack of boards that caught my eye.

There was Sophy Howe, her back to the wall, skirts up, her pink-stockinged legs wrapped around the agitated buttocks of some man in a red coat in a display of agility I would not have credited her with. Both grunted steadily away. Distantly, I noted the red and gold coat was a footman's livery.

Sophy saw me. Although her eyes were heavy-lidded, there was no mistaking how she looked right at me. Just as there was no mistaking the triumph in her smile. Robert, too busy at his task to be bothered with anything else, did not so much as pause.

I fled. I did not think. I did not reason. Disgust, shock, and a whole host of other feelings wrenched me around and sent me blundering across the cobbles. I could not seem to see straight, and tripped repeatedly over the catshead stones until I fetched up hard against the corner of some brick outbuilding and had to stop, because although I was but lightly laced for the morning, I could no longer breathe.

What is happening to me? I pressed my face into my hands. *I am losing my mind. I must be.*

I was no prude. I had spent more than one summer in my uncle's country house. One occasionally came upon an energetic tryst in some corner of barn or stable. Whatever this was boiling now through my veins, it was not some Puritan's outraged propriety. It was something else, something more violent and less comprehensible.

"Lady Francesca?"

I lifted my head to see Matthew Reade standing in front of me. He'd clearly pulled on his coat in haste and had not even properly laced his shirt. "Lady Francesca, are you well?"

I confess that I entirely failed to return a polite answer to this gentle inquiry. My readers will surely understand how this could have come to pass and forgive the lapse. In point of fact, I suspect I gaped like a fish.

Another young man—a stout, dark-haired fellow with a square and stubbled chin—peered over Matthew's shoulder.

"It's all right, Burke," Matthew said. "I'll take care of this. Weren't you just on your way out?"

Mr. Burke returned an unkind leer, but also put a tricorn hat on his head, tugged it low, and strolled out into the courtyard, tucking shirttails into breeches as he went. Matthew took my elbow firmly and ushered me through the door.

The dim workshop was filled with tables that were in turn filled with the tools for preparing paints, canvas, and frames. It smelled strongly enough of sawdust, turpentine, and other unsavory compounds to set my nose itching and my eyes watering. The shutters were closed, which was a mercy. I did not want to be seen by any more people than necessary.

"What's happened?" Matthew pushed a battered cane-bottomed chair toward me.

"I, erm, nothing. Nothing, really." Except it was not "nothing" that had so disordered my wits. I could find no name to put to the distressing internal phenomenon that had overtaken me. It could not possibly be, for example, jealousy. Jealousy would be nonsensical. But a single day ago, Robert had professed heartbreak and self-harm—at least to the girl he thought I was. I had believed those feelings to be genuine. For the briefest moment while I was with him, my fickle and lonely heart had wished in vain that I were Francesca, who could command such feeling in a man. Now I found my oh-so-clever self deceived, and I was angry, shocked, and frightened all at once. None of this was lessened by the fact that he was with spiteful, snippy, petty, pretty Sophy Howe. She had been gone yesterday. Where? Had Robert been with her? What had they been doing?

But surely I wondered that because of the wager and because Robert was so very concerned with keeping Sophy quiet. I was not in the least jealous. Oh, no. That could never be.

A far more vital fact dropped like ice into the center of my heated emotion. Robert had clearly lied about his regard for Francesca. His declaration that he intended to take me — her — safe away from here to his friends in the North could be yet another lie. He could have used her for some Jacobite purpose and then killed her when that use was done.

If Robert was her murderer, he knew I was a counterfeit. He could have told Sophy the truth in a bawdy scene that ended in the flagrant display I had happened upon. He and Sophy together could be planning how to finish me off.

For a moment, I genuinely thought I was going to faint.

"Tell me what this is about," said Matthew. "Please, my lady."

I looked up at him helplessly. I took a strangled breath. I had already made the choice to trust him, but now that the moment had come to do so, I found it absurdly difficult to begin.

"There's no drawing of Lady Francesca in your portfolio," I said at last.

I was walking blind. I might have just ended everything
short of my life. But Matthew Reade's troubled gray eyes
remained steady. When he did turn away, it was only to
kneel by one of the two cots standing in the far corner of the
workshop. He pulled out a clothes press, raised its lid, and
lifted up its trays. From the bottom, he drew a paper. This
he handed to me.

There was Francesca, very much as she had been in Mrs.
Abbott's miniature: cheerful, mischievous, looking at her
cards as if she meant to tell a delicious secret. But there was
another study too, this one drawn in profile. In this, Francesca gazed at some distant point, and I felt the fierce and
desperate hunger in that gaze. No, more than hunger. Matthew had drawn Francesca with an expression of pure and
unadulterated greed on her lovely face.

The sight of that greed touched a nerve deep within me,
and I shuddered. I did not doubt for one instant that this was
genuine; some unguarded moment witnessed by a person who
was overlooked because he had no name or power. It took
a long moment for me to see beyond that and to note how
clearly one could see the differences in the line of my jaw and
Francesca's, and in the slant of our cheekbones. These were
distinctions that powder and paint might obscure, but not
completely hide, and that no amount of lost weight could
explain.

Matthew Reade had known I was not the person I

claimed to be, probably from the moment of our first meeting in the gallery.

I moved to hand the paper back to him, but he waved it away. "You keep it. My gift to you. You should perhaps burn it, though."

I looked at it, and my throat constricted. "It is too fine a piece of work for that."

Matthew's smile sparked a fresh light deep within his eyes. "Never fear. I've another. One that I think is much better done." And he handed me a second paper.

This new sketch showed my face as clearly as my glass did on any given morning. Matthew had drawn me without powder or patches. Lines of concentration etched my forehead, and a tiny smile curved my lips. I was planning something or about to make a telling argument. It was like Francesca's portrait, but not quite. My eyes were harder than hers, but less showily saucy, and my features less refined and coy. It was not perhaps a completely flattering portrait, but I could not deny it was true to the original.

I swallowed, and reluctantly laid both drawings down on the table beside me, face-down, so I did not have to see either pair of eyes.

"Why didn't you tell anyone?" I asked.

Matthew shrugged. "What do I care for who does what among the fine folk of the court? Their intrigues are nothing to me."

His words struck home, but perhaps not in the way he meant them to. I was reminded that he was an apprentice, with a place to maintain, one that he could lose as easily as I could lose mine.

"You're right. Of course you're right. I'm sorry. I don't want to cause you trouble. I'll go now." I started for the door.

"Wait. I . . ." He stopped. "I don't even know your name."

"Margaret," I said, with my hand on the latch. "Margaret Preston Fitzroy. Peggy, mostly."

"Peggy Mostly Fitzroy," he said, and I smiled weakly at the jest. "It was not Lady Francesca I offered friendship to, you know."

I couldn't turn around. I did not dare. If I turned, I would see his gray eyes and kind face. I would see the man I had so very much hoped would be my friend. "You don't know who I am." The words tasted of gall as I forced them out. "Not really. You should keep your friendship for those who won't drag you into trouble."

"I thank my lady for her advice," Matthew replied with tremendous dignity. "But as a freeborn son of England, I'll bestow my friendship where I choose."

I blinked. "You read poetry, don't you?"

"What of it?"

"Nothing. Nothing at all." I took a deep breath. I should not do this. He deserved so much better than to be mixed up in . . . in whatever this morass would ultimately prove to be. Yet, even now, he offered his friendship and offered it freely. I might not know him any better than he knew me, but I knew the value of such a gift. How could I disdain it now?

"I did come to ask for your help, Mr. Reade."

"I'll do what I can." He stopped again. "As long as you don't require me to deliver a love billet or some such."

In that moment, he sounded so much like a peevish boy, I laughed. "Nothing like that. I promise. But I do need a letter taken to St. James's Square as soon as may be."

"What about your maid?" He stopped. "No, I've seen your maid." He paused, considering. "Your timing is good, at least. Mr. Thornhill requires some additional supplies for the princess's ceiling. Possibly I can arrange to be the one commissioned to fetch them."

It was a less certain answer than I would have hoped for, but my choice of messengers at this time was strictly limited. There was a torn paper and a charcoal pencil on the cluttered table. I appropriated both and wrote quickly.

To Lady H. Not the Thames bridge Friday. Hampton Court Palace, the king's courtyard, Thursday.

"This is for the maid of the house, Templeton. Tell her it is from the cousin." I folded the paper and scribbled down the direction. I could not possibly risk the message going directly to Olivia. Uncle or Aunt Pierpont might very well be having her letters watched. Perhaps I was being overcautious. Perhaps palace intrigue had begun to taint my blood, but I did not want to take the chance. "You can read it if you want," I said boldly as I handed it to him.

Matthew was looking at me oddly. Sizing me up, perhaps, so I could be rendered once more into charcoal or pastel. What would that new sketch show, if taken at this very awkward moment? But whatever he saw or thought as he eyed me, he still put my note in his pocket, unread.

"What happened to her?" he asked. "Lady Francesca?"

"I don't know." I faced him squarely. I had gone this far. There was no turning back. "But I think she was murdered. I'm trying to find out who did the thing and why."

Matthew's hand moved in an uncertain gesture that ended in him brushing his hair from his forehead and then pressing a knuckle to his mouth.

"You don't have to go on," I told him. "I can just leave now. I know you won't give me away."

Matthew lowered his hand to his pocket and shook his head. "No. I'll take your note, and a promise as well." I held my breath and waited. "As soon as we can make shift for time, you will tell me the whole of your story."

"I promise." I fumbled with my sleeve where Francesca's sketch waited. "Indeed, I—"

But I was too late. The workshop door opened, and Mr. James Thornhill, resplendent in a blue coat and black velvet breeches, strode into the workshop. He extended his long arm toward Matthew, his mottled finger pointed and ready to accuse. It was only after he opened his mouth that he recognized me.

"Why, Lady Francesca! Good morning to you!"

The mask of maid of honor came down with dizzying speed as I made my curtsy. "Mr. Thornhill. I was hoping I might find you here."

My smooth greeting caught him entirely off-guard.

Clearly, he and this Burke had been expecting a very different sort of scene. "Then I am sorry to have kept you waiting," Mr. Thornhill said stiffly. "Indeed, I was already at work when I received word"—he glanced over his shoulder at his unshaven and much-chagrined apprentice—"that Mr. Reade was entertaining a woman in my workshop. There was no mention that it was *you*, my lady." These words held the clear implication that the offending tale-bearer would be grinding paints for at least the next week.

I dipped my gaze modestly. "I wrote to my physician, you see, about continuing my drawing lessons. Sadly, he is of the opinion my eyes must still be weak from the fever and I am not to tax myself with drawing just yet. I must wait another few weeks before making the attempt." I made sure my smile was filled to the brim with delicate regret. "I came here to tell you as much, Mr. Thornhill. Of course I should have realized such a scrupulous and industrious artisan as yourself would already be at your work. Mr. Reade had just made the very gracious offer to convey my message to you and save me the extra trip."

Mr. Thornhill sighed and made a fine show of distress. "I see. Well, we must bow before your physician's commands. It would not do for those lovely and delicate eyes to be in any way harmed by overmuch work."

Mr. Thornhill smiled graciously, and I smiled back, then turned to Matthew. "Thank you for your offer of assistance, Mr. Reade," I said, hoping he heard that these words were genuine. "I am most grateful."

Matthew made his bow. Truly, it was a fine and graceful bow and showed a very good leg, I now noticed. "Your servant, my lady."

I very much wanted to say something more, to make certain he understood that what had passed between us before was my genuine self and this politesse was the pretense. But there stood Mr. Thornhill, with Mr. Burke fidgeting behind him. I could only delicately gather my skirts and smile as the men bowed for my passage.

Outside, underneath lowering clouds, I dodged builders, milkmaids, goose girls, laundry women, provisioners, and men on horseback on their way out for an early gallop. This time, though, my heart was light, and my slippers tripped easily, even gracefully over the stones. I had a friend. A true and steady friend, and if I thought on his lively eyes and handsome face as well as his generous offer to assist me in my time of trouble . . . well, I am but a frail girl, after all, and cannot be blamed for that.

I was still in danger. I was still in doubt, but I was no longer alone. Surely after this, all things would become easier.

But when I opened my door, it was to see an oblong man clothed entirely in black turn away from the fire where he'd been warming himself.

"Where have you been out so early?" asked Mr. Peele. "And where the devil is Mrs. Abbott?"

CHAPTER TWENTY-THREE

IN WHICH OUR HEROINE DISCOVERS

SHE IS NOT THE ONLY ONE

RECEIVING UNWELCOME NEWS.

There are times in one's life when all training in deportment and manners fails. One is then thrown back on mother wit.

"I . . . erm . . . I don't know." I looked about the room, which was indeed deserted, except, of course, for Mr. Peele.

"You don't know where you've been?" Mr. Peele sneered. "Oh, don't bother. I do know what you meant. You don't know where Abbott is. Come in here and shut that door."

I did as I was bidden, closing the door carefully. I advanced a few steps into the room, but not so many as would bring me within arm's reach of Mr. Peele. I had been thinking far too much on murder, and a cloud of anger surrounded him. It filled his rectangular face and keen eyes up to the brim. I did not plan to enter further into that miasma than was absolutely necessary.

Mr. Peele did not fail to note my hesitancy, and snorted in impatience. "Well, young woman? I asked you more than one question. Where have you been?"

"Walking in the gardens."

"It is remarkably early for a courtier." One of his fine hands reached out and touched the clock on the mantel, running his fingers over its polished silver sides and the smooth glass of its face. Neither of us could fail to note it had not yet gone on eight o'clock.

"I am following the example of Her Royal Highness as to the importance of fresh air and exercise," I said, remembering to draw myself up as I did. "To what do I owe the honor of your visit, sir?"

Rather than answer, Mr. Peele reached into his coat and brought out a letter. This he handed to me. I noted that it was not one of my nightly dispatches. This was some other missive. The messengers and postmen had clearly been busy over the past day or so. It was a wonder they had not all bumped into one another in the courtyard.

This letter was in French, and written in a clumsy, block-letter hand I knew I had seen before. Slowly, I realized it was the same hand that had labeled the myriad jars on my dressing table.

Sir:

> With this writing, I leave your employment. But in partial payment for your many kindnesses to me, I render you this last service. I warn you your protégée has once again entered into

communication where she should not. Remove her at once from
this place before further harm can be done.

  A.

I leave your employment. I stared about the empty room. It
was not possible. Mrs. Abbott was committed to the scheme.
Unhappy, yes, but committed. She had gone so far as to help
me by following Robert the night before.

The night before. She followed Robert; she told me
what she'd seen. Then she vanished. Completely and entirely.

Forgetting Mr. Peele's presence, I hurried to the little
back room that kept her bed and things. I had not thought to
do this before, because it had not even occurred to me that
she might have left for good. But now I stood and stared at
a room stripped quite bare. Only the cot, dresser, and chair
remained.

I do not need you so much as you may think, she had said. And
then there was Sophy's little aside about stealing her away.
Had Mrs. Abbott gone to work for Sophy Howe?

Why? What on earth would Sophy want with her? That question, at least, had a simple answer. Sophy wanted her for
gossip. So she could learn something that might be turned
against me.

"Struck dumb, my lady?" Mr. Peele retrieved the missive
from where I'd dropped it and stowed it once more in his
pocket. "That is most out of character."

"Mrs. Abbott sent her note to you?" I asked, as confused

about this point as any other since I walked into the room. "Not Mr. Tinderflint?"

Mr. Peele shrugged. "Perhaps she does not trust our Mr. Tinderflint to be as firm with you as is required."

I whirled around. Mr. Peele's visage was still and calm. This was the same blank mask he donned at the card table. It was meant to reveal nothing to the opposing player, but in this it failed. For it said he played a game with me now and was surely lying about how that letter had come into his hands. I found I had moved several steps away from him without entirely realizing it. I was afraid of Mr. Peele. I was afraid of his unmarked hands, and the strength of his anger, and the fact that we were quite alone.

"What is the communication to which Mrs. Abbott refers?" asked Mr. Peele. "What have you done and with whom?"

I showed him my own bland mask, the one he himself had taught me how to fashion. "I have no idea what she's talking about."

"You're lying."

I did not let my eyes so much as flicker at this accusation. Mr. Peele turned again to the contemplation of the clock. He opened the glass facing and touched the wrought silver hand, lightly of course. So as not to disturb its motion.

"Perhaps Mrs. Abbott is correct," he said to the clock. "Perhaps you should be removed."

He waited then. The ticking of my little silver clock filled the space between us. A stick cracked in the fire, falling into the ashes with a sad rustle. Mr. Peele continued to wait, to see if I would protest or beg.

I did neither.

"It is, of course, up to you whether I stay or go," I told him. "Or, rather, as Mr. Tinderflint is known to be my guardian, it is up to him." Mr. Peele shut the clock facing. The click sounded very loud, as if he were laying down a coin on the table. I had surprised him.

How is it gentlemen think we maids do not know who rules us? We who serve, whether we stand or sit to do it, know very well the workings of power, especially when they affect us directly. I had lived too long under my uncle's thumb not to have a mathematically precise understanding of who was in charge of what in any given house and how far that power stretched.

Mr. Peele remained silent, fully aware that play had passed to me and I had not yet finished my bids.

"You should be aware, sir, that if I am ordered away by my dear guardian, I will protest to Her Royal Highness. She has taken a liking to me, you know, as has her daughter Anne." This was a bit of a bluff, but not too great a one, I hoped. "I will say my guardian, Lord Tierney, is most unkind and ask her to intercede for me." I paused there to be sure that Mr. Peele had time to take note of this entire speech. "I wonder what Mr. Tinderflint will do when faced with a royal request."

Mr. Peele's eyes narrowed a fraction of an inch. "You are daring a great deal, my girl."

And yet I did dare, despite the danger, despite the murder done and the very real possibility it might be done again. I had to. "You want something here, Mr. Peele. You don't have it yet, or you would already have ordered Mr. Tinderflint to take me away." My voice hitched as I said this, but I forced myself to continue. "I must conclude that, despite all, I remain your best chance of acquiring whatever it is. Possibly even more so now that Mrs. Abbott has deserted you." I was not fully cognizant of this truth until the words had left my mouth, but I knew my words to be correct.

"Do you know where she has gone?"

"I don't know," I said.

"Why would she choose now to leave our merry band?"

"I don't know," I repeated, and though I had my suspicions, I truly did not. She could be anywhere and doing anything. She could have lied to me from beginning to end about what she'd seen when she followed Robert. That thought tightened my throat with fear and anger, but at the same time, I wondered at Mr. Peele's questions. It had not until that moment occurred to me that this careful, inscrutable card player might not compass the motivations of the other members of his conspiracy. Perhaps he tested me only in order to discover how much I knew. But his hand had strayed back to the clock. Its silver legs had been worked into the likeness of little lion's paws, and he tapped his fingertip against one now. It was a telltale gesture. The first I had ever seen from him. Mr. Peele was nervous.

"The fool," he remarked, but at the same time, he took

hold of the clock's paw with two long fingers, to pinch it tight between them. "She knows—" He stopped, becoming aware of his own words and his fingers pinching the unfeeling clock at the same time. He released the clock and came forward to stand directly in front of me.

"Why are you still here? You have been left all but unguarded with money and jewels enough. You could have helped yourself and made your escape at any time. But you have not. Why is that?"

"I like it here," I answered, using all the strength of nerve I had to keep my voice and gaze steady. "The life of Lady Francesca suits me very well. Why are you still here, Mr. Peele?" I asked in return. "What is it you still hope to gain by having a Lady Francesca at court?"

"Why would you think I would tell you that now?"

"Because keeping me in ignorance has not achieved your ends, so it might be time to employ a fresh stratagem."

"What a clever girl," he murmured. "Very well. I am still here because I have not made enough money from this proposition yet."

"How could two hundred pounds a year ever be enough for you?"

He snorted and waved his hand. "You already know the salary to be a mere blind. No, I am after much bigger fish with infinitely deeper pockets."

"And the letters I've been writing with their descriptions of the card games, these will give you access to those pockets?"

Mr. Peele returned nothing but silence then, but one word still hung clearly in the air between us. Blackmail. Cheating at cards was an unpardonable offense among the ranks of aristocrats and other gentlemen. A card cheat himself, Mr. Peele would know this. With my descriptions of the games and the parties and the gossip, he would extort money from the players. Be a man ever so titled, an accusation of cheating could result in ruin. It could even bring a messy death in a cold meadow at an uncivilized hour. Such was the importance of honor among gentlemen.

Mr. Peele considered the clock once more. It ticked and it tocked. One silver hand lowered itself a fraction of an inch.

"Why do you need me for this?" I asked, a little frightened and at the same time a little piqued. I should have guessed this was what was happening, but with all the revelations about spies and Jacobites, I had given up on money being the root of any of the firm's diverse machinations. "Why not go to some gaming house yourself and play?"

A smile and a slight shake of his head demonstrated Mr. Peele's amusement with such naiveté. "Some of our finer gentlemen are surprisingly fastidious about those they enter into play with. They fear to be cheated." He let the word fall lightly, as if he had no knowledge at all of such sordid matters. "I do not present a pleasing exterior; neither do I turn a good phrase or sketch an elegant bow. Therefore I cannot, as others do, pass for a true gentleman, let alone one of the noble sort. Nor do I particularly relish being caught at my trade. I am a tolerable shot, I assure you, and passable with a sword, but bloodletting in a duel is something I choose to avoid. Also, I was indiscreet a time or two, and gained a certain . . . notoriety that has made things difficult in recent years." He shook his head at his own folly. "So, I am forced to use other means, and other hands."

I did not answer at once. Something here did not ring true. It was . . . too complex a scheme. Mr. Peele was too careful a man to conceive of a plan that involved so many confederates, especially when he did not know them as well as he might. He was still lying.

"So, what is it you thought Mrs. Abbott was doing here?" I asked this to goad him, to see how much he would dare say.

Unfortunately, Mr. Peele seemed to have regained his customary steely self-possession. "Mrs. Abbott is no longer part of this discussion. It is you I am concerned with. It is time for you to leave."

"I've already told you, I will appeal—"

"Oh, you are not leaving through the front door, my dear," he said. "You are going to take advantage of the jewels and money and leave by the back, very, very quietly."

What was he doing, suggesting such a thing? But a moment later, I understood him. If I stole away, quite literally the thief in the night, I could never tell where I'd been and what I had done, not if I wanted to keep my neck out of a noose.

Mr. Peele smiled, a small smile indeed, but all the more chilling for the amount of triumph distilled into that tiny, precise curve.

"You have already contacted your cousin. Well and good." He folded his hands behind himself, and for a moment he looked enough like my uncle that it raised goose bumps all down my arms. He might have been guessing about who it was that I had entered into communication with, but it was not a difficult guess to make. "Let her help you to a swift retreat with as much as you can contrive to carry."

"Why?" I asked him. It was the only question I had left in me.

"Because with Abbott's departure and what I have seen now in this room, it is clearly time for this nonsense to end," he replied calmly. "And because if you do not, I will take it upon myself to expose you for the fraud that you are." He paused, as if some new and unexpected thought had just occurred to him. "I would take the garnets, if I were you. I believe they are valued at five hundred pounds."

He walked out of the room and shut the door. I sat down in the chair nearest the fire and stayed there for a very long time. I waited for fear to set me trembling, as it had so many times during my rash adventure. But no tremors came. Instead, bits and pieces of understanding dropped into place, slowly, like coins falling at the card table.

Of them all, Mr. Peele really was in this scheme for the money. Mr. Peele was threatening me, yet again. He wanted me frightened, and yet he did not want me to stay and be obedient. He commanded me to be gone. He might well be having me watched to make sure I complied. A blackmailer would know whom to bribe, and when and how to receive news of me. He could be watching for the moment when I fled the palace, presumably under cover of darkness, with Francesca's jewels and money, especially those garnets valued at five hundred pounds. He might even take it into his head to follow me as I made my way down deserted roads to some secure country retreat. He was a "tolerable shot," and "passable with a sword," but preferred to leave bloodshed to others. But even I knew that men who had no such qualms could be hired in the less reputable quarters of London town.

Would even Mr. Tinderflint stop one moment to wonder at the robbery and death of a girl who had turned thief? Of course he would not. No more than he would question the death of his nervous and exhausted ward when she fell low with a fever.

This whole time, my eyes had been lowered, taking in the details of my hems, the toes of my slippers, and my work-basket. Slowly, I remembered kicking that basket underneath the chair when last I pulled out Lady Francesca's sketch. Now, however, it rested tidily beside the hearth.

I lifted the basket up. I removed the cloth and colored threads. And the padded bottom I had added, and the layers of tissue.

I removed nothing else. Because there was nothing left to remove.

CHAPTER TWENTY-FOUR

IN WHICH POISON IS REVEALED

TO COME IN MANY FORMS.

There you are, Francesca! Oh, you poor dear!"

Those were the words Molly Lepell greeted me with as she walked, wholly uninvited, through my chamber door two hours later.

At that time, I was kneeling in the midst of a mess of embroidery thread and unmended lace, staring at the dying fire. I had madly searched through Mrs. Abbott's empty chamber and my writing desk, even turned over my pillows and bedsheets, in case in some fever dream of a moment I had moved the sketches to another location. But there was nothing. All Francesca's sketches, save for the one I still had tucked into my sleeve, were gone. They had been there this morning. They were not there now. Mr. Peele had taken them away.

Molly sank to her knees beside me, her bright blue skirts

billowing around her, and grasped my hands. "I know every-thing. And it's abominable!"

Molly's words speared through the cloud of despair, and they drew a swift, and loud, response.

"You KNOW!"

"Of course I do! Sophy is practically parading her through the palace. Fran, you mustn't let this dishearten you!"

I stared at Molly Lepell. She stared at me. "What are you talking about?"

"What do you think I'm talking about? Sophy Howe has stolen your maid."

I opened my mouth. I closed it again. I realized I had better do something else, if only to disguise the fact that I currently bore a striking resemblance to a madwoman.

"Oh, Molly!" I flung myself into her arms. "She just did it to be spiteful. I'm sure she did!"

"Why else does the Howe do anything? Fran, you ninny, you should be thanking her!" Molly grabbed both my elbows and raised me to my feet. Apparently so it would be easier to give me a solid shake. "The woman was plaguing your heart out."

I blotted at my eyes with the back of my hand. The fact of Mr. Peele finding and stealing Francesca's sketches had driven out of my head all consideration that Mrs. Abbott might have turned her coat. Now, as my thoughts struggled to right themselves, I saw it made perfect sense. Sophy had threatened to steal her, and Mrs. Abbott had declared shortly after that that she did not need me so much as might be thought. One of them, or both, had been planning this for some time. The question was not why did the Abbott leave the firm of Tinderflint and Peele at this moment, but why did she leave at all? What did she hope to gain in Sophy Howe's employ? Did she think she could use Sophy to get to Robert? Why would she need to? Mrs. Abbott and Robert were servants together. Involving our silken set in spying or quarreling between them would only cause complications.

"Here, sit down." Molly guided us both over to the sofa and, being Molly, returned at once to essentials. "You look a mess, Fran. Have you had anything to eat this morning?" I shook my head, and she got up at once in a great flouncing of muslin and lace and left the room. She returned a moment later. "I've sent my woman down for a breakfast. In the meantime, I will play lady's maid for you. The weather's cleared, and Her Royal Highness will be walking this morning, so we have to be ready."

"I don't think I can, Molly," I made myself whisper. "I shall have to have a headache." A headache is among the most versatile tools available to a delicate lady, nearly as useful on a moment's notice as "feeling faint."

"You can't have a headache," she told me. "You would be leaving Sophy alone with the other ladies. Within five minutes, everyone will believe you're looking for a way out of your wager, or that you've worked out a way to cheat."

"Everyone?" I looked at her pleadingly.

"Sophy Howe talks enough to qualify as everyone, and you know it. Come, now." Molly threaded her arm through mine. "I can have you decent in a trice." She towed me toward the dressing room with that strength of purpose and arm she was capable of displaying. "Let's just see what you have."

I sat in front of my mirrored table with hands clasped while Molly sorted dresses with an efficiency that would have done credit to Mrs. Abbott. "Here. You shall wear the light green damask." She held up the mantua for my approval. "It will do nicely with the petticoat you already have on. Then we'll sort out that hair of yours."

Molly tutted and exclaimed but asked no awkward questions as she unlaced my simple dress, pulled my stays tighter, and generally forced me into a gown much more suited to being seen in the train of Her Royal Highness. I admit I was scarce listening to Molly's words. The questions drumming in my thoughts quite drowned out her chatter. Where was Mr. Peele, and what was he doing with the sketches? Would they mean anything to him? If he did understand them, what then? What would he do when he found out Mrs. Abbott was with Sophy Howe? She had to know he would do so. Whatever she had planned, he surely wouldn't leave her much time to finish it. But what was she planning, and why, and why did she need Sophy Howe?

And what was I going to do about it? Or indeed, about anything at all, now that I had Mr. Peele waiting for me to take my abrupt and felonious leave?

". . . and honestly, I don't know what's gotten into you since you've been back, Fran," Molly was saying overhead.

"Sneaking about, staying up until all hours, deliberately pulling Sophy's nose. You never behaved so before. Keep still," she ordered as she took up my hair brush.

"I barely remember what I was like before," I said to our reflections as Molly brushed my hair back and dipped her rosy fingers into the pomade jar so she could form and arrange the curls.

"Well, you laughed much more, for one thing. You and Mary were quite impossible once you started into a fit of giggles. You weren't at all interested in the princess's philosophical gentlemen, either." Molly paused, as if on the brink of some great revelation. "Mother always did warn me that overmuch reading was bad for a girl, and I think you're the proof." She looked at the two of us there in the glass. "What are you doing to yourself, Fran?" she asked with sudden, soft solemnity.

I couldn't possibly answer that. So I asked an entirely different question, and one to which Molly might just know the answer.

"Why does Sophy hate me so? What have I done to her? It can't be because of Robert. It simply *can't*."

"No, I rather expect it's because of the money."

Money? My jaw dropped open until I was executing a fine imitation of a codfish. Molly rolled her bright eyes again.

"Honestly, did you think no one would find out? Especially as this is Sophy we're talking about." She sighed deeply. "Oh, Fran. You're so good, and so kind. That's why I tried to warn you against Sophy. She's no one's friend. She's only out for what she can get."

"Aren't we all?" I murmured, forgetting my role for a bitter moment.

"Yes, of course, dear. But the problem with the Howe is she enjoys it too much. The rest of us . . . well, we just do as we must." Molly busied herself with the brush for another few moments. "Sophy is one of those contrary sorts who is convinced people only do her favors so they can humiliate her later. She expects you to make some demand on her and is going to try to ruin you before you can. I can't think what you were about."

Neither could I, of course, so I settled for the obvious response. "I thought she'd just pay me back."

"Well, that was your mistake, wasn't it? Sophy hasn't got a bean, and for some reason, she can't seem to find herself a protector, which surely has nothing to do with her amiable and forthright temperament."

We both paused long enough to provide a silent acknowledgment of this twist of irony. But inside, I thought how this might be what drew Mrs. Abbott to take service with Sophy Howe. If the Abbott had found out Francesca had lent Sophy money, she might easily believe Sophy Howe had some hand in her daughter's death. She might even have discovered Sophy had some hold over Francesca, perhaps through Robert, or beyond Robert, all the way to those friends in the North.

A shiver ran through me, and I realized I had let the silence linger far too long.

"I can't believe Sophy told anyone about the loans," I said. "She's so proud."

"What makes you think she told me?" exclaimed Molly. "I can put two and two together, Fran, and so can plenty of others. In fact, a number of us were surprised that it was you who left court, and not Sophy."

Indeed, it was lucky for Francesca that there was this business of the money and Sophy Howe, I thought wearily. It was so obviously the cause of her troubles that no one would look far for another reason behind her flight from court, such as dealings with the Jacobites who were then on the march. It really couldn't have worked out better if the sweet creature had arranged it.

"There. Much better." Molly gave the thick curls lying against my shoulder a final twist. "But really, your eyes are like burned holes in your head. At least your maid's left you your cosmetics. Now, where . . ." She rooted among the forest of jars and bottles that Mrs. Abbott kept on the table. "Oh, don't tell me . . ." she muttered. "Never mind it, I'll get mine."

Molly bustled away, and I stayed where I was. I found myself rather jealous of Molly Lepell. She knew her place, and if she played a game, it was for herself alone.

When Molly came back, she carried with her a small brown bottle.

"Tip your head back," she commanded.

The bottle had a glass dropper, and as I put my head back, she dripped something cold into my eyes that stung abominably. Tears formed instantly. Molly dabbed at my face with a kerchief and told me I could sit up. I did, but I could no longer see clearly. The whole room was very much blurred, and a glowing halo surrounded each candle.

"What is this stuff?" I blinked hard, trying to clear my sight.

"Belladonna, of course."

Of course. It was a favorite tincture for brightening eyes. It also stung like the devil.

"If you're going to continue staying up to all hours and following that up with crying fits, you'll want your new maid to lay in a supply."

But I wasn't listening. I was on my feet without entirely realizing I had moved. "My maid . . . I must go . . . I . . ."

I ran from the room, almost upsetting the table the maids and footmen were laying out for breakfast. I scurried through the gallery, blinking in the dim light, trying to count doors. Finally, praying I had found the right one, I yanked it open and threw myself inside.

There was Sophy Howe standing in the middle of a stuffy, overfurnished chamber, letting Mrs. Abbott fix a pair of sparkling jewels to her ears.

"Why, Fran!" said Sophy in a tone that clearly meant *What took you so long?* "What an unexpected surprise!"

I didn't bother to answer. I seized Mrs. Abbott's hand and dragged her from the room. I strongly suspect it was only the fact I had caught her completely unawares that enabled me to do so.

"Have you gone mad!" Mrs. Abbott reasserted her strength and yanked her arm back so I was forced to spin and face her.

"I know what you're doing, Mrs. Abbott! I—"

She smacked me straight across the cheek with the back of her work-hardened hand. Before I could recover from this outrage, she yanked me farther away from Sophy's door. Off the gallery there was a blue chamber hung with a broad tapestry of great antiquity portraying a hunting scene. Mrs. Abbott shoved me inside, hard enough to set me stumbling. She shut the door and looked for a bolt to shoot home. Finding none, she strode so close that our noses almost touched as she loomed over me.

"What are you talking about?" she whispered hoarsely.

"You think Sophy Howe's responsible for Francesca's death," I whispered back. "You mean to poison her for it, with belladonna."

I don't know what sort of reaction I expected, but it was certainly something more than Mrs. Abbott pulling her nose back a bare half inch from mine. "Belladonna? What's given you such an idiotic idea?"

"There's none on the dressing table." I spoke the words slowly. They were, after all, my coup de grace. "Of all the cosmetics, *that's* the one you've taken with you."

Mrs. Abbott reeled backward. Her head bowed, jerkily, until her brow rested against her palm. For a moment I knew a cold and bitter triumph. She meant to do murder. She always had, to revenge her lost Francesca, and I had prevented her.

Then, slowly, rustily, Mrs. Abbott began to laugh.

I looked to the door, wondering what I would do if, in her hysteria at being discovered, she attacked me. Once again, I had failed to position myself near the fireplace irons at a critical moment.

I was just about to begin sidling toward them when Mrs. Abbott lifted her streaming eyes. "There is none on the dressing table because I don't use it, you little fool! The stuff discolors the white of the eye."

My throat made a strange little hiccoughing noise.

"*Peste!*" Mrs. Abbott hurried to the door and listened there for a minute before returning to me. "Why are you even still here? Mr. Peele has been and gone."

I did not even bother to ask how she knew that. "You thought he'd take me away," I croaked.

"Why else would I notify Tinderflint of your foolishness? You are only a danger to yourself and should be gotten away from here."

Of all the things she'd said yet, this was the one that awoke the full depths of my confusion. "Why would you care what happens to me?"

Mrs. Abbott stared, her eyebrows drawing tightly together to form one wrinkled, dark line across her forehead. "You truly believe me to be such a monster? I would endanger one girl, I would murder another, for my vengeance? Good

God, I would not have your heart for all the world. Go away." She pushed me backwards. "I am done with you."

"But . . ." I could manage nothing more. I had been wrong about Mrs. Abbott. Entirely, completely, fatally wrong. It had never once occurred to me that the reason she so opposed my every move might be to try to protect me. But now I could see it plainly. If she could derail the schemes of Messrs. Tinderflint and Peele, no other girl would be in jeopardy, as her daughter had been. When that had failed, she thought if I stumbled early in my impersonation, I might just be sent away before I did something truly dangerous. Like gamble too deeply. Like lie through my teeth to the Princess of Wales. And when that failed, she took service with Sophy Howe so she could stay to unravel her mystery while I was taken safely out of here.

"Abbott? I trust there is no problem?"

Sophy stood framed in the doorway and spoke in her most composed voice. I could not see her clearly, thanks to the belladonna in my eyes, but I could picture the lift of her brow and her pert nose that would come with the question.

"But no, Miss Howe," replied Mrs. Abbott. "There is no problem here. I thank you for your offer, my lady." This she said to me, not bothering with the curtsy. "I am most contented with my new place."

Sophy stepped aside so Abbott could leave and moved to follow.

"And what do you want, Sophy?" I said to her back. I

wasn't even aware I had spoken aloud, until Sophy turned her head to look over her shoulder at me. I could more than picture the smile of victory on her face—I could hear it in her voice.

"What on earth are you talking about, Fran?"

I should have remained cool and coy. I should have wrapped my meaning in layers of innuendo and obscurity. But standing there amid the ashes of my own failed perception, I found I could not stomach such evasions. "You've stolen my maid, and you're trying to steal Robert. Why? Do you think I'll forgive your debt in order to buy them back?"

Sophy laughed. It was a brittle sound, gliding like glass shards against my skin. "That fever truly did addle your brain, didn't it? Pretty little Francesca." She grew darkly serious all in a moment. "One of the Sparkling *Three*. Did you hope I'd just let you go on as if nothing had happened? Frankly, I'm astounded you had the courage to come back." She reached out one hand to pat my cheek. Her hand smelled of rosewater, and her breath smelled of almonds and wine as she leaned in close to whisper. "Let me speak plainly, Fran. Nothing has changed. Cozy up to a thousand princesses, if you will. Flirt with a thousand apprentices to try to make Robert jealous. I still know all about you and your lover, and so, my dear little Fran, I own you forever."

"Fran? Sophy?" said another voice from the doorway. "What's going on here?"

Molly had found us, and she was standing in the

doorway, her hands on her hips. "Sophy, what are you doing to poor Fran?"

"Oh, yes, poor Fran," sneered Sophy. "Did you fix her hair this morning, Molly? With your usual skill, I see." She adjusted the curl on my shoulder. "I'll just leave you two to finish up. I know it takes Fran such a long time to get anything right—everything right, I mean, of course."

Sophy sailed past Molly. I stood there, numb, wondering how I'd ever find the courage to move again. Those ashes of perception had reformed themselves, and the new picture that filled me now was as disturbing as the last. It was also one I should have seen before. Indeed, I should have uncovered the possibility the moment Mr. Peele started talking blackmail. Because while Mr. Peele might or might not be blackmailing Mr. Tinderflint, Sophy Howe was most definitely blackmailing Francesca.

Somehow, Sophy had discovered Robert Ballantyne was a Jacobite. She had extorted money from Francesca in return for her silence on the subject of Robert's loyalties. Francesca had paid Sophy whatever she asked. Possibly because she was good and sweet, and loved Robert. Possibly because she understood that if Robert was exposed as a traitor to the Crown, she risked being brought down with him. She had his promise they would be fleeing to join their friends. She had gone home in order to make ready, but the rebellion had been put down, and no flight was possible.

I had been afraid all this time that Francesca had been

murdered. But as Molly took my arm to steer me back to my room and the breakfast she had arranged, it began to occur to me that, faced with debt, exposure, the failure of her plans, and a faithless man for whom she had sacrificed so much, Lady Francesca Wallingham might not have needed assistance to end her life. She might have done it all herself.

CHAPTER TWENTY-FIVE

IN WHICH THERE ARE UNWELCOME
CONVERSATIONS, BUT WELCOME ARRIVALS.

T he remainder of that day passed in relative quiet.
I walked with the princess. I stood with my sister maids
and waited as she argued with Dean Swift and some other
gentlemen whose names escaped me. For once I was relieved
that custom did not permit conversation on the part of us
maids. For one thing, it kept the amount of playacting I had
to do to a minimum. For another, it kept Sophy's mouth shut.
Not that she didn't try her best to be communicative. It was
truly astounding to see how many variations on the theme of
"smug" one young woman could settle on her features.

Molly kept her eyes rigidly ahead, attempting to ignore
us both. Mary glanced from me to Sophy and back again. I
had the feeling she was laying wagers within herself as to

which of us would be the first to explode from so much suppressed feeling.

At nuncheon, His Royal Highness joined his wife and her maids and ladies for venison pasties, potatoes, and greens, as well as a huge trifle with blueberries and a rich custard redolent with vanilla and cinnamon. Afterward, there came more standing and waiting as the princess met with several lords of parliament to hear the status of some dense bill being put forth involving, I think, corn, or possibly the colony of Virginia. Or possibly both.

To say that my mind was not fully diverted by these important and improving matters would be to state the case mildly indeed. Even as I seethed under variation number 683 of Sophy's smug gaze, my heart was wrung out imagining a thousand dramatic scenes involving Lady Francesca. I saw Mr. Tinderflint sobbing that Francesca had ruined them all. I saw her fond and secret mother trying in vain to suppress her anger that Francesca had bankrupted them trying to keep Sophy Howe silent. I saw Francesca with a brown bottle in her hand such as Molly resorted to for the brightening of my eyes. Any apothecary could have supplied the poison, and none would have questioned a young lady's desire for it. Did she put it into some wine, or did she drink it straight from the bottle? Did it hurt?

I alternated these scenes with firm reminders that I had no business conjuring any of them. I listed my own proven inadequacies as a reasoner, and that list was depressingly long.

For example, I had been patently mistaken about Mrs. Abbott. I had been almost as entirely mistaken about Mr. Peele. I could not even begin to decide what to believe about Mr. Tinderflint.

How long did I have before Mr. Peele played his next card and exposed me? There was no way of knowing. Could I write to Mr. Tinderflint and warn him what had happened? But that would do no good. I already knew Mr. Peele was intercepting his partner's letters. Even if a letter did reach Mr. Tinderflint, I had little expectation that he would raise a hand against Peele. I had already seen how Mr. Tinderflint responded to threats against my person by that estimable gentleman.

The only support I had left during that whole long, agonizing day was the hope that Matthew would be assigned the commission to fetch Mr. Thornhill's supplies from town. A water taxi such as had brought me here could accomplish the trip in two or three hours, if the weather was fair. My message might reach Olivia today. She would understand it at once. But even if Matthew did not succeed today, tomorrow would be soon enough. Surely it would be. Mr. Peele could not expect me to leave tonight. He said I should have Olivia help me. He would at least wait until she arrived. I still had time. I must have time.

I fear that hope of Mr. Reade's speed and efficacy felt very frail, drowning as I was under the weight of my mistakes, accompanied by visions that alternated murder with self-murder. So crowded and distracted was my mind, in fact, that I almost failed to notice when we were dismissed to rest and change for that evening's gathering. By then, my head was aching in truth and I was ready to claw out my blurred and itching eyes. If ever I found the opportunity to speak again with Mrs. Abbott, I would thank her for sparing me belladonna's ravages.

Mary Bellenden left our fine flock first when we maids of honor reached the top of the grand staircase. She strode into her room calling ostentatiously for her maid. "Bring me a powder, Mellon. *Something* has soured my stomach terribly!"

"So delicate, our Mary," remarked Sophy. "I should send Abbott to her. The woman brews the most wonderful tisanes. Oh, I'm sorry. Was that indiscreet?" She smiled and picked up her skirts to skip quickly away, which was probably just as well. I'd been aching to kick something all day, and her ankles were a tempting target.

"Don't worry, Fran." Molly laid a hand on my arm. "I'll bring Jessop to you. Have you seen her yet? She's very keen. I've often thought she would be an excellent lady's maid for someone. She'll make sure you're beautiful this evening." She hugged me and whispered in my ear. "And for God's sake, *don't* let Sophy tease you anymore. You'll get a crease in your forehead if you keep looking like that."

I murmured back something that I hoped would pass for a promise and went into my room. There was clean water in the ewer on the dresser, and a towel beside it. I bent over the basin and bathed my eyes quickly and lavishly until the itching eased.

I was still dripping when I heard a soft scratching at the door. I almost asked Mrs. Abbott to open it, before I remembered she was not there and I must shift for myself. But I had no time to start forward, because the person on the other side took it upon himself to open the door and walk in.

It was Robert.

"This is for you," he announced brusquely, and thrust his silver tray at me. A tiny scrap of paper lay in its center.

I unfolded it. A brief note had been written out in a firm hand I did not recognize. *On my way. Will return tonight.*

"It's from that 'prentice, isn't it?" Robert demanded.

"How should I know?" I answered back, in no mood to coquette. "It's unsigned. Where did you find it?"

"I passed by your door in hopes of stealing a word with you, and it was tucked into the latch."

You read my note! Anger flared bright and innervating.

"What are you doing with that fellow, Fran?" Robert was asking.

"What are you doing with the Howe behind the timber pile?" I snapped in answer.

I expected vociferous denial. What I received was an impatient sigh that was flavored most distinctly with regret. *He should go on the stage,* I thought as I watched Robert hang his head. *I've never seen such a performance.*

"I wondered if we were going to come to that," he said, much more to the toes of his buckled shoes than to me. "Fran, how many times have I told you? You are not to mind anything I do with the Howe. I have to keep her quiet, that's all."

"She didn't seem very quiet this morning," I muttered.

Robert did not seem in the least surprised that I should speak in so direct a fashion. Doubtlessly Sophy had made sure that he knew they'd been seen, and by whom. Indeed, I could imagine her speculating out loud on what I might be doing hurrying down to Thornhill's workshop so early in the morning. That had been another mistake on my part. I should never have assumed that all the important and noteworthy eyes would still be sound asleep when I took my little jaunt.

"It changes nothing, Fran," said Robert, slowly, making sure each word was clear and distinct. "As long as Sophy believes I am her creature, she will not make extra difficulties for you."

A laugh escaped me then, and another, and another, until I was lost in a torrent of joyless noise. My knees buckled, and I collapsed backwards onto the sofa. If this was the Howe not making extra difficulties, then heaven help me if she ever did truly concern herself with me.

"Hush, Fran, hush." Robert knelt at my feet and grasped both my hands. "You must calm yourself. Someone will hear!"

What did it matter? So the Howe would hear that Robert had been in my rooms. I wiped at my streaming eyes. Thought and sense reeled, and I could bring no order to them. What could I do? What could I say? All I had to fall back on at this moment was Francesca's much reported sweetness of character.

What would a kind, good, silly girl want to know from this man now?

"Do you love her?"

Robert stood up. He walked over to the window and lifted the edge of one velvet curtain to peer out. I don't know what he saw, but I suspect it had nothing to do with the fact that it had begun raining again.

"I thought I did," he said, "once upon a time. Isn't that how the stories go? She was so witty and so sure of herself. I was . . . flattered when she singled me out." He turned toward me once more, and when he spoke again, a strength filled his voice. "That was before I ever met you, Fran. Before I understood true love belongs to the true heart." He came back and rested his hands on my shoulders. "Remember what I told you? God has given me a second chance. I do not mean to waste it. Whatever you've seen, Fran, whatever I've done, it was for us. So we can be together." He put his hand under my chin and tipped my face up so I had to look at him.

"Do you remember that night we watched the fireworks? When you stole away to meet me in the fountain court?"

I took Robert's hand and removed it from my chin, slowly and keeping gentle hold of his fingertips, so it would not seem I rejected his touch. All the time, my mind worked feverishly. "You tell it, Robert. I want to hear you."

Robert smiled in fond amusement at this. "When I saw you coming up the lane, like a queen, your cloak billowing in the breeze, I was struck dumb. I couldn't believe one man could be so lucky," he murmured. "Just to sit with you by the fountain was a moment of perfection. I remember how delighted you were that we could see the fireworks twice: first in the sky and again in the fountain basin. It was like being lost in a world of light, you said." He smoothed back a crease in my glove's silk from my fingers, to see the shape of them better. "If I'd died right then, I could have been happy." He spoke these words to our joined hands. "I would have left the cause for you. I couldn't believe I felt that much, even as I was saying it. But you wouldn't let me leave. You always understood how important it was to be loyal. I'll never forget . . ." His voice faltered. "When you spoke about all the damage you'd seen from the ones who deserted what they'd sworn to uphold." He squeezed my fingers gently. "You thought that's what I'd done this morning, didn't you?"

I nodded mutely. My envy for Francesca returned in force. For a sweet, silly girl, she always seemed to know exactly what to say. She was lucky too, the way her troubles conspired to hide one another. At least until the end.

"Set your heart at rest, Fran. Please." Robert kissed my knuckle and smoothed his palm over the slight damp patch the gesture left behind. "What Sophy's doing . . . she's jealous, Fran. She's discovered I don't love her, but she's like a child who can't bear to let go of a toy. She has to try to keep all of her hold over me, and for now, just for now, I have to pretend, or she'll have me dismissed before I can complete my task. Remember our night by the fountain. You even wept for her. I couldn't believe it. She'd been so spiteful to you, and you wept for her, lamenting how hurt she must be to behave in such a fashion."

I closed my eyes so they would not widen in pure and

unsullied disbelief. What sort of saint could weep for Sophy Howe? There was naive and good, and there was inhuman. It could not be true. Love was not only blind, it was playing tricks with Robert's memory.

Suddenly, it all seemed too much. I could not bear any more of this litany of the other Francesca's impossible perfections. What I really wanted to do was fling the fact of her sacrifice back in Robert's face. I wanted to scream at him that she was dead because of him and his errands and his loyalties. Dead and in her grave because of all that he had dragged her through.

I am a girl in love, I reminded myself strenuously. *I believe what I am told.* "I cannot bear this much longer, Robert."

"I have one last errand to complete. Then we go." He caressed my cheek once more. "Will you be able to keep your nerve just another few nights?"

"I don't know." I drew my fingers out from between his and rubbed my tired eyes. "I'm so very good and so very simple. Are you sure I can be trusted that long?" I bit my lip, but the words were already out and the shock of them showed in Robert's eyes.

"I don't understand what's come over you," he murmured. "This business with that apprentice, and now you don't even say thank you for my getting rid of that dragon for you —"

"You? You did that?"

"Who else? Fran, I've been putting the idea to Sophy for the past week. Now you're free of her spying and—" He stopped. "You really didn't know this was my doing, did you?"

"How could I, Robert?" The feeling of dark and still water closing overhead engulfed me. I had strayed too far from my role. "You said nothing, and it's all been so upsetting . . ." I blinked rapidly, trying to work some tears up into my eyes.

Robert was a long time answering. "Yes, yes, of course. I am sorry." He paused again. "I need to ask a last favor of you, Fran." His face was drawn, the way it got when he was worried. The words he spoke came slowly, as if they had to travel a great distance to reach his lips. "I didn't want to . . . I don't want to . . . This is the last and only thing I will ever ask of you. I need you to keep something for me, and keep it quite safe. Could you do that?"

I wanted with all my heart to refuse, but I had tripped up too many times during this conversation. "Of course I will." I hoped any hollowness in the smile I turned up to him now might be attributed to weariness.

Robert pulled a packet of papers from inside his coat. They were tied in blue ribbons and sealed with plain blue wax. "Fran, I know how hard this has been." He laid the papers in my hands. "I have been dying inside these past weeks, seeing how you've suffered for what I've had to do. Just a little more time is all I ask. Then I'll be able to deliver what I keep to its destination, and we'll be safe away. To Edinburgh, or perhaps even to Paris. Would you like to live in Paris, Fran?" He gave me a smile I'm sure was meant to be encouraging. "They have the finest dressmakers in the world there. I'll fit you out like the queen among maids that you are. We'll be married in the heart of the city, with all the cathedral bells ringing."

"It sounds too beautiful to be true."

"I will make it true. I'll wrap Paris in a silken ribbon and lay it at your feet, as I always meant to do." He took my face in both his hands. "For you are my true, my only, and my dear one. That is what you are and all you are." He closed my fingers around the packet and smiled, but that smile was strained, and when he spoke again, it was to the papers, not to my eyes. "All will be well. God is good, and He has not deserted us, or our cause." There was a ferocious hope in those words, the kind that one lays on most thickly when one is seeking to bury an equally ferocious doubt. "Our success will prove it. You can manage Sophy. I know you can. Just be your own sweet self with her. She was starting to come around before you took ill. She even sent you that box of bonbons, didn't she?"

Sophy sent her rival a box of bonbons? That was almost as likely as her putting herself out to win the loyalty of a footman who hadn't any more pennies in his purse than she had in hers. Still, now was not the time to argue this point. I made myself smile once more, and let Robert kiss my brow and my cheek, and steeled myself to protest as I felt his hand glide down my shoulder while he leaned in closer.

Someone knocked at the door. Robert cursed and jumped away. Our eyes met for a moment, before he snatched up the silver tray and strode to the door. By the time he was there, he was the personification of the perfect palace footman.

He opened the door, bowing smoothly as he did so.

Matthew walked in, shedding rain from his hat and cloak. With him walked a woman in a hooded, rain-spattered black cloak that showed about an inch of mud-stained hemline beneath. The cloak was opened just far enough that I could see she hugged a huge wicker basket tight to her chest.

Robert straightened up. His eyes met Matthew's, and the two men stared at each other. I had a sudden vision of pistols and drawn swords passing back and forth between their imaginations.

"What you sent for, my lady."

The young woman came forward with her basket and dropped a curtsy. I lifted the basket's latch. In the next instant, a river of white fur and barking exploded in every direction.

"Oh, merciful God!" I cried.

It wasn't one dog, it was the entire fluffy flock, and they were now scattered all about my room, barking and wagging and growling at everything that did not get out of their way.

"Is something wrong, my lady?" murmured the young woman, lifting her face just a tiny bit.

Just enough so I could see I'd been right. Olivia had not sent a maid to bring her dogs to me. She never would do such a weak-kneed thing. She'd come her own self, and she grinned at me now.

CHAPTER TWENTY-SIX

IN WHICH OUR HEROINE INDULGES IN FOND
REUNION AND DISCOVERS FRESH COMPLICATIONS
INVOLVING PAINT, POWDER, AND SMALL DOGS.

Thank you, Robert," I said as calmly as I could manage. I did not look at him. All I could see was Olivia's eyes, shining with merriment at the success of her adventure. All I could hear was relief and joy singing their exultant chorus in my heart. I forgot all other dangers and difficulties. I forgot that my rapport with Robert was in a most precarious state. Olivia was here, and all that mattered was that I must remove his prying eyes as quickly as possible. "You may go."

"If you're certain, my lady," said Robert. Even deafened by my own relief as I was, I heard the suspicion in his voice. I made myself glance toward him and give him a smile meant to convey reassurance. It probably would have had a more significant effect if Matthew had not been there with us and if I had not I still been clutching the papers Robert had entrusted to me.

"I believe the lady was quite clear," said Matthew, exercising that male privilege of speaking for any female present.

He and Robert sized each other up again. I ground my teeth together, largely to help suppress my urge to box both their ears. I did, however, take that moment when their attention was so focused to lay the papers on my writing desk, where they would at least be less conspicuous.

Unfortunately for Robert, there was only one way this challenge of masculine wills could end. He held the lower rank, at least to all appearances, and so he must bow, and with a final wary, warning glance in my direction, must leave. I let my eyes shift toward the now hidden papers, hoping to reassure him, but he was out the door before I could be certain I had succeeded.

Matthew shut the door. I whisked around and ran to Olivia, shoving back her cloak's hood so I could see her clearly.

"Cousin!" I did not care that I shrieked. I could have shouted from the rooftops and danced down the lane in my petticoats and not cared one jot.

"You're all right!" Olivia cried as we embraced. "Oh, Peggy, I've been so frightened! But you're truly all right!"

I will gloss over the kissing and crying that followed. I mustered enough rationality to divest Olivia of her sodden cloak and lead her to the fire, where she could begin to dry her soaked and too-short hems, but no more. For this blessed moment suspicion and decorum both were forgotten. I could even forgive the dogs their whining and wagging and dodging between us while I embraced my best and truest friend tightly, reassuring myself that she was indeed here with me.

"But . . . but the palace!" spluttered Olivia when emotion's tide had ebbed and we were both finally able to talk sensibly again. "I saw the advertisement, of course, and the original direction for Thames bridge, and then when Mr. Reade brought your message . . ." She glanced toward Matthew, who had moved to the sofa and had the dogs clustered around him. He'd brought out a piece of cake from somewhere, possibly his pocket, and was busy making friends with the greedy creatures in the most direct way possible, all the while studiously pretending to ignore us. Olivia didn't believe the pretense any more than I did, and drew me to the farthest corner of the room. "Peggy, what have you done?" she whispered.

Of course I understood her fear. Olivia knew as well as I did that there existed few routes by which a girl might quickly increase her wealth and consequence. Most of those ended in some man's bed, and probably not as his wife.

"It's all right, Olivia." I squeezed her hand. "And you can speak freely in front of Mr. Reade. He's a true friend."

Matthew looked at me from under the fringe of copper hair that slanted across his brow. His smile was entirely in his eyes, but I felt it distinctly. In answer, my heart performed an odd and not unpleasant little flip directly beneath my rib cage. This was not something I concealed successfully, for

Olivia was looking from Matthew to me. Briskly, she picked up the nearest dog and plumped herself down on the sofa, right next to Mr. Reade. In her plain maid's dress and old-fashioned cap, she looked very much like a chaperone during a social call with a niece whose decorum she did not entirely trust. "You'd best tell me everything."

I opened my mouth to begin, but was interrupted by a swift knock at the door. Just as swiftly, it opened and Molly Lepell sailed in with a plump, brown-haired maid in tow.

"Now, Fran, here is Jess . . ."

She never finished the sentence. The dogs formed into a shaggy phalanx and charged, barking to break their tiny warrior hearts at these new hems that had suddenly appeared to jeopardize the well-being of their mistress.

"Fran, what on earth!" cried Molly as the dogs converged on her. The maid—Jessop, I presumed—squealed and retreated to the wall, which only set off a fresh round of barking.

"Hello, Molly. Oh, back, you silly things." I waded in, prodding and shooing to clear a path for Molly to the fireside. She came, but slowly. The dogs had faded from her attention as she took long and careful notice of Mr. Reade, still sitting on the sofa with Olivia, who also received cool and suspicious perusal.

"Lady Hannah Applepuss's pure white hounds, I presume," said Molly, flicking a finger vaguely toward the dogs, but not taking her attention from Matthew and Olivia.

"Well, yes." This was not good. It was dangerous in the

extreme that yet more people were seeing Matthew Reade in my room with only the highly dubious chaperonage of an unknown girl in a maid's costume. Molly was no talking fool, but I knew nothing about this Jessop, who was still pressed back against the wall, as if she feared the fluff flock might assemble itself into one great wolf and devour her messily.

"I thought the dogs weren't arriving until Friday," Molly was saying. "I had heard, in fact, that there were great plans for a welcoming party on the bridge."

"The stage was early. It's all this good weather we've been having," I replied blandly. We were silent for a minute, listening to the rain drumming against the window.

"This is Templeton. My guardian sent her to take Mrs. Abbott's place." I gestured toward Olivia, who belatedly realized she should have been on her feet already. Any working maid would have been. Jessop had gotten over enough of her fright to turn her attention toward Olivia, and it was very close attention indeed. She made clear and special note of everything about my cousin, from her too short, muddy skirt, to her cap with its strings dangling. She was quite obviously not impressed. A fact that Molly Lepell did not miss.

"Well. How very prompt. And Mr. Reade is here to make sure this important moment is memorialized on canvas?" In that moment, Molly sounded distressingly like Sophy Howe.

Matthew, quite sensibly, executed one of his famous bows, murmured some excuse that none of us could hear, and retreated. I envied him.

Molly waved Jessop out of the room as well, and then pushed the door shut. She faced me again with folded arms and a face as sour as old vinegar. I wondered if she had small siblings at home on whom she had practiced that particular frown. "Fran, what are you playing at?"

"Nothing, Molly. Nothing new," I amended, retrieving the smallest of the small dogs, who had found a bit of loose thread on Molly's skirt to growl at and looked to be working his way up to a lunge. "I wanted to make sure Sophy wasn't able to interfere with the dogs' arrival, so I had them brought by an alternate route. That is all."

Molly's cheeks colored, and it was not in amusement, or a maiden's lively blush. It was anger. "Did it never occur to you that if you lost this silly bet, Sophy might relent a little?"

"No," I replied honestly, handing the dog over to Olivia. "It's not in her nature."

Molly sighed, a sound that was both strangled and resigned. "Well, I expect you're right." She looked again at the fluff flock. Worn clean through from subduing the entire room, the majority had collapsed in a panting heap in front of the fire. "They are darling little things, aren't they?"

"Thank you," said Olivia, forgetting I'd just introduced her as a maid. Molly stared, affronted. Olivia stared straight back. Then she did duck her head and curtsy, but it was too late.

Molly stalked over to my cousin and pulled on her cap. Olivia snatched it back, but her wealth of gold hair, along with several silver pins, had already tumbled down. Molly grabbed her hand, examining first the perfectly kept nails and then, upon turning it over, the absolute lack of calluses on her palm.

"Who are you?" Molly demanded, but she did not wait for her answer before she rounded on me. "Fran, what are you *doing?*"

"She's my cousin," I said. "She's here to help me."

"By masquerading as your *maid?* Have you taken leave of your senses?"

Very probably, but I could not say that to her. In point of fact, I needed to end this conversation now, before she could be driven to ask any more questions, however valid they might be. "I have my reasons, Molly. Please, please, don't say anything. That's all I ask."

Molly looked at me, and the dogs, and Olivia. I read anger deepening in her, and regret. I read the death of a friendship under the weight of one deception too many. "I came to make sure you'd be ready in time for Mr. Handel's concert tonight," she said coolly. "But as I see you have made your own arrangements, I leave you to complete them." She curtsied to me in a most formal manner. Then without another word, she walked out the door and let it shut behind her.

I'm afraid my ladylike and well-bred response to this was to curse, at length, using a number of phrases and variations I had overheard from my uncle's grooms. I liked Molly. She had been nothing but kind to me and my predecessor. She had been both friend and ally, and I had not guarded that friendship sufficiently.

But just as bad was the understanding that even if Molly kept her mouth closed, the maid Jessop surely would not. The news of Matthew being in my room would spread all through the court. As would the news that the dogs had arrived early. There might even be mention of Olivia.

Olivia, however, was not attuned to these nuances of my —our—position. Her attention was elsewhere. "Good heavens, Peg, that was Molly Lepell, wasn't it? She's a maid of honor! One of the Shining Three! She called you *Fran*. You haven't been . . . you're not   "

For the first time in my life, I saw my cousin at an absolute loss. She plumped back down onto the sofa and stared wide-eyed up at me. "How did you even get here, Peggy?"

I sat beside her and took her hand. It had gone cold, and I looked into my cousin's genuinely worried eyes. I couldn't blame her for that worry. There was certainly enough cause for it. There'd be even more once she knew my long, immensely convoluted story.

Which I had no time to tell her. The silvery bell of the mantel clock was striking seven, and I was expected to be in attendance on Her Royal Highness very soon. If I was not, there would be yet more questions I could not answer.

"Olivia, please tell me my aunt thinks you are visiting a friend for the night," I said.

"Do you think I'm simple? Charlotte Maidstone has suffered a severe disappointment, and I am there to hold her hand and make sure she has plenty of violet water and strong tea."

I squeezed my cousin's hand tight. Of course she had thought of that. It was just like her. "Then I promise I will be able to tell you everything, but later. Right now I need your help."

"Anything, Peggy, you know that."

"I need to get ready to wait on the Princess of Wales."

It is perhaps an odd thing, but even when one spends much of one's life being dressed by others, one does not often stop to think of the range of skills and the amount of patience required on the part of the dresser. Olivia and I had, of course, laced each other's stays and straightened ruffles and even painted faces. But that was for more ordinary occasions, and with clothes that had been sufficiently cared for and carefully laid out. The complexities of court dress, with its extra pinnings and lacings, the yards of additional ribbon, the weight and type of paint, and the bewildering variety of brushes and sponges was foreign to us. As were the exacting requirements involved in securing the exasperating puzzle pieces of the wig into place over hair that was lumpish and uncertain under its own mass of pins and netting. I was delighted to have my cousin with me, exerting all her energies to help me in this hour of my greatest need. But at the same time, I regretted Jessop. I missed my little dark-haired Libby. When I looked in the glass and saw my crooked cheeks and my misplaced patch and felt the awkward shifting of my wig on my scalp, I positively mourned Mrs. Abbott.

"It will be fine," I said, in an attempt to reassure Olivia, and myself. "It's one of Mr. Handel's concerts tonight. No one will be paying me the least attention."

Except, of course, everyone was. When I entered the princess's apartments, where the select several dozen had gathered to refresh themselves and enjoy one another's company prior to the music, every eye turned toward me. They all knew something had happened, and they looked to see its effects. What they saw was me, turned out clumsily, moving with caution so as not to dislodge my wig, and missing my fan. Especially Sophy saw, as clearly as I saw Molly standing beside her. Mary, who was engaged in some evidently highly witty conversation with Mr. Danforth, looked at me and shook her head in open pity.

There was nothing to do except brazen it out. I lifted my chin and pulled all my borrowed airs about myself as I crossed the vast expanse of that chamber to where Her Royal Highness sat. There, I curtsied, carefully.

"You're late, Lady Francesca," said the princess coolly. "I was about to send someone to make sure that you had not fallen ill."

"My apologies, Your Highness," I said. "I found myself at the last moment in receipt of an unexpected message."

"Did you?" The frost in my mistress's clear blue gaze did not thaw in the least. "It must have been very important."

"From Stemhempfordshire, madame. I believe Princess Anne will find it most welcome. If I may have permission to speak with her about it, tomorrow . . . ?"

I kept my voice low. Only Her Royal Highness and the nearest three ladies of the bedchamber would hear. And Lord Blakeney, of course, who had already arched his brows and put on a grin of such width as to say he'd just won a sizable wager. Word would spread in a murmur about the rest of the gathering. The grand finale of the Maids' Puppy Wager had commenced. Speculation would attribute any lapse in my appearance or deportment to that fact, or so I most fervently hoped.

"I see," said the princess. "You will have to take up the matter with Lady Portland, but I am certain you will be able to persuade her that Anne should pay you a call tomorrow."

I murmured my heartfelt thanks and was waved away so Her Royal Highness could return to her conversation with the Lords Stanhope and Edgemonte. I retreated, carefully. As word of the wager's conclusion rippled out through the splendid crowd, I was saluted with raised glasses and sly winks. It would be too bad to spoil this moment by losing my hair.

"Well, well," said Mary Bellenden brightly as I joined her by the window where she sat with Molly and Sophy. The night had cleared outside, and the moon was just beginning to rise above the distant trees. "It looks as though our Fran has won after all."

Molly said nothing. She did not even look at me. She contemplated the rising moon. There was a ring around it, a sign a storm was surely coming.

"Has she won indeed?" murmured Sophy. She stood

behind Molly's chair, her gloved hands curled around the carved and painted wood. "Because I must say, for someone who has achieved victory, Fran, you look awful."

I bit my lip and fixed on a polite smile, but I also said nothing. At that moment, seeing Molly's turned head and Sophy's knowing smile, I was not at all sure of my success. I consoled myself by contemplating the fact that Olivia was safe and snug in my room upstairs. We were together again. There was nothing even Sophy Howe could dream up that Olivia and I could not face.

CHAPTER TWENTY-SEVEN

MOST UNNATURAL MURDER.

I expect the concert was lovely. Court musicians are in general highly praised, usually because no one wishes to be seen faulting the taste of the royal patron. But Mr. Handel's music was in truth excellent. Tonight, however, all I wanted was to fly back to my room, where I could sit with Olivia and tell her everything. Sophy's repeated remarks from behind her fan about how truly ill I was looking did not help the time pass any more swiftly; not during the concert, nor during the reprise the Prince of Wales unexpectedly ordered, nor during the dinner that followed the music, nor the drinking and card playing after that.

I was all but shaking with impatience by the time Her Royal Highness announced her intent to retire. Molly had not spoken one word to me all night, and more people than Mary were noticing. If Sophy had been preening any more openly, I could have hired her out as one of the parkland peacocks. Her insouciance at the whispered news that the puppies had arrived had me wondering what hidden card she thought she carried. This only worsened my impatience. Something was going wrong. I was sure of it. Sophy knew what it was, and I couldn't even guess at it.

Through what I can only describe as sheer force of will, I lingered in the lower gallery to say a protracted good night to Mr. Danforth. Poor man, I think I gave him the impression I cherished a *tendre* for him, but in truth, I just wanted to let my sister maids go ahead of me so I would not have to endure yet more remarks from Sophy regarding how sickly I looked. At last, I submitted to a kiss on the cheek and made my escape alone up the stairs and down the gallery.

I had almost reached my door when movement caught my eye. I jumped near out of my skin. I recovered in time, though, to see the door to the tapestry room ease back just enough to show a sliver of candlelight, and Matthew Reade.

I put my fingers over my mouth to smother my exclamations and looked sharply left and right. But we were alone, and all the doors nearby were closed. I beckoned Matthew forward. He came swiftly, and close. We smiled at each other like guilty children, and I grabbed up my hems to hurry toward my chamber.

That was when I heard the crash and the high-pitched, terrified howl.

✦   ✦   ✦

I don't remember running the rest of the way down the corridor or bursting into my room. I only remember seeing Olivia, stretched out on the floor, her eyes staring, her mouth open, and her arms flailing weakly. She gasped, a hoarse and painful sound. Around her, the dogs yipped and wailed in frantic confusion. There were the remains of a meal with its plates and tray scattered all over the floor, including a shattered glass and a pool of sherry spreading beneath Olivia's hand.

I don't know if I screamed. I don't know if I didn't. The world seemed to be proceeding in fits and starts. One moment I was in the doorway. The next, I was on my knees beside my cousin. The next, I held her arms and called her name.

"Olivia! Olivia! What's happened? My God! What's wrong!" But my cousin only groaned. Her eyes rolled madly in her head. She was cold to the touch, and her mouth and hands had taken on a terrifying blue-gray tinge.

Matthew was on his knees with us. He snatched up the glass and sniffed at it. Then he dipped his finger in the spilled sherry and tasted.

"She's been poisoned," he said. "Belladonna."

"No," I said uselessly. "My God, no!" I did not doubt him for a minute. His father was an apothecary; he would know.

"We've got to get it out of her. We need an emetic. Christ!" he shouted as he jumped to his feet. "I don't know where anything is in this place!"

"Get Mrs. Abbott!" I said without thinking. "Three doors down on the left. *Hurry!*" Olivia convulsed in my arms again.

Matthew ran. I was weeping now. Olivia choked. I prayed and babbled and rolled her on her side so that she would not swallow her tongue. I scrabbled at her dress to loosen her laces. She choked again, and I wrapped my arms around her stomach, pressing hard, crying more and willing her to vomit.

She was going to die. Olivia, my cousin, my friend, was going to die because someone had meant to poison me. Out in the corridor, someone laughed. Someone else remarked at all the terrible noise and how if one was going to have dogs, one should keep them under control.

It was a thousand years before Matthew reappeared with Mrs. Abbott beside him. "Get her on the bed," she ordered as she strode straight past us and vanished into the dressing room.

Matthew and I struggled to obey. Olivia had gone terribly, terribly still. Her skin was clammy and stone cold. Her eyelids flickered wildly, and her eyes were nothing but twin black holes in her white, white face. The dogs sniffed and whined about us, and I kicked them ruthlessly out of the way. We laid her on my bed, and I climbed up beside her, to hold and warm her, for all the good it would do.

Mrs. Abbott emerged from the dressing room with an array of bottles and a fresh basin. Matthew grabbed up a clean glass from the table beside the sherry decanter so Mrs. Abbott could pour some concoction into it. She attempted to pass it directly to Olivia, but Matthew snatched it out of her fingers, sniffed it, tasted it, and nodded.

I would later marvel that Mrs. Abbott permitted this, but all she said was "Lift her head."

I tried to obey. I had been a nurse to friends, and my uncle's aged mother. I knew how to lift a patient's head and cradle it so broth or medicine might be spooned into a mouth. But this was different. This was Olivia, and she was dying of poison, and my hands were shaking so terribly I could barely do anything at all.

"Open, Olivia. You must. Please, please, please." I gently prised her jaw apart. She tried to struggle. She choked and wheezed. Her breath smelt sweet and foul. Mrs. Abbott, grim and silent, poured the entire glass of greasy-looking brown liquid down Olivia's throat, clamping her mouth and nose ruthlessly shut so she must swallow.

I waited one heartbeat. Two. Three. A dozen. Olivia convulsed again. She gagged and shook. I rolled her onto her side, and Matthew took her shoulders to help hold her steady. Mrs. Abbott held the basin. Olivia vomited.

When at last she finished, she went limp in my arms. "Olivia?" I whispered. She was cold. She was still. Her mouth was blue, and it should not have been. No living flesh ever wore that color. I squeezed her hand as tightly as I could. "Olivia!"

Matthew had gone white. Mrs. Abbott left us, and I barely noticed. When she returned a moment later, she had a hand mirror with her. I was weeping continuously now as I lifted my cousin's head so Mrs. Abbott could hold the glass in front of Olivia's mouth.

A heartbeat. Another. An eternity and an instant. Matthew's strong, warm hand on my shoulder.

A faint silver mist formed on the glass.

She's alive. The words thundered through me, but I could not speak. I slumped backwards and would have fallen against the headboard if Matthew had not been there to catch me.

Mrs. Abbott drew the mirror away and then gently lifted one of Olivia's lids to peer into her eye. She laid her hand against Olivia's chest and then pressed her ear there.

"Alive, yes, but weak. Her heart is not steady. You are sure it was belladonna that did this?" she demanded of Matthew.

Matthew indicated the fallen glass, which, I now belatedly realized, the dogs were sniffing around. My God, what if one of them had drunk . . . ? Olivia might live, but if one of her dogs was harmed, she would certainly kill me.

Mrs. Abbott retrieved the glass and, as Matthew had, she sniffed and she tasted. Her face went white as sheets and paper, and she strode to the table where the sherry decanter sat. For a moment I thought she was going to smash the crystal bottle, but she only unstoppered it and sniffed again.

We saw by her expression that this was where the poison waited. Not that she turned toward us. She stayed there, facing the poisoned wine, her head bowed.

"This is how it was done," she whispered. "It was poison for my Francesca as well. And I did not see. I did not think. I was so sure it was fever. I . . ." She choked on the grief that swelled beneath her words.

But then Olivia stirred. Her eyes flickered and opened. "P . . . Peg?" she breathed.

It was a long time before I could stop crying.

CHAPTER TWENTY-EIGHT

‑ⰓⰅ✦ⰋⰓ‑

IN WHICH MYSTERIES AND DRAWINGS ARE
EXAMINED, AND SOME ANSWERS ARE DISCERNED.

I pray sincerely that I never know a night worse than that one. Olivia vomited three more times. Twice more she fell into a stupor, breath and pulse both faltering. Each time, I was certain she had died. I sat on the bed beside her and held her in my arms and babbled at her, begging that she live. I don't know if I was begging Olivia or God, and I don't suppose it mattered much.

Matthew kept the fire blazing, even as night gave way to a clear dawn. He drew the window curtains shut against any possibility of draft.

As dawn brightened into a hot morning, Mrs. Abbott worked. She all but forced me into the dressing room to get me out of my court clothes and into day things. She brought hot bricks wrapped in flannel to place at Olivia's feet and sides, and clean water to moisten her mouth and wipe her face. She mopped up all trace of the spilled sherry and put down more clean water for the dogs.

At eight o'clock, however, Mrs. Abbott left us. She had to return to Sophy Howe to avoid rousing her new mistress's suspicions. She promised she would tell Sophy that Lady Francesca had indeed fallen ill again, and she would send one of the reliable palace maids up with brandy, bread, and broth.

She stood by the door as she said all this. Her eyes were red with unspent tears, and her voice harsh as any crow's from weariness and a fury I could finally begin to understand.

"Thank you," I said to her. It was all I had to offer. "You saved her life. Thank you."

Mrs. Abbott's eyes glittered, and for all my new understanding, I could read nothing in her hard face. She turned and softly closed the door behind her as she left.

I tried to send Matthew away as well, but he would not go. "You'll lose your position," I warned him.

He shrugged. "It's lost. I've been seen with you under dubious circumstances, and I've stayed out all night. Mr. Thornhill will not tolerate such behavior."

"I'm sorry," I whispered miserably.

But Matthew took my hand. "I'm not."

The morning wore itself away into afternoon. Mrs. Abbott did send up the victuals she promised. I fed Olivia broth and brandy. Matthew and I and the dogs shared out the bread and some biscuits. Sometimes Olivia lapsed into sleep. Other times she woke, her eyes dull, but focused.

At those times I talked, telling Olivia and Matthew the whole of my story, from my first meeting with the firm of Tinderflint, Peele, and Abbott, to my training to impersonate Lady Francesca, to finding the drawings that my predecessor had hidden. I told them how Mrs. Abbott deserted me to take service with Sophy Howe and why she'd done it. I talked about Mr. Peele stealing two of the three sketches and ordering me to turn thief and to get myself out of the palace without delay. Finally, I told them both about Robert, and the Jacobites, and the papers he had left in my keeping.

"Are they still here? Those papers?" asked Matthew.

I felt my blood drain from my cheeks. Matthew went to my writing table and, after a moment's search, found the packet with its blue ribbons. It seemed a very small thing just then, but it was a sign of hope. Perhaps.

"What about this sketch? May I see it?"

I squeezed my eyes shut. I could not do this now. Not with Olivia still hovering so close to the abyss. But something was touching my hand. I opened my eyes to see Olivia looking at me from under her heavy lids. Her one finger tapped at my hand restlessly. No, impatiently. When she saw she had my attention, she croaked a few syllables and jerked that finger toward Matthew. And then fell back against the pillows, her breath ragged from the effort.

It was so like her, I thought with awe and exasperation. She might be near dead, but Olivia still had not lost her sense of drama. She wanted to hear the end of the story.

I left her side and unearthed the last sketch from my workbasket, where I'd stowed it. Matthew cleared the round table beside the bed and brought over a candle for extra light. We needed it. The sketch had become well smeared from all the folding and unfolding and being carried about in my sleeve. Matthew bent close and squinted at the lines. Then he lifted it, holding the paper in one hand and a candle in the other, examining the drawing in silence, his ruddy cheeks slowly growing pale.

"Do you know what this is?" he asked.

"It's a parody of the ceiling in the princess's new apartment," I said. "But I can't understand why the couple there on the rocks is dead."

"Look at them again." He passed me the paper and then went and pulled back the curtains so the bright daylight flooded the chamber. "Look closely."

I did look. Perhaps I could have seen, had not so much of my attention kept darting back to Olivia to reassure itself she was still breathing.

"That's His Majesty King George there, dead on the ground," said Matthew quietly. He was right. I'd passed the king's portrait a thousand times in the dim gallery, but had only seen him in person the day he left, and then only his shoes. "This one, mounting the chariot instead of Apollo? That's James the Pretender. I've seen his portrait elsewhere," he added quickly, but I heard afresh the north country burr in his voice and wondered at that. "He's here again, in the medallion where His Royal Highness's portrait is on the original. I can't tell who the woman standing in for the princess in the other medallion is . . ."

I peered closely. I'd stared at this sketch more times than I could count, but I'd been in the twilight of my room, either in the mornings before anyone was about, or late at night when I couldn't sleep. Flickering firelight and classical dress in the sketch, and paint and powdered wigs on the originals had obscured the details that broad daylight and Matthew's artist's eye revealed. "God in Heaven. That's her. That's Francesca." Francesca had filled in her own face in the place where the Princess of Wales belonged.

"No." Matthew leaned in until his nose almost touched the sketch. "Yes. You're right. And Leucothoe here? That's Sophy Howe."

I stared at the figure who was trying to bar the Apollo figure from his conveyance. "And the charioteer . . ." recognition came over me slowly. "That's Robert Ballantyne, and Sophy Howe is holding James the Pretender back from climbing into the chariot. Robert Ballantyne is the Pretender's charioteer, and all of it, over His Majesty's dead body." Everyone said Francesca was so sweet, but no sweet girl put herself in the place of a princess, beside a man who meant to retake the throne his father had lost. I thought on another sketch, the portrait Matthew had drawn, and of the greed he'd captured in Francesca's face. "What was she playing at?"

"What about the other two drawings?" asked Matthew. "The ones that this Peele took. Describe them to me."

I did. I told him about the death of Queen Anne with its addition of the monkey, and the man with the paper beside the secret panel in the fireplace. I could not help but remember that Robert had pulled the papers he had left with me from another such panel. I also told Matthew about the floor plan for the great house.

"Queen Anne died in Kensington Palace," said Matthew slowly. "Could this floor plan have been for Kensington?"

"It could have." In fact, it was a wonder I had not considered this before. I told myself I had other demands on my attention, but this did not make me feel any less a fool. I took up Olivia's hand again. Did it feel warmer, or was that just hopeful imagination? Olivia's eyes flickered again and opened a hair's breadth. She was watching me, us. She listened closely, although she could not speak. My heart swelled.

"So, when Queen Anne died, a monkey and a man hid something in her bedchamber," said Matthew slowly. "But what? And why would it be worth murder?"

Matthew shook his head and frowned at the picture of the ceiling, tracing its lines with one finger. I gripped Olivia's hand and listened to her breathe. I tried to think. If this were a game, if this were the two of us in the breakfast parlor laughing over an advertisement or cartoon, Olivia would already have the whole storyline laid out. She'd have it all making perfect sense from beginning to end.

How would Olivia think about this?

"There are two houses," I said slowly to her. Olivia's mouth opened, and closed. She gave a little jerk of her chin. *Go on,* she was telling me. *Go on.* "There are two houses. The town house, and the palace. Suppose one intrigue for each house. In the town house, there are the plans of this trio of Lady Fran's. In the palace, there are the plans of the spies. What bridges them? Lady Francesca." I answered my own question. "Lady Francesca is raised in the Jacobite palace of Saint-Germaine, surrounded by plots and counterplots." I eyed the door uncertainly. I wondered what Mrs. Abbott was doing at this moment. I didn't dare think what Sophy Howe was doing.

Matthew noticed my distraction and took up the narrative thread for me. "So, she is a courtier as a girl, with no idea her kind guardian is a spy, or that he is setting her up as a pawn in his game when he plucks her from the Jacobite court to send her to the Hanoverians. There, romantic that she is, she fails to fall in love with any of the wealthy and titled gentlemen who would make her fortune. Instead, she loses her heart to the poor footman who dreams of bringing his king home from across the water. Perhaps he even found out she had been at Saint-Germaine and sought her out—"

"But how would he have done that?" I asked. My head was aching. Something was wrong. Something had been wrong this whole time. Olivia parted her lips again. How could I even be thinking about this? I reached for the damp cloth and patted her lips. But I had to think. It was only at the end of this labyrinth that I'd discover who had meant to poison me and found Olivia instead. "No one knew Francesca had lived at Saint-Germaine. She was supposed to be from Dover. That's what Mr. Tinderflint told everyone."

"Robert Ballantyne's a spy." Matthew waved my words away. "Spies find out things. It's their primary occupation. This Robert, a dedicated Jacobite, finds out about Francesca's other life as an exile in the court of the Pretender and goes to her. They talk. Both are lonely and are filled with the fervor of the cause. Their love burns bright, and he tells her his plans—"

"Except he didn't," I reminded him. "He's been keeping things from her, for her own safety."

Matthew evidently could not think of any answer to this and lapsed into silence. I sat holding Olivia's hand and wishing in vain for the other two drawings—the death of Queen Anne, and the floor plan of the unknown house. What did those mean, and what were we missing now? I stared at the drawing in front of us. I thought about Lady Fran—described by her lover and her sister maid as so sweet and selfless—making so many sacrifices for love of her footman and his cause. I touched the self-portrait Francesca had put in place of Her Royal Highness's visage. I thought about how this sweet girl always knew what to say, and how her troubles folded together so tidily, like a well-made fan.

Then I thought how there was one person in this mystery who had never called her sweet, let alone simple. That was Mr. Peele, the cheat and blackmailer. The man who had come into this room and had thought to search the workbasket. Which was one of the places Francesca had in fact hidden her sketches. I'd gotten the idea from her, because that sweet girl was also very good at hiding things.

These thoughts slid across the floor of my mind, and it was as if a prop had been kicked away. The whole unruly pile of bricks that were the events of my life and Lady Francesca's toppled. But instead of falling into a heap, they landed in the tidiest pyramid imaginable.

"We've been wrong," I said softly. I lifted my eyes to the twin expressions of confusion that had fallen across Matthew and Olivia's faces. "Sweet, good Lady Francesca. She fooled us all."

CHAPTER TWENTY-NINE

WHAT DID HAPPEN?

T his is what happened:

Francesca Wallingham grew up in the court of Saint-Germaine, the bastard daughter of an upper servant and some French noble or other. She was quick, and she was clever, and she knew to a nicety who held the reins of power in that palace of exiles. She watched the men come and go, knew all the hiding places and overheard all the whispers. She learned how to laugh and flatter and use her big, dark eyes to best effect. She learned how to appear innocent and sweet. So sweet, in fact, that the conspirators would be convinced she was stupid beyond belief, and either ignore her or try to make use of her.

She watched her mother earn money by passing messages. Maybe she even learned the trade, whether her mother knew she did or not. By the time Mr. Tinderflint came along in his guise as Mr. Taggert, she was very good at this, too. She was greedy and jealous of the ones who would always have more than she. In front of her mother, she sighed and lamented about England, about how well they both would do there. Her mother made a bargain with Mr. Tinderflint, and the two of them escaped across the channel.

Mr. Tinderflint housed them. He coached Francesca as he had coached me, grooming her patiently for her role. He wrote letters as necessary, and when George of Hanover became King George of Great Britain, he had his sweet protégée installed in the palace, intending to use her as a source of news and gossip, just as he had used my mother.

But Mr. Tinderflint had no idea how adept Francesca was at overhearing things, nor how well she was able to keep what she heard to herself. Being from Saint-Germaine, she knew the codes men spoke in and the secret names the Jacobites used to refer to their leaders and their king. She discovered the would-be traitors among the courtiers and the servants. She found the one who could not resist her, and she used him. Oh, poor Robert, how she used him. She made herself into his dream of a girl, a beauteous maiden with a pure soul and lofty spirit. She found out what he guarded. She made her own coded copy of the pertinent information so she could find it herself when she was ready. She paid off Sophy Howe—not to protect Robert, but to protect herself until she had all her plans in place. Then she left the court, feigning nervous exhaustion. Her intent was always to recover this treasure of Robert's to take it back to Saint-Germaine herself and present it to the Pretender.

That was why none of what I'd unearthed made sense before. That was why the three people I'd been calling "the firm" seemed to have such separate and conflicting motivations. The conspiracy did not belong to Tinderflint, Peele, and Abbott. It belonged wholly and solely to sunny, sweet, pretty, false Lady Francesca. In the end, though, it was not the swiftness with which the uprising was put down that ruined her schemes. It was death.

This was what I explained in a great rush to Matthew. I was so lost in the story, I did not notice for a long time that he had ceased to look at me. He gazed over my shoulder. My back was to the door. When I turned, I saw Mrs. Abbott there.

"Go on," she said as she walked farther into the room. She deftly flipped the counterpane up from the end of the bed and felt the cloth-wrapped bricks at Olivia's feet. "Go on."

"I'm sorry, Mrs. Abbott," I whispered.

She smoothed the coverings back in place. Olivia's eyes had fallen closed. She still wore a sickly, waxen pallor, but the blue tinge was gone from her lips, and her breathing was much easier. Mrs. Abbott watched her for a long time.

"I think I knew," she said, finally. "But I did not want to believe. I think I came into this new foolishness because I wanted to prove my own suspicions wrong. I wanted to lay them to rest, to save for myself, at least, the memory of my child."

It was indecent that we should be here for this. No one should have to make such a confession to strangers.

"But she—Francesca—couldn't do all this alone," said Matthew. He was speaking as gently as he could. "A woman can't travel alone. She can't make the arrangements and pay out the money on her own. She'd be taken for a . . . well . . . a . . . courtesan."

"She wasn't alone. She had help, or she thought she did. Mr. Peele." I said this to Mrs. Abbott, and as I spoke, the last bits of understanding fell into place.

"Tinderflint used Peele," said Mrs. Abbott dully. "Bought his information and made use of his less savory contacts. I would have warned Tinderflint against him. If a man will cheat at one thing in life, he will cheat at many. But I did not think it was my place. I did not think I needed to care."

She did not instantly blame Peele for corrupting her daughter. The time for such protestation was over, even for her. I wished I had comfort to offer.

"Did Peele have a hold over Mr. Tinderflint?" I asked.

"He was a blackmailer. What would keep him from blackmailing the man who was already paying him for information?"

"Mrs. Abbott . . ." I hesitated. "Mrs. Abbott, which side is Mr. Tinderflint on? Is he Hanoverian or Jacobite?"

"When one is building one's plans around a spy, it is best to know as few of his secrets as possible. He does not tell me. I do not ask." She added this last in a whisper.

"Still, whatever we are dealing in, it is important enough

to cause a professional scoundrel like Peele to turn his coat," said Matthew.

"Oh, it is even more important than that." I took the ceiling satire from him, and pointed to the medallions where Francesca had substituted herself for the Princess of Wales and the Pretender for the prince. "Whatever it is, it is so vital to the Jacobite cause that Francesca thought the Pretender would marry her for it."

Mrs. Abbott swayed, just once, then she gripped the foot of the bed. "She is blinded by this plot of hers. She bribes Mr. Peele with the promise of wealth and reward when it succeeds. She gains the trust of this footman, or he gains hers. They are discovered, at least in some measure, by the Howe and attempt to purchase her silence." She stopped, and I saw her knuckles turn white where they clutched the footboard. On the mantel, the clock's bell chimed four. "And now Robert Ballantyne has fled."

Matthew and I both stared at her.

"Fled!" I shouted.

Matthew was more practical. "Why? Where?"

Mrs. Abbott shook her head, slowly. "No one knows. This is what I came back to tell you. All below stairs is in an uproar. He was here this morning, but sometime since noon, he left off his livery and took his bundle and vanished. There is a horse missing from the stables as well."

"But . . . but . . . he wouldn't have just left. Not without these!" I snatched the packet of papers he had given me off my writing desk. "These are the papers he got from the chapel."

Mrs. Abbott took that packet from me. Without hesitation, she broke the seal and ripped it open. She stared grimly at what she found and then passed it to me.

It was a stack of five pages. Every one of them was blank.

The worst of it was, we could not even say for sure what had happened. Was this packet the original Robert had left with me? If so, he had come to the room suspicious of his dear, sweet Fran and this was meant as a distraction, or a test, which I failed. Infuriated, he had left the poison.

Or had someone else delivered the poison and then substituted the packet of blank papers for the original? It could have been anybody, in almost any disguise. Olivia had meant to retreat to Mrs. Abbott's closet if anyone came in, but even if she had faced a visitor, how would she know the false courtier or servant from the genuine? She was a stranger here.

But it almost did not matter who had brought the poison, or when, or how. There was only one course left to us, and we must follow it at once.

"We have to go to Kensington," I said. "We have to find whatever is hidden there before Robert does."

"No," said Matthew.

"Ridiculous," said Mrs. Abbott.

"Then what?" I demanded. "What are we to do?"

Matthew leveled his most serious gaze on me. "Go to Her Royal Highness. Tell her everything. Show her—"

"Show her *what?*" I was shaking. I had cause. Olivia was nothing like out of danger. Sophy was at the very least going to be wondering what Mrs. Abbott was up to. She might even now be calling down the palace guard because she'd heard God-alone-knew-what from Robert about me. That was if she wasn't busy designing a new dress for my funeral because she was the one who'd poisoned my wine. To top off the matter, I had a flock of increasingly restless dogs in my room. "I am to go to the princess with a tale of murder and spies, and she's going to believe me because of a blurred sketch and some blank paper?"

"But if you explain . . ." began Matthew

"I explain? Who am I? I'm an impostor! I've already defrauded the court with the intent, you'll remember, of robbing the Crown. I've seduced an apprentice and corrupted a servant." I did not look at Mrs. Abbott as I said this. "It's well known I'm conducting an affair with Robert Ballantyne. I might be a jilted lover trying to smear his name. I might be *anything.* I cannot go to Her Royal Highness with tales of a Jacobite conspiracy and no proof."

"What about this proof?" Matthew pointed to Olivia. She'd fallen asleep again and stirred only faintly as we raised our voices. "There's proof enough of poison for any with eyes to see."

"But no proof as to which hand put it here," said Mrs. Abbott slowly. "It could have been done by any of a hundred people. The whole of the court was at the concert. Anyone could have roamed the halls unseen. Until the cousin is well enough to speak, we will not have the least conception of who might have done this. By then, Ballantyne will have claimed his prize and be on his way to the borderlands, or even to France."

"It doesn't even have to be a member of the court or its servants." Fear and fury strangled my words. "Anyone who wears the right clothes and the proper attitude can walk in here as easy as 'please' and 'thank you.'" I could state this with confidence. After all, I had done almost exactly that.

"Which may be true, but won't be any help to us at Kensington," said Matthew. "Mr. Thornhill said it's shut up until spring." Mrs. Abbott and I stared at him, and Matthew shrugged. "The king is talking about redecorating Kensington as well, and Thornhill's doing some sketches for the ceiling in the cupola room."

My mouth had gone dry. "If he's been designing for the palace, then he must have a floor plan. One that might show where the old queen's bedroom is?"

"Yes," said Matthew softly. "Yes, I believe he does."

"That is a good thought," said Mrs. Abbott, and as a mark of how very much things had changed, I did not hear any trace of her old reluctance in this acknowledgment. "That is how we must think now."

"Robert has a head start," said Matthew with the air of a man making a last stand. "And a horse. Even if the roads are poor, we'll never catch up with him now."

I bit my lip hard. That could not be the end of it. We could not be stopped by so mundane a thing as a stolen horse and a few hours' head start.

"Then it will have to be by water," said Mrs. Abbott. "I will go to the bargemen at the boathouse and speak to them for you. This will require a very large bribe."

I got my purse out of my desk and handed it to her, cursing the fact that I had let Sophy win so much from me the other night. Then I turned to Matthew. I meant to tell him he could go. I meant to thank him for all that he had done and how I was so glad to have known him. I would be firm. I would not endanger him further. He did not deserve it. This plot and all its entanglements were none of his doing.

But he simply leveled his steel gray eyes at me, and all those fine and honorable intentions died a death that was as sudden as it was complete.

"I'll go pack," he said. "You cannot go alone."

‐ͺͺ⟶⟶•⟵⟵ͺͺ‐

IN WHICH MUCH IS ACCOMPLISHED
IN DARKNESS, BUT NOT QUITE ENOUGH.

I have a warning I wish to impart most urgently to all young ladies of delicate breeding who wish to embark upon lives of adventure:

Don't.

Adventures, as it happens, are universally uncomfortable things, and as near as I can determine, are frowned upon by Nature and Nature's God. We had not been on the river yet half an hour before it began once more to rain: a steady down-pour of determined drops such as would worm their way under all layers of cloth to leave me soaked to the skin and cold to my bones.

Neither was that the only inconvenience regarding clothing. It should be obvious to even the most casual and disinterested observer that a lady cannot go adventuring in her mantua. Matthew, who had already sacrificed so much for this mad venture, went further yet and lent me his spare set of clothes. Nothing fit, from the boots to the coat, and having my legs exposed to the view of the entire world, even though encased in breeches, was much less comfortable than I had dreamed it would be.

It was not made any more comfortable by the fact that this was no royal barge that carried us. We rode in a battered rowboat so slender and low that the Thames regularly lapped over the gunwales. One sour, tobacco-spitting man plied the oars. Another stood in the bow by the lantern, watching the way and cursing the rain, the river, the dark, and anything else that came to mind. Matthew and I huddled together on a lumpy sack. On this small and makeshift sofa, my all but naked leg pressed up close to Matthew's. My side, which was innocent of stays for almost the first time since I had turned eleven, pushed against his.

The true agony was that I had no strength of heart or mind left to enjoy this position. Quite apart from the rough river and the freezing damp, I was half dead with worry over Olivia. Mrs. Abbott swore she was out of danger. Matthew said the same, but how could she be? She was still in the palace. The murderer still roamed freely somewhere.

Olivia's only real hope was for Matthew and me to reach Kensington ahead of Robert, find this hidden Jacobite thing, and bring it to Their Royal Highnesses. We had a chance at that. Even in good weather, Matthew assured me, it was more than eight hours' hard ride from Hampton Court to

Kensington. And this was most decidedly not good weather. The roads would be rivers of mud. We still had time. We still had a chance.

If there was any good to be had from this, I thought miserably, it was that I was obeying my instructions. I had left the palace by the back door. I had even turned thief. I hoped Mr. Peele, wherever he might be, was satisfied or, at the least, confused and delayed.

It was full dark by the time our little slip of a boat pulled up to the Kensington dock. There we were met by the frustrations of a fresh delay while Matthew first found us a stable, and then while he banged on the door and shouted to wake the fat, surly, unshaven owner, who smelled of horses and onions. The remains of my coinage eventually convinced him to hire us a cart, and Matthew's stern eye eventually got us a horse that wasn't swaybacked or broken-winded. I appropriated a stool to load into our cart when the stableman wasn't looking and didn't feel the least twinge of guilt. After all, he was trying to cheat us, and we would be bringing it back. Probably.

Thus it was we forsook our long, wet, cold ride in a rocking boat for a long, wet, cold drive in a rickety cart. Even though the rain relented, the moon remained lost behind the clouds, and the cart's lantern sputtered dangerously. Mud became our enemy. Our hired horse would only pick its way slowly along. We held our breath when the wheels stuck and stuck again. If we broke a wheel or an axle, we were lost. If this old, mended conveyance overturned, we might add broken bones to the night's adventures. I was several times afraid we'd be forced to stop somewhere to wait for dawn. By then, Robert could have easily gotten to the palace before us and made off with . . . whatever it was.

I could have gotten Olivia near killed, could have lost Matthew his place and walked myself to the gallows, and it might still be all for nothing.

We finally limped up to the grounds of Kensington Palace on its eastern side, where it stood hard by the narrow, muddy country lane that branched off the king's highway. Matthew quite sensibly pointed out that it would not do us any good to try to enter from the main road, as we might be seen by those who kept the lodges and gatehouses. He was right, of course, although I found I doubted the existence of such creatures. The world seemed to have entirely emptied of people. The only sounds were the rush of the frustratingly cold wind in the hedges and the hoot of owls warning one another to keep away. The moon had probably passed its zenith, but the clouds still gathered so thick and hung so low, there was no way to be sure.

A high green hedge separated the lane from the palace grounds. Matthew lay flat on the ground and wriggled between the crooked hornbeam trunks, pushing the pierced tin lantern we had taken from the cart ahead of him. He twisted hard and smothered several curses along the way. Despite all our difficulties and dangers, I felt a grin spreading on my face. I ducked myself down and snaked straight through. Even pulling my stolen stool with me, I was on my feet again while he was still up to his waist in hedge. Matthew glowered as I held out my hand to help pull him the rest of the way.

"Country summers," I whispered. "Olivia always said I could turn poacher if I had a mind to."

I realized slowly that neither of us showed any inclination to let go of the other's hand. And that for once in my life, I was not wearing gloves, so we touched skin to skin, as cold as those skins might be. Matthew touched the corner of my mouth. His eyes shone with far more than lantern light.

We both let go in the same instant and turned away before such thoughts could get the better of us. In silent accord, we started across the vast lawn as swiftly as we dared. If all our plans failed because of a twisted ankle or knee, it would be a most sorry end. And possibly a deadly one, if Robert and his confederates found us before honest help did. Of course, that honest help would probably be those lodge keepers Matthew hypothesized, and they might not be inclined to look with gentle amusement upon our antics.

Kensington Palace was a sprawling building, mostly L-shaped, with three stories and enough chimneys and windows for a good-sized village. We fetched up against the red brick wall and stood there, panting. Matthew shielded the lantern with his hat, and we both listened, straining our ears. There was nothing. Nothing in all the world save us, the

wind, and the night creatures. Matthew nodded, and I nodded in reply, and we turned to face the palace we meant to
plunder.

All the windows were shuttered. There was no hint
of light to be seen, no human sound to be heard. The wind
whistled mischievously around the eaves and chimneys as if it
sought to rouse them from their slumbers. Inside its tin housing, our lone candle flickered fitfully.

"This will do as well as any." Matthew set the stool
beneath the sill of the nearest window. We both had canvas satchels slung over our shoulders for carrying a few items
we'd deemed might be useful for this venture. I had brought
rope and a tinderbox. From his sack, Matthew took out an
oiled leather wrapper filled with an array of delicate tools,
most of which seemed to be knives. They were for carving
wood and plaster, he told me, as well as mending other tools.
And they could, in a pinch, be used to lift a latch.

The doors would all be barred, but the shutters should
only have a single latch. I wanted very much to ask how he
was so sure of this detail regarding housebreaking, but held
my peace. If we were successful, there would be time for such
revelations later. If we failed, they would not matter.

Matthew selected a palette knife and murmured either
a prayer or an apology. I held the lantern as high and steady
as I could while trying to look over my shoulder the whole
time. There were hooves sounding on the road, imagination
told me urgently. That was not just my heartbeat. That was
hooves, and they were thudding louder. The riders would see

the light. They already had. It was the lodge keepers. It was the city watch. Did the watch come out this far?

"There." Matthew folded one shutter back to show the glass glimmering in the lantern light. "Now for the panes. Hold the light closer."

Even with the stool, Matthew had to stand on tiptoe to slip his knife between the casements. The stool shifted on the mud and gravel below, and he cursed. He wriggled the blade, cursed again, and wriggled the blade some more. I tasted blood where I was biting my lip to keep from begging him to hurry. Finally, there sounded the soft and infinitely beautiful scrape of metal on metal. Matthew settled back on his heels, staring, as if he could not believe what he'd done. But he dug his fingers between the casements, and the window swung smoothly outward.

We grinned at each other and gripped our hands. Matthew made one of his fine bows, and then laced his fingers together, making a cup for my foot. I let him boost me inside.

I landed awkwardly, and my ill-fitting boots sounded like thunder on the floor. I crouched beneath the sill, straining with all my might to hear past the fading echoes of my own ungainly entrance. I heard the night noises, and the wind overhead. These were accompanied by a low, slow creaking in the walls as the great, empty house settled itself for the night. There was nothing else, except an annoyed hiss from Matthew.

He passed me the lantern and the stool, and scrabbled in over the window ledge. While he caught his breath, I pulled the shutters closed and latched the windows again. Matthew shone the lantern about the room. It was a large chamber, made larger by the fact that it was absolutely empty. There was no plan for the court to return to this residence until next spring, so the vast majority of the furnishings and draperies had been removed to other palaces or to storage. The walls were decorated with dust cloths hung over the few paintings that had been permitted to remain.

We exited that room by the only door and found ourselves in a gallery that might as well have been the center of the earth, it was so dark. Beyond the tiny sphere of illumination our candle made, there was nothing.

Was Robert here? Had he been and gone already? There was no way at all to tell.

Matthew reached into his satchel again and brought out a thick and much-folded paper. He opened it and squinted at the ink and pencil lines. "This way. I think."

In popular dramas, there occur frequent instances of players slipping through a darkened house. Thieves, mad monks, desperate heroes, and all such personages manage it with ease. I can now speak the truth and say it is in no way as simple as it sounds. My too big, too stiff boots thumped against the floor, no matter how softly I tried to move. Each breath, each rustle echoed off walls we could not see, until it seemed we traveled with an entire regiment shadowing us. Claws scrabbled about the wainscoting as the rats fled our light. The wind found its way inside at least as easily as we had and curled in damp drafts around our already frozen ankles. The darkness gave us no limits for our eyes, and our fingertips grazed the walls and the occasional piece of furniture that had been left behind. Once, in a racket fit to split the world in two, I banged against a set of fire irons. We both jumped and froze in place, but there was nothing to follow that horrible, ringing crash. Nothing, that is, except for an extra flutter from the dust cloths that hung over the paintings, making shadows across our pitiful puddle of light and setting my mind thinking far too much on ghosts.

Adding to these burdens was the fact that I kept stopping us in our prolonged slink through the empty chambers and galleries. Not once, but again, and again. My heart would not slow, neither would my breath, and I could not fight the growing certainty that we were being followed. There was another shadow here, another pair of footsteps. Something pattered against the wood, and it was not the rats. Somewhere, the wind brought a fresh scent, like mud and damp wool. I was certain of it. Robert was already here. Or a confederate.

"Peggy, stop it," snapped Matthew finally. "You'll ruin your own nerves."

"It's already done," I muttered back. But I clenched my fists and my jaw and let him take us around another corner. We passed through yet another antechamber with its fireplace irons keeping a lonely watch beside the empty hearth. From there we came to an open room with curving walls. A grand staircase rose to one side. A chandelier encased in gauze netting hung from the high, vaulted ceiling. For one moment, it looked like a web spun by gargantuan spiders. In the next moment, I wished desperately I had never thought of that. The rats sneaking with us through the dark were quite bad enough. I did not need to go inventing other large vermin.

"I know this place." Relief filled Matthew's voice. "This is the cupola room, and that's the king's staircase. This is where Thornhill means to put the new ceiling tableau." He squinted again at the floor plan he carried, turning it this way and that while turning himself in a tight circle to get his bearings.

Something cracked sharply, and I jumped, knocking against Matthew. The lantern guttered, and my heart stopped. The thought of losing the light now was nothing short of terrifying, even though we had a tinderbox—I had felt a dozen times in my satchel to make sure it was still there. I listened again, willing myself to hear only what was there. Just the sounds of an empty house, nothing more.

Rain rattled the shutters, adding their noise to that of my maddened heart and harsh breath. Tears pricked the backs of my eyes. Fortunately, anger rose up to beat them back. I was no child lost in the dark. I would not give in to night terrors. I folded my arms and tucked my hands into my armpits to try to warm them. If I inched closer to Matthew in the process, it was purely by accident.

"I have it," said Matthew, and I have never heard happier words in the whole of my life. "Up these stairs and at the end of the rightmost gallery."

We hurried. I don't know if my fear infected Matthew or if the dark and draft and rain had finally begun its work on him, but we could not seem to slow the pace as our echoes chased us through the empty galleries. It was only at the last minute that we pulled up short of the wall where the gallery ended and turned toward the closed door.

Neither of us asked what we would do if that carved door was locked. It was not to be thought of. I reached out to the brass handle. A draft brushed my shoulder and my bare hand. I prayed, and pulled.

Nothing happened.

I cursed, myself and the darkness. I took the handle again. This time I pushed.

The door came open, and I slumped against the wall, limp with relief. I thought Matthew would berate me again, but he just took my hand in his, and together we entered the chamber of a dead queen.

Matthew lifted the lantern high. There was nothing to mark this place as different from any other room we had passed through, and yet my eyes seemed to fit in the outlines of the figures Francesca had drawn. In that dreamlike space of dark and imagination, I saw the ghosts of quarreling men and the old queen in her bed, trying to signal her last orders to her ministers.

Matthew, being Matthew, did not waste time on such reflections. He took the lantern over to the great hearth. Looking on it, my heart sank. The fireplace was broader than I was tall, and framed with an amazing bulwark of carved plaster that had been worked with beasts and birds and flowers and even letters—mostly H's and A's knotted together.

The hairs on my neck prickled. I stared at the thousand, thousand decorations and crenellations. Somewhere in this vast stretch of ornamentation, there was a hidden panel. Matthew set the lantern on the mantel. Methodically, he began to run his dexterous artist's fingers across the flowers and vines, seeking a latch, or hinge, or a join between panels. But I couldn't see where to begin. We did not even know for certain any such panel existed.

I gathered all the strength I had left to me, and one slow inch at a time, I shoved the panic back. I forced myself to think only of what I had seen. I made my mind work over all the mysteries and all the intrigues that turned on whatever had been hidden in this room when Queen Anne died. In the dark of my mind's eye, I saw Robert as I had seen the silhouettes from Francesca's sketch. I placed him in the Queen's Chapel as Mrs. Abbott described him—kneeling in front of the hidden crucifix, his head bowed in prayer.

I put my hand on the right corner of the fireplace. I bent as close as I could to the plaster, seeking with eyes and fingers. And I found it.

There, among all the other decorations, was a Catholic cross so twined in ivy and perched upon by birds as to be almost invisible. I pressed it. There was a click as latch and spring released, and a slender door opened beneath my hand, its joins hidden by the straight trunk of one carved tree. It was scarcely thick enough for me to get my fingers into so I could draw out the piece of parchment folded inside.

Matthew brought the lantern and himself close so we could both read. The missive was in Latin, and had been written large in a bold, flowing hand.

I stared at the elaborate lettering, fighting to translate the words. My heart was beating hard enough to shake my hands, but slowly the meaning settled itself into my mind.

"Know all men by these presents that I, Anne, by Grace of God Queen of Great Britain and Ireland," I read, "after much prayer and reflection and in deepest desire to right the grievous wrong which by our hand and action we did set seal to . . ." I fumbled the next few words, but then picked up the thread. "Do hereby declare our sole and proper successor to be our brother James Edward Stuart, son of James II and VI of England and Scotland, and—"

"God in Heaven," whispered Matthew. "It's the succession letter. The Jacobites always said it existed, but it was supposed to have been burnt when she died, in order to make way for King George . . ." We stared at each other.

"If this is genuine, the Jacobites could use it to prove the Pretender is the rightful king," I said. "They could start another civil war. Robert's father was a footman here, and he was here when Queen Anne died. I'll bet he told Robert about the letter, and Robert told the Jacobites—"

"Yes," said Robert behind us. "And you're going to tell me who in the hell you are."

CHAPTER THIRTY-ONE

In which violence, deception,

and murder hold sway in darkness.

It is odd what fear does to one's powers of perception. As Robert Ballantyne came forward to the edge of our circle of light, the first thing I noted was that he had abandoned his footman's livery for the dress of a plain gentleman—a dark coat and breeches, white stockings, muddy boots, simple gloves, and unpowdered hair. Truth be told, in the flickering lantern light, he looked a bit like Mr. Peele.

I'd been right. We had been followed, but I derived no satisfaction from this triumph of my perception. Especially as I could now see that as a plain gentleman, Robert had brought with him a light sword, which he pointed directly at me.

"I asked who the hell you are." Robert's words grated across my skin. "Because you're not Francesca. Francesca is dead." His eyes were bright with an emotion as far beyond anger as the sun was beyond our feeble lantern.

Matthew straightened and stepped in front of me in one smooth motion. "This is none of your business, Ballantyne."

"You're wrong, Master Paint Dauber. This is very much my business." I could not tear my eyes away from Robert's sword Neither could I stop myself from remembering that the only armaments Matthew and I carried were the tiny knives securely stowed in Matthew's satchel. "She is my business, as is what she's got hold of. Give it here." He held out his free hand. "Or I'll slit your gullet open."

"What have you done, Robert?" I asked slowly. Matthew was tensing, I could feel it. In his careful way, he was gauging distances and angles between himself and Robert, and between me and Robert and the glimmering tip of his sword. I had to play for time. "Who is your paymaster?"

"Of course such a one as you would think of money." Robert sneered. "I should have known from the beginning that you were not my Fran, you conniving bitch. She was sweet, kind, open. She couldn't have deceived anyone to save her life. That's why they all used her. She—" He stopped. "You took her name and her station, and you're not fit to kiss her shoe."

I considered reminding him that he had mistaken me for his dear Fran for a number of weeks now, but decided antagonizing him so would not help us. Although what I did say was perhaps not much better.

"Who killed Francesca, Robert? Who poisoned her and left her to die?"

The only answer I received was strained silence. "She was going to betray you," I said. "You found out. You thought she was going to tell someone." I sincerely doubted this gallant romantic understood Francesca meant to leave him flat as soon as she got her greedy, pretty hands on Queen Anne's letter. "Did you decide to kill her on your own, or did you have orders?"

"I never harmed her!" cried Robert. "I never would!"

"You poisoned her." My anger boiled through each word. Robert Ballantyne was a fool, a traitor, and a murderer. He would confess. I would make him confess. "Or you know who did. You poisoned that box of bonbons you said came from Sophy. You tried to poison me when you realized I wasn't Fran, but you missed. You almost killed an innocent girl, you—"

Matthew jumped. He tackled Robert, and the two men went down in a thunderous heap, tumbling from light into darkness. They hollered and swore and set up the sound of fists against flesh and bone. The sword skittered across the floor, and I raced after it. Matthew straddled Robert's chest, raining blows on his head, while Robert cursed and struggled. I caught the sword up and swung around awkwardly. It was not so very heavy, but I was unused to it. My pathetic stab into Robert's shoulder caught only the thick cloth of his coat, so he cursed and jerked away hard, which in turn loosened Matthew's grip. Robert twisted and threw Matthew aside.

Faster than I would have believed possible, Robert was on his feet. I slashed at him, but he charged underneath my swing and grabbed my wrist, digging his fingers hard into my tendons. My fingers went numb, and the sword fell. Matthew hollered and lunged again, grabbing Robert about the knees. Robert toppled over, but kept tight hold on his sword. The lantern was on the floor, guttering badly. I ran for it and snatched it up. Without light, we were truly lost. Matthew seized hold of my arm, dragging me out the door and into a run. Blood dripped down the back of his hand and smeared his cheek. Robert, still cursing, raced behind us as we tore through the gallery. We had to lose him, but we never would, not as long as we carried the light.

I yanked Matthew around a corner, and another, pulling us both back so our shoulder blades pressed against the wall. I lifted the lantern and blew hard on the flame. Darkness was immediate, thick, and absolute. Matthew squeezed my hand. I heard him struggling to control his breathing, and his grunt of pain. I couldn't ask where he was cut, or how deeply, because I did not dare make a sound. I tried to take comfort in the strength of his grip. If he could hold me this tightly, he could not be too badly hurt.

There came a soft shuffling from out in the gallery. It grew slowly closer, bringing with it the rustle of cloth and the scrape of heels against the floor. Robert was out there, moving cautiously forward in the dark, listening for us as we listened for him.

The footsteps stopped, but the rustling continued. Then there was the distinct sound of flint against steel. A spark flared, and blossomed into candlelight beyond the threshold. Naturally, Robert had also brought a lantern, and he lit it now. I shrank back, trying to melt into the wall, but Matthew squeezed my hand again, warning me to be still. From our awkward angle, we saw the barest edge of the light spreading along the wall of the farther antechamber. Robert's elongated shadow spread with it as he lifted the lantern high and walked.

Walked away, taking the light and leaving us once more in darkness.

I wanted to run. I wanted to scream. I wanted to do anything except what I must, which was stay here and be silent. My head and ears ached from straining to hear each noise. I hated the palace and the blood I was sure still ran from Matthew's wounds. I hated the dark. I hated my fool self and all the Jacobites in all the world for bringing us here. Tears wet my cheeks, wrung from me by fear and tension, and I was grateful Matthew could not see them.

After what was surely an eternity, the last of Robert's footsteps blended with the drumming rain. I leaned toward Matthew, so close my lips brushed the warm edge of his ear.

"He won't leave," I whispered. "We have the letter. He's still here."

I felt Matthew nod. "Boots off," he breathed, and I

understood. In bare feet we would be able to move more quietly. I obeyed as best I could, freezing in fear at each small sound I made.

Matthew's hand was on my shoulder, and it trailed down my arm to my hand. Gently, he unfolded my fingers and pressed something against my palm. It took me a minute to realize I held a knife's handle.

"Follow," he breathed, "Wait for signal of three. Eyes down so the light won't blind."

He kissed me, soft and warm and swift. It lasted just long enough for the ache of it to shoot through me and then his warmth was gone, although not far. Still, I understood. This moment, this acknowledgment of hope and feeling, was over. To find out what might come next between us, we needed to live through the night.

I tucked the knife into my coat pocket alongside the queen's letter, stuffed my stockings into my boots, and took Matthew's hand. The floor was cold and smooth under my bare feet as we slipped forward, one painful inch at a time. We crept through the first doorway and around the first corner. Around the outer chamber, following the wall, slowly, softly, hearts racing. To the second threshold.

My toe touched Matthew's bare heel. He'd gone still. He squeezed my fingers. One, two, three. I dropped my gaze to the floor. Matthew let go of my hand.

And threw his boot against the far wall. There was a thunder of noise as it hit. Light flared beyond the threshold. Matthew took off at a run in the opposite direction down the long gallery. Robert, with his sword and lantern, flashed past the doorway. I ran after both men. And instantly, tangling my feet in folds of cloth, fell in a loud and undignified heap.

Robert skidded to a halt. He turned and saw me wrestling myself away from what proved to be a man's coat. He must have used it to cover his lantern. He growled an oath and lunged for me.

I scrabbled to my feet and threw the coat in Robert's face. He swung the sword and batted the flying bundle away, but Matthew leaped at him from the side and drove his knife into Robert's arm. Robert screamed, and the lantern fell. I snatched at it and screamed in pain as the heated tin burned my palms. Robert swung around, tearing the knife from Matthew's hand, and I jumped out of his reach. The candle guttered but stayed lit, so I could set it down and still see. So I knew where to run and how I should leap on Robert's back, loop my arm around his throat, and drag him backward.

But Robert stomped the heel of his shoe onto my bare toes. Pain exploded in my foot, and I screamed. He snatched the satchel off my shoulder and ran.

I screamed again and moved to stagger after Robert.

"Let him go!" gasped Matthew. "We have the letter, need to get out."

He was right. We might have only a minute, just until Robert found out I hadn't been so careless as to carry the letter in the satchel. I lifted the lantern, Matthew wrapped his arm around my shoulders for support, and we staggered awkwardly in the opposite direction from the way Robert had run. The pain in my foot redoubled with each step. It took my breath as effectively as a corset could have, but I grit teeth and fists against it and kept moving. We struggled down yards of empty gallery, trying to watch in front of us and behind at the same time. After an eternity, we reached the top of the king's staircase.

Movement caught my eye and I swung around, lantern high. Robert's sword, aimed for my head, swept out from the darkness and clanged against the tin housing. The force of the blow ripped the lantern from my hand. It hit the floor and sputtered into a bare spark. I dropped to my knees, frantic to right it, to breathe that last spark back to flame. Matthew and Robert closed overhead. The light flickered and flared again. Matthew had his hands around Robert's wrists and was struggling to keep the sword over both their heads.

Robert's knee came up and planted itself in Matthew's groin. Matthew went still for a heartbeat, and then he fell, but not alone. He dragged Robert with him, and together they toppled down the stairs, all the long way down to the landing where the staircase turned.

"Matthew!" I forgot Robert, forgot the pain in my foot, the lantern, the letter, and danger altogether. I forgot every-thing except flying down the stairs to where Matthew lay sprawled on his back and horribly still.

"Matthew, wake up, wake up!" Blood ran freely from his hand and his head. "Oh, God, please, please, please. . . ." I pressed my hand against his chest, against his throat, feeling desperately for some sign of life. Robert had fallen half a step farther and was sprawled on his back, his head and hands both bloody, his chest still. I disregarded him. I cared only for Matthew. He had to live. He had to.

Matthew's eyes fluttered open. Joy and relief stopped my breath. Slowly, his mouth shaped one word.

Run.

- ⟨ᴏ⟨ᴏ⟩•⟨ᴏ⟩ᴏ⟩ -

IN WHICH OUR HEROINE IS
PROVED RIGHT ONCE MORE.

But before comprehension or fresh fear had time to penetrate the whirlwind of my thoughts, I felt the warmth of another body behind me. A single frantic heartbeat later, I felt the bite of cold metal against my spine, just above my collar.

"Get up," ordered Mr. Peele.

So. I had been right, again. Robert did have a confederate with him. Why could I not have been right about something pleasant and useful?

On my knees, I turned. The sword's edge slid slowly against my skin, not quite hard enough to break it, until the tip rested right over my collarbone. Mr. Peele had the lantern in one hand and the sword in the other. He'd had plenty of time to retrieve both while I tried to discover if Matthew still lived.

"Please," I croaked. "He's hurt. They're hurt," I added. "They need help."

Mr. Peele glanced from Matthew to Robert, who hadn't moved at all, despite being in a most awkward and uncomfortable position. Mr. Peele took one step forward, and another. He rested the tip of his sword against Robert's bosom. I screamed and lunged, but not in time. Mr. Peele stabbed deep. Blood welled out, dripping down the stairs, and Robert convulsed once.

Mr. Peele turned to me. "On your feet, young woman, or I'll serve your apprentice just the same."

I could not believe what I had seen, and yet I had seen it. Robert Ballantyne was dead. Poor, loyal, romantic, deceived Robert was dead, and the man who had killed him loomed over Matthew and me.

"I said, get up, Peggy Fitzroy."

Matthew's face had gone dead white. Blood ran down from a gash in his forehead. The angle of his sprawling right arm was wrong. He'd broken a bone, at least. He mouthed *Run, go, run*. But I couldn't. Mr. Peele would do as he said. I couldn't leave Matthew to be killed.

I climbed to my feet and turned to look into Mr. Peele's bland, calm eyes. Then and there I hated him with as pure and cold a hatred as was ever given to womankind. If I'd had the power in that moment to cast him into the fires of hell, I would have done so, and done it cheerfully.

"Why are you doing this?" I asked. "What does it matter to you who's king?"

"Nothing at all." He smiled his thin smile. "But it matters very much that there are plenty of men who will pay a great deal of money for the letter in your pocket."

I thought for a moment he was going to stab me as he'd stabbed Robert. I almost wished he would. If he moved, if I could dodge, I could grab him, grapple away that sword. This time I would not strike so weakly. If I just had the chance, I'd drive that blade straight into his murderous heart.

"You killed Francesca," I said. "You worked out that she meant to take the letter to the Jacobites and leave you behind. So you killed her and convinced the others that this business with a substitute could be made to work. But once you'd gotten hold of the sketches she left, you didn't need me anymore. You knew where the letter was hidden. You tried to get me to leave, but it didn't matter if I obeyed, because you'd poisoned the wine in my room."

"Just in case," said Mr. Peele mildly. "Then either you'd be dead or in chains as a murderer. You are a clever girl, Peggy Fitzroy, but very headstrong. And yes, you were my idea, and I will say you played your part quite well. You flushed Francesca's secret lover out into the open. I had only to expose you to him and to play the loyal Jacobite. Now, clever girl, you will walk down the stairs. No tricks, or I swear I'll strike your lover dead."

I had done many difficult things since I made my decision to become Lady Francesca, but none so difficult as fixing my eyes ahead of me and walking down those stairs. My bare foot stepped into Robert's cooling blood, and my nerve almost failed me. I carried that blood with me now. With each painful step down the staircase, the sole of my foot stuck to the wood and peeled away again reluctantly. Mr. Peele followed me, his sword resting against my spine.

Behind us, Matthew moaned in his pain, but I could not let that distract me. I could not even look back. I had to look ahead, only ahead. I had to think. I must get Mr. Peele away from Matthew. I must find some way to fight back. I didn't know where my knife had gone. I had only my bare hands and my wits, and both felt hollowed out by fear and exhaustion. I believe that without my anger over Matthew to sustain me, I would have fainted dead away.

As soon as I thought this, an idea blossomed in my mind. Complete and perfect, it filled me, from the soles of my bare and bloody feet to the crown of my head. Perhaps it was a gift from my mother, who waited in the portion of Elysium reserved for good spies. The splendid irony of it all was that here I was, finally dressed as a male, and yet I was about to act as the worst of all possible females.

"Please." I swallowed my bile. "Please, don't kill me."

"Oh, I won't. Not yet, anyway," said Mr. Peele calmly. He cared nothing at all for the possibility that he had reduced me to tears.

"No, please. I'm frightened. Don't." So much emotion flowed through me, it was surprisingly easy to work my voice into a fever pitch. And something of an odd relief, after all the time spent holding my fear at bay.

"Pathetic," he sneered. "I suppose it was inevitable you should break in the end."

"I can't do this. I can't!" I let myself limp, as if the pain was joining with the fear, each making the other worse. "Please, please, don't hurt me!"

"Save your breath."

"No, no, please, I'll do anything!" *Forgive me, Matthew.* "Anything you want! I'll say I'm for King James. Anything. I hate George and all the Hanovers. I was only pretending to be on their side. Please!"

We were on the main floor now. The cupola room opened around us, its ceiling soaring into shadow, its cocooned chandelier seeming to hover in midair.

"I'll do anything! I swear I will!" Tears fell from my eyes far too easily, and I thought I was going to be sick from anger and guilt. Matthew could hear me. I just had to trust he knew it was all a lie. Except for the tears. The tears were genuine.

"Keep moving, and never mind your oaths." Mr. Peele pressed the sword harder against my spine and I stumbled forward, another few steps. Another few steps was all I needed.

"I can't . . . I can't. Oh, Matthew! Oh, God! Help me! Help me!" I screamed and staggered away, exaggerating my limp, trying to run, but plainly—oh, frail female creature that I was—too weak to truly flee. "Save me! Please, someone save me!"

"Get back here, you stupid bitch!"

Come after me, I begged in my mind as I limped and wailed from the cupola room to the chamber beside it—where there was a fireplace. I remembered passing it. *Come after me, Mr. Peele. I can't move that quickly. You can catch me. It's not worth it to go back to threaten Matthew. It's not. Come after me.*

Mr. Peele cursed. His boots slapped the floor as he stomped up behind me, calling me names I should have very much resented if I hadn't been expending all my energy on not looking back and keeping up the truly pathetic wailing. I was at the hearthside now. I slumped and sagged forward, clutching at the mantelpiece and weeping wildly.

"Stop that at once!" He set the lantern on the mantel's corner. He sheathed his sword and moved forward to kick me or push me with his free hand. I never found out which.

Because I grabbed up the poker from the fire irons and struck him on the arm, then, with a backswing to the chin, snapped his head back.

Mr. Peele crumpled, rather more slowly than I would have expected, and thudded onto the floor. He was bleeding hard from his jaw, and I was panting, and suddenly the poker felt terribly heavy in my trembling hand.

There was a noise. In the other room. A banging, rattling noise and a man's shout, much muffled by stout doors and falling rain.

"Open! In the name of King George, open!"

Moving on little more than instinct, I walked into the cupola room. I fumbled with bar and latch, one-handed, because I couldn't seem to make myself put down the poker. I grasped the ring and pulled open the heavy door. On the other side, mounted on a pale horse of truly astounding proportions, sat Mr. Tinderflint.

CHAPTER THIRTY-THREE

IN WHICH THERE OCCUR SEVERAL MATTERS
OF LIFE AND DEATH.

W"here's Peele?" Mr. Tinderflint asked with commendable brevity as he dropped from the horse's back. He also drew an enormously practical-looking sword. If I had been anything other than numb at that moment, I would have been afraid. But the night's adventures seemed to have inured me to the sight of swords. Or anything else.

"Where is Peele?" demanded Mr. Tinderflint again.

I pointed to the antechamber and only belatedly noticed that I did so with the hand holding the poker.

"Oh, dear," he murmured. "Dear, dear, dear."

Mr. Tinderflint ran to the next room, his cloak flapping behind him and showering me with raindrops as he passed. He knelt beside Mr. Peele, who still had not moved. He cradled his former confederate's head in his hands. I heard him grunt, and I heard a sharp, short, terrible snap.

Mr. Tinderflint stood up and turned away from where Mr. Peele lay.

"Perhaps I should take that." He gently removed the poker from my unresisting hand. At the same time, he peered closely at me, looking me up and down to ascertain whether I was all there. I could not have given him much reassurance on that point. "There will be some soldiers with us soon, and we do not need extra questions. No, we do not. Now, my dear, where is Mr. Reade?"

"Matthew!" I swung about toward the staircase. I had forgotten Matthew. How could I have forgotten him, even for a moment?

There was movement in the shadows surrounding the great staircase. In the faint light of the two lanterns, I saw Matthew, on his feet, cradling his arm and leaning heavily on the banister, but he was upright, and he was awake, and our eyes met.

I was not to remember anything more for a long time after that.

CHAPTER THIRTY-FOUR

THE ENDING, WHICH, AS THE SAGACIOUS READER
WILL KNOW, IS ALWAYS A BEGINNING.

It can be further said of adventures that their endings are very protracted things. The soldiers did eventually arrive, and Mr. Tinderflint gave many orders concerning myself and Matthew, as well as the corpses of Mr. Peele and poor, de-ceived, traitorous Robert. The soldiers, being soldiers, were familiar with broken bones and banged-up skulls, and were well able to bind Matthew's wounds and pour quantities of brandy down his throat until he was almost as dazed as I was.

A cart filled with straw and equipped with warm blan-kets was acquired from somewhere to transport Matthew and myself to the docks and the boat that waited to carry us back to Hampton Court.

Somewhere in the whole business, amid the orders and

the bustle, my coat, with Queen Anne's letter still in its pocket, went missing.

We were not taken back to the palace directly, but rather to a stout cottage somewhere on the grounds. There we were looked after by a mostly deaf and entirely ancient man and his equally deaf and ancient wife. One redcoat soldier lounged by our door, and another around back. I had the bedchamber, which I shared with Olivia, who had been brought down, along with all the dogs. Matthew was stowed in the attic. I was allowed to sit with him all day. He slept a good deal. When he woke, we talked over what had happened. Once he could stand, we went downstairs and sat with Olivia in the parlor. We talked over what had happened some more, the three of us. We tried to guess what would happen next. We wondered whether any word had been sent to Olivia's parents regarding her whereabouts and health, and if so, if that word bore any resemblance to the truth.

Of Mrs. Abbott there was neither sign nor word.

Our confinement lasted two days before the front-door solider stepped into the parlor, where the three of us were just finishing up a breakfast of kippers and porridge, and announced I had been summoned to Her Royal Highness.

Olivia, still pale and weak, blanched more than was good for her. Matthew pressed my hand and met my gaze steadily. I brushed my skirts down and took my leave of my companions quietly and without too many words. What was there for me to say?

Resignation is a very freeing thing, and I sank into it now. I would either live or I would die. All had been done. There was nothing left but to meet my mistress and learn my fate.

I did finally get to see the back stairs, which were not, in fact, a single staircase. Rather, they were a dank, dusty, and unpainted labyrinth branching throughout the entire palace. They were also crowded with all manner of servants and courtiers racing up and down heavily shadowed corridors that reminded me far too much of that horrible night in Kensington Palace. I hadn't slept at all well during my residence in the cottage. Robert Ballantyne had developed a disconcerting habit of turning up at the foot of my bed, his waistcoat covered in blood and his long face drawn and haggard as he looked down at me with sad, accusing eyes.

I was much relieved when my soldier opened a door in the wall, stood aside, and gestured for me to pass him. I walked, blinking, into the clear daylight that filled Her Royal Highness's apartments.

The great room was all but empty. Two footmen I did not know stood at rigid attention beside the main doors. The only other occupant was the princess herself, sitting in the carved and gilt chair beneath the canopy of state. This woman was not my kind and clever mistress. She was Her Royal Highness Caroline, Princess of Wales, and she looked at me with cold, clear, blue eyes and waited.

The door clicked shut behind me.

I approached Her Royal Highness, because it was what I must do. I tried not to look at her hard face. I failed in that as badly as I failed to keep my legs from trembling as I made my curtsy.

Her Royal Highness gestured once for me to rise. I did so. I stood there for a long time, my gaze directed toward the floor. The parquet was scuffed. I'd never noticed that before.

"You will want to know that your Lord Tierney has been this morning to see His Royal Highness," said the princess.

I thought to say he was not my Lord Tierney, but that would not have been true.

"That conversation has reached a satisfactory conclusion. Although my husband did say he believes it would be wise for his lordship to be absent from court for a while. It has been left to me to deal with you." The edge to the royal voice could have cut glass. "A scandal of this nature while the king is in Hanover could very easily upset some delicately laid plans. I cannot be at all sure Mr. Walpole will be able to intercept all the . . . unfortunate letters that will be sent."

I said nothing. What on earth could I have said?

"As regards you, Margaret Fitzroy, I had initially thought your case would be a simple one. But it turns out you have several persons pleading for you. Beginning with my daughter Anne. Although I am not sure whether it's you or those blasted dogs she wishes to save."

I swallowed.

"I am given to understand you speak German?"

"Yes, ma'am," I whispered.

"*Sehr gut*," she said. "You will use it now," she continued in harsh and heavy German. "You are now given one chance, and one only. Tell me the truth. How do you come to be in my house?"

I told her. It took a very long time. So long, my throat and my feet began to ache, especially the one Robert had stomped on. But the princess did not allow me to sit or to have a drink of the wine that waited at the royal elbow. She just sat as still as a painted portrait, absorbing each syllable, every single intonation and tremor.

At long last, my well of words ran dry, and I stood trembling as badly as I had after my battle with Mr. Peele. I had no excuses to offer, no plea to make. I was entirely at this woman's mercy. If she raised her hand, I would be imprisoned or transported. Hanged.

Slowly, the princess nodded. "That sorts with what his lordship has said. Now. I have one more question for you, and I urge that you think most carefully before you give your answer." She paused, making sure I had adequately understood this. "What do you think of me?"

I hope my readers will believe me when I say there is not a more complicated question one's sovereign lady can ask. Especially when one has been implicated in the death of two men and as fine a piece of blatant fraud as was ever committed within palace walls.

I swallowed. I knotted my fingers together. I prayed to God Most High. And I told the truth.

"I think, madame, you are a very intelligent woman who

watches over her husband and loves her daughters, and I would not have your place for all the gold in Spain."

She was silent for a long time.

"You may sit down, Margaret Fitzroy." She gestured, and one of the waiting men brought a chair forward.

I did sit. Actually, I plumped. Because all the strength in my knees gave way at once.

"You knew," I breathed. "Your Highness," I added quickly. "This whole time. You knew I wasn't Francesca."

She did not answer, not directly. "I was not happy to come to England, you know. The idea of my husband being heir to a disputed throne in a country that saw us as outsiders, if not actual invaders . . ." She shook her head. "It did not calculate to please. But now that we are here, it is my work to make that throne secure and to see that it passes smoothly from my father-in-law, to my husband, to our heirs. That is the whole of my business, you understand this?"

"Yes, ma'am."

"It is good. It is known, of course, there are Jacobite spies at court. They have many reasons to justify their treason. Loyalty and religion, these might be laudable, but they can also be very dangerous because they are hard to change. Greed or caprice or revenge, these are dangerous because they may arise in an instant, but those who hold them may also be more easily persuaded to change sides.

"I have been watching you carefully since you came to us. I believe you to be an intelligent young woman and one who understands the ways of the world, far beyond the immediate rewards of the card table and the gossip's feast. I put it to you now, Margaret Fitzroy, that it is best for all concerned that we find who this Robert Ballantyne worked for and with, in order that these persons be brought before the bar of His Majesty's justice to pay the full price for what they have done."

"Yes, madame." It occurred to me I was not to die. It occurred to me that I might, in fact, be allowed to live.

"I put it to you that you are uniquely situated to aid in this endeavor."

"Madame?"

There has never in my life occurred anything so wholly unexpected as that moment when Her Royal Highness looked at me, Peggy Fitzroy, and smiled.

"Will you aid me in this, Miss Margaret Fitzroy? Will you be my eyes and ears among the courtiers and find who leads this plot within my own house?"

It was a royal command. A commission for king and country of the sort given only to great heroines. As a loyal subject of the Crown, I answered in the only way I could.

"I . . . but . . . but . . ."

My mistress rolled her eyes. "But what?"

I bit my lip. In flagrant violation of courtesy, decorum, and good sense, I met the gaze royal. "But I will require the help of my friend, and my cousin."

Mr. Tinderflint was waiting in the antechamber when I emerged from my audience. He leaped to his feet from the velvet cushioned bench and bustled forward, lace and ribbons fluttering madly.

"Well? Well?"

"I am to be maid of honor," I told him. "Maid Margaret Fitzroy at a salary of two hundred a year. She will speak to Mr. Thornhill about Matthew's place. She . . . I . . ." I swallowed against the joyous riot of confusion and remembered I still had business with this man. But it was not only that. When I looked at him now, I remembered that sharp, clear snapping sound I had heard as Mr. Tinderflint, Lord Tierney, bent over Mr. Peele. And now Mr. Peele's hold over him was finished. I'd thought this ugly act over very carefully during the past couple of days.

He must have seen something of this in my eyes, because he kept his distance. "I think, perhaps, we should talk."

Mr. Tinderflint had clearly anticipated the conflict between my desire to speak with him and my reluctance to do so. He walked us down to the riverbank, where we came upon two conveniently placed chairs but also a cluster of soldiers and a pair of maids stationed a discreet distance away. This was obviously for my benefit. He wanted me to trust him. He was always so very good at getting me to trust him.

"Now, Peggy." He sat and folded his hands over his ribboned walking stick. "I may call you Peggy, mayn't I? Ask your questions." He spoke quietly and in Latin—I presume to keep the witnesses from comprehending our conversation.

"My lord—"

"Tush, Peggy." He smiled. "You may call me Tinderflint. I've grown rather accustomed to the name and find I like it."

"Mr. Tinderflint." He enjoined me to ask my questions, this man who had planned an enterprise that had nearly gotten me, and my cousin, killed. He had tracked me down, ruthlessly placed me in danger, and killed a murderous, blackmailing traitor with his bare, fat, many-ringed hands.

Where on earth could I possibly begin?

"How did you find me?"

"I'd a missive from Her Royal Highness summoning me back to court." He smiled at my surprise. "Yes, yes, my dear, I am also employed by the Crown. But it was Mrs. Abbott who told me where you'd gone. I made shift to follow as quickly as I could. I'm only sorry I was not faster." I could have sworn he meant it, too.

"You must have seen the letter of succession," I said. "You must have taken it. Was it genuine? Did Queen Anne write it?"

Mr. Tinderflint lifted his brows and dipped his chin. It was a surprisingly owlish look. "What would you do if I said yes? Turn on your mistress? Abandon your new post?"

"I don't know what I would do," I said to the river at his back. "But I want to know, all the same."

The smile he gave me then was a gentle one and filled with understanding. "You have a good heart, Peggy Fitzroy, and a clear head. I don't know why I should be surprised to find how good and how clear. So I will tell you the truth." He took a deep breath. "No. The letter was not genuine. It was a very good forgery that the Jacobites were originally planning to 'discover' as soon as they'd received certain promises of men and arms from France and Spain."

"But . . . wasn't that the northern uprising? They failed."

"I can only assume they mean to try again, and to keep on trying until they have their way, and damn the consequences to their nation or her people." He colored a bit under his face paint. "I should beg your pardon for my language."

I had heard and used much worse, but now was not the time for digressions. "That's what Her Highness thinks."

"Her Highness is a very intelligent woman," he replied. "But then, you know that."

"Why did you send Francesca to court in the first place?"

"Poor Francesca." This was another moment when I was sure I glimpsed the man beneath the ribbons and posturing, and that man was filled with regret. "Another sin for which I will surely have to answer when all is said and done. Her story was much as Mrs. Abbott related to you. I did take her as my ward after one of my visits to Saint-Germaine."

"Mrs. Abbott said she was Francesca's mother."

"And so she is. It is the common tale. Pretty words and a turned head, and a man who took what he wanted and left it to his lady fair to pay the price. She's gone home, by the way," he said. "Back to Paris. She thought it best to leave before too many questions could be asked."

I nodded. It made perfect sense, but I was sorry not to have a chance to say farewell. She had done her best in so many ways. I owed her a great deal.

"It was truly my intent to give Francesca some security and a place in society, where the circumstances of her birth might be conveniently buried under fashion and fortune," Mr. Tinderflint was saying. "That it might one day become useful for me to have a pair of eyes and ears among the ladies was something I considered by the way, and did not even mention to her." He shook his head until his chin wagged. "Now, Peggy, I must interrupt your questions for one of my own. What happened to her? To Francesca? Exactly what had she become involved in?"

I told him, both what I had learned and what I guessed, of Francesca's plotting, of her intent to use Robert and Peele to return in triumph to Saint-Germaine, to present the proof of kingship to the Pretender, and from there to work her wiles upon him.

Mr. Tinderflint listened in absolute silence. When I finished, he looked into the distance for a long time. His eyes were brighter than they had been. I held my peace and gave him time to find his voice again.

"When she turned up on the doorstep, I thought little of it," he murmured. "I thought perhaps she had been disappointed in a love affair or had simply wearied of the rigors and confinement of court life. It wasn't until Peele came to me with his proof that Fran had been a courier for the Jacobite faction that I even suspected she had been murdered." His voice grew bitter, and he wiped at his eyes. "At least I was able to pay Peele back for that much."

I swallowed and looked at my hands. I did not know

what to think of this revelation. I wished I did not have to think of it at all.

"We searched her rooms for hints as to what she'd been up to at court," said Mr. Tinderflint in a more conversational tone. "We uncovered nothing. Where did you find that extraordinary drawing?"

"Sewn into the curtain."

"Very clever, very clever. Ah, me. Perhaps I am too old a dog for these tricks." He shook his head once more.

"But who are you?" I asked him. "What is your part in this, Mr. Tinderflint?"

He sighed and looked at the grass at our feet, at the palace, at the willow branches overhead, and finally at me. "My full name is Hugh Thurlow Flintcross Gainsford, Earl Tierney. I am the heir of an aristocratic estate and a heritage that goes back in a line so straight it shows up the meandering heritage of the English Crown for the mess it is. Tierneys have had their sticky fingers in every disputed succession since the first prudent scion of our house met with a representative of William the Conqueror one dark night in 1065 to discuss remuneration for assisting with a landing at Hastings."

"But whom do you serve?"

"My king. Ah." His eyes twinkled with a mirth I in no way felt inclined to share. "I see you are about to ask who my king is. Well, now, Peggy Fitzroy, I will tell you. I will. I have been to France. I have met James the Second, before he died, obviously. I have met his son the Pretender since then. I have no love of our Hanoverian Georges, and I see trouble ahead with that family. The prince is already growing impatient for the chances the king denies him . . . but they are at least better men than the ones my father helped depose. And it is my belief that it is better for this nation that things should remain as they are now. Yet another war can do us no good at all."

That was it, then. I twisted my hands together and asked the important question. "And my mother? What of her?"

"Your mother was an agent for Her Majesty Queen Anne, Peggy, as was your father. She was as trusted as she was secret. We were able to help each other from time to time." He smiled at some distant memory. "She did not trust me much, I'm sorry to say."

My mother. My beautiful, wonderful mother was a trusted agent of the Crown. Not a secret Jacobite. Not a secret courtesan. My mother was loyal and true and clever, and . . . and . . . a royal spy. So was my vanished father.

Oh, just wait till I tell Olivia! She'll expire from envy. I pressed both hands to my mouth. I knew I was being ridiculous, but it was the thought that came to me in that sunlit summer moment.

"There, now. That's better," said Mr. Tinderflint. "You should not be pale, Peggy, my dear. It does not suit. No, it does not."

I set aside this bit of fine news. I had other questions, which might yield less pleasant answers, but I was determined to ask them, nonetheless.

"Do you know where my father is?"

The question seemed to take him aback. "I am sorry to say I do not. There are others who might, but I do not think they will be glad to have even his daughter know the truth."

He looked at me. I looked at Mr. Tinderflint. "You owe me a debt, Mr. Tinderflint," I said.

Mr. Tinderflint, who was Hugh Templeton Flintcross Gainsford, Earl Tierney, nodded. "I would be a petty man not to acknowledge there is a debt, and it is a deep one. Very well," he said. "I will find out what I can regarding Jonathan Fitzroy. This may take some little time."

"You will always find me at home," I told him solemnly.

At this, Mr. Tinderflint laughed out loud. "Oh, very good! Very good! And in return, my dear Peggy, whenever you find yourself in need of a friend, you have but to call on your Mr. Tinderflint." He stood and took my hand and bowed deeply over it. "May I escort you somewhere?"

"No. If you don't mind, I think I'd like to go alone."

"I understand. I do." He took up his cane and bowed once more. "Fare you well, Peggy Fitzroy. You're a fine young lady. However sorry I might be as to the circumstances, I am very glad to have met you."

He took his leave of me and strolled down the gravel pathway toward the palace. I watched him for a long moment before I turned away.

For a time, I did nothing more than walk slowly on the riverbank, grateful that whatever instructions had been given to the soldiers and the maids, they did not include shadowing me, at least not so I could see them. My thoughts meandered here and there, dazzled by the turn of my fortune as much as by sun and summer warmth. I mourned Lady Francesca then, for the greed that ruined her chance at a good life. I mourned Robert Ballantyne and the trust and love he'd so badly misplaced.

And what of Peggy Fitzroy? What had I gotten myself into? Sophy Howe would be waiting for me when I returned to the palace. I was still not at all sure I'd plumbed the depths of her malice. And there was the mess I'd made of my friendship with Molly Lepell. Last but not least, there was the fact that I had been charged with ferreting out any remaining Jacobites in the court. How on earth was I to do that?

Olivia would try to talk me out of this. As would Matthew. But they would fail. Whatever else happened, I had truly made a life of my own, and I would live it.

I took a deep breath and turned in the direction of the cottage where Olivia and Matthew Reade waited for word of what was to become of me. Of all of us.

And I began to run.